REWRITING
OF TIME

SEQUEL TO *CHILDREN OF THE GODS*

KONRAD KOENIGSMANN

outskirts
press

This book is dedicated to my parents
for their unceasing support.

TABLE OF CONTENTS

Prologue

A SEMBLANCE OF NORMALITY

Just as on any other day, my alarm went off at 6:00 a.m. I had had a late night and all I wanted to do was catch a few more minutes of sleep, so I yawned and turned over in my bed. Noticing this, my alarm tone became higher-pitched, penetrating more deeply into my half-awake brain. Perceiving the onset of a mild headache if I continued to lie in bed, I grudgingly left the comfort of my cool sheets and stumbled to the bathroom.

As my toothbrush, guided by the robotic arm extending from my medicine cabinet, flew into my mouth following a quick snap of my fingers, I tapped my interactive mirror with my other hand and brought up the daily weather report. Another gesture, and the mirror began to read it out to me. "The weather in New Berlin is expected to be partly cloudy today," it intoned in a sweet, feminine voice. "Later today, some rain is expected as part of the Europan government policy of rainwater collection. Please remember to carry an umbrella and set up your collection bucket before leaving. The temperature is expected to hover around a balmy twenty-six degrees

Celsius." I waved my hand at the mirror, and a new readout appeared on the screen. "Given the weather conditions and traffic patterns," continued my mirror, "your daily commute is expected to take twenty-four minutes and thirty-five seconds today. To ensure a timely arrival at your workplace, it is suggested that you leave your home in thirty-two minutes and seven seconds."

I finished brushing my teeth and prepared to get dressed. "What sort of style would you like to wear today?" asked the same voice emanating from a hidden speaker in my closet. "Casual but with a collared shirt," I replied. Almost immediately, a low "chunk" sound was audible as the pistons embedded in some of my clothes hangers decompressed. An assortment of clothing flew out of my closet and laid itself out on my bed. Walking over, I took off my pajamas and started pulling on underwear and the jeans that my assistant had selected for me.

"What would you like for breakfast?" interjected the voice while I finished buttoning up my shirt.

"Some eggs would be nice. Sunny-side up, and add a slice of toast while you're at it."

I walked into my kitchen to find the toast sticking out of the toaster, with a jar of marmalade open on the counter. The eggs were just about ready on the stove, and even as I walked to the refrigerator to grab a glass of orange juice, the stove beeped and turned off. The frying pan suddenly pivoted, lightly tossing the eggs into the air. At the end of their trajectories, the eggs found a clean plate waiting for them at the table. I sat down to eat quickly, glancing at the headline of the *Berliner Zeitung* that had been laid next to my seat. "Do me a favor," I said between mouthfuls of the delicious eggs. "Save the newspaper for when I get home this evening."

"As you wish," replied my assistant. "I would also like to remind you that you now have nine minutes and forty-two seconds until it is suggested you leave for your workplace." I nodded absentmindedly, forgetting for a moment that my assistant was not a real person and couldn't see what I was doing, at least not directly.

In the hall, after putting on my shoes, I pulled a remote out of my pocket and pointed it at a wall panel near my front door. I pressed a button, and the panel slid to the side noiselessly. Behind the panel was a series of buttons labeled with several different icons. I pressed the button that was adorned with the image of a giant bucket and heard a faint whirring noise as my rainwater collection system deployed. With another press of the same button on my remote, the panel closed itself again. I fished my personal communications device out of my shirt pocket and opened the car application. Lo and behold, as soon as I stepped outside my door, a car pulled up to meet me, even obligingly opening its door for me.

"Please fasten your seat belt and insert your Autopass in the appropriate slot on the dashboard," said a masculine voice. I did as instructed and heard the car door shut behind me. "What is your destination today?" asked the same voice. "Alexanderplatz," I replied quickly. "The *Energieforschung* complex." The car pulled smoothly away from the curb.

"Enjoy your commute," continued the voice. "Would you care for some music as you ride?"

"Yes, please. Bach, Goldberg Variations, the 1955 recording by Glenn Gould." Without further prompting, the soft notes of the theme began to fill the car as it whizzed along in the morning traffic.

I pulled my personal communications device back out and went to the e-reader app. "Feynman Lectures on Physics," I muttered under my breath. The app went to my latest bookmark, and I resumed reading through the lecture on quantum physics that I had been reviewing. It seemed as if no time at all had passed when the music shut off. I looked up to see the car pulling up in front of a nondescript glass edifice.

"You have arrived at your final destination," declared the masculine voice. "Enjoy your day at work, and don't forget to take your Autopass with you. Your total charge of fourteen euros and twenty-three cents will be added to your monthly bill."

The door of the car opened as soon as I unbuckled my seat belt, and I clambered out quickly, noticing the car rapidly speeding away out of the corner of my eye. Glancing around, making sure that no one was looking in my direction, I surreptitiously touched my personal communications device to the palm of my left hand. There was a small beep, and a red glow began to emanate from my palm. Quickly, I touched my hand to the surface of the door. There was a buzzing noise and the door opened. Simultaneously, the glow in my palm disappeared. I walked through and stepped into the line for the security checkpoint.

I began to empty my pockets as I neared the front of the line and left my business case open for inspection by the guards. "Hey there, buddy!" greeted one of the guards, a well-muscled, stocky man with a severe buzz cut that failed to match his personality. "Having a good morning so far?"

I smiled, enjoying the camaraderie. "Always the best of

mornings for me, Martin," I replied with a chipper tone of voice. "I hope you haven't succumbed yet to the dullness of your job." Martin laughed, the expression making prominent the laugh lines permanently carved into his face. "I'll never do that," he replied. "We both know I'm too good for that." He waved me forward. "You know the drill. Step into the fermium-255 detector for me, please." I walked forward, entering a tightly packed chamber filled with detection instruments. The door shut behind me with a hiss, and I felt rather than heard a faint buzzing touching my body. After a few seconds, the door opened behind me. "You're good to go," I heard Martin say. "See you in the afternoon!"

"See you!" I called back, replacing the items I had taken out of my pockets and stepping forward to pick up my inspected business case.

As I rapidly crossed the dank, bare, underground lobby of the building, another feminine voice, deeper and more perfunctory than my assistant's, became audible. "*Willkommen*, Pierre Hartford," it began. "It is Day Four of Cycle Sixty-Two of the year 2073. Please be advised that you have a meeting in Conference Room Seven at 9:30 with Mr. Benton. You have twenty-three unread messages, of which seven have been labeled urgent. You will be able to access them once you reach your office." I walked into the waiting elevator tube and braced myself. Soundlessly, the tube sealed itself, and I suddenly shot downward, reaching my destination in mere moments. I stepped out, heading down the hallway until I reached the fourth door on my right. Opening it, I entered my office.

A whirring noise immediately became audible as my desk shot out of an opening in the floor before me, bearing with it my work computer. I ran the tip of my index finger over the lid of the computer, hearing the internal components humming to life as I placed my business case on the other side of it. Opening the case, I pulled out something resembling a translucent wafer of plastic. After folding it in on itself twice, I stuck it to the edge of my now-open computer screen. A popup informed me that the files my portable disk had been holding had been transferred.

Going to my messages, I quickly scanned all twenty-three of them, creating a mental checklist in my head to plan out my day. Quietly humming the Goldberg Variations, I set about to do as much work as I could before my meeting at 9:30. Yet again, it seemed, there were production delays at the fermium reactor. Would they ever learn how to accurately fire helium atoms at a californium target? Apparently not. At least the fusion reactor finally was delivering consistent results. Would this be the year that it exceeded its break-even point, yielding more energy than was put into it? One breakthrough would be nice by the end of the year. After all, if it was thought that my department was putting an undue strain on company resources, things might turn...unpleasant.

A single chime sounded in my office, warning of my imminent meeting with Mr. Benton. With a flick of my wrist, my computer closed itself and flew into my hand. I walked toward the back of my office, taking care not to bump into the glass wall I was attempting to reach. From a distance, it would seem as if I were pressing my palm against thin air, but in fact I was touching the cold, near-invisible glass pane that marked the beginning of the back wall of my office. Soundlessly, a red light flashed once more in the palm of my hand and the glass melted away before me, leaving in its place a narrow passageway leading to another elevator tube. "Conference Room Seven," I called out, stepping into the tube.

A small, wizened old man awaited me when I stepped out of the tube into an opulent room resplendent with wood paneling and state-of-the-art clerium plating. Though he did not look it, Mr. Benton, the CEO of Energieforschung GmbH, was one of the most dangerous men on the planet. Concealed in his ordinary body was a mind of boundless cunning and ruthlessness. He had accrued a vast empire of energy businesses by being willing to take the steps no other man would, even undercutting his own products to secure any possible competitive advantage on the global stage. He was responsible for the energy revolution that had swept the world the past three years, and his inventions had allowed Energieforschung to go beyond energy research and become something akin to a multinational state, controlling the lives of millions through cheap energy. Truly the leader of an empire within an empire.

"Mr. Hartford," began Mr. Benton, his slightly upturned mouth the only indication he was aware of my being twenty-seven seconds late. Even his voice was icy, piercing the silence between us like a shard of glass. "I am the bringer of great news today." His voice mellowed slightly. "I believe that today I have made the biggest score of my long and illustrious career." He paused, obviously inviting me to say something. "What would that be, sir?" I asked after a moment, filling the expectant silence that had cropped up.

Mr. Benton smiled, a thin, wan sort of grimace tugging the upper corners of his lips and accentuating the hard lines of his mouth. "Tell me, Mr. Hartford," he continued, "you have xiv •

heard of the recent meteorite strikes, have you not?" I nodded. "Good, good," he replied. "Then you will be pleased to hear that Energieforschung has taken possession of the valuable extraterrestrial materials these meteorites have given us. I will be granting you sole discretion over these materials, as I think they will be most useful for projects *Wandlung* and *Entdeckung*."

My right eyebrow twitched. Mr. Benton was giving *me* sole discretion over the new meteorites because he thought the antimatter and wormhole projects would best benefit? Talk about more responsibility being heaped upon my shoulders. Mr. Benton's roving eyes missed nothing, and I saw his mouth become that much more of a thin line as my eyebrow moved. "Mr. Hartford," he said, his tone becoming icy once more. "I want you to understand something. I am placing a great deal of trust and resources into your pet project especially. Fail me, and the consequences will not be pretty. I want results, and I want them fast. Nothing less than undisputed success will be accepted. Is that understood?"

"Loud and clear, sir," I replied, successfully keeping the sarcasm out of my voice. *As if anything else would ever be accepted*, I thought. The perils of flirting with danger on a daily basis.

Sometime later, my assistant informed that the building was closing down for the day. A small vial soundlessly rose out of the center of my desk, adorned only with a label marked Fm-255. Unscrewing it, I downed the whole vial in one go, immediately gagging upon swallowing. I mentally sighed to myself again. Mr. Benton's paranoia knew no bounds, it seemed, if he would even go so far as to dose his employees with a mildly radioactive substance. It was an ingenious security measure. Fermium-255 has a half-life of roughly twenty hours, and moreover, was only produced at Energieforschung, which ensured that only those who took daily doses would be allowed back into the building on a regular basis. The taste, however, reminded me of a pair of moldy socks and was frankly quite bothersome. Energieforschung had fundamentally changed the world many times over and found itself at the forefront of technological innovation, but it couldn't find the time to develop a compound that was not utterly rancid?

I left the building, stepping through the fermium detector once more, and entered Alexanderplatz. Stepping into the car I had called, I headed across the city toward the bar *Quelle der Hoffnung*. Entering it, I made a beeline for the table around which three familiar faces sat: Robert, the boisterous Englishman with a ruddy face and friendly expression who worked for the diplomatic corps in the Americanian Relations branch; Maximillian, or Max, quiet, German, but always ready with an insightful, sometimes sarcastic comment, who worked for AI Development at the Siemens plant; and Luka, the Czech, always with an intelligent look in his eyes, scanning his surroundings with a hunger for knowledge, who was the special aide to the Environmental Counsellor of New Berlin. "Oh, look who decided to grace us with his presence," boomed Robert's voice, with his mild English accent giving the words haughty undertones.

"How kind of you to join us," said Luka smoothly, mirth sparkling in his eyes.

"Find another way to blow us all up yet, Pierre?" inquired Max, struggling to hold in his laughter.

"As I can see, you three have lost none of your humorous instincts," I replied sarcastically. "Don't worry, I'll still save

you when the time comes. You can definitely count on that."
The three of them laughed uproariously.

Robert waved his hand, and the robotic barkeep whizzed over to our table. "Another pseudo-beer and currywurst for my friend here, please."

"At once, sir," replied the robot, whizzing away immediately. I glanced up at the holoscreen set into the wall behind us. Another Bundesliga match going on, Hertha BSC vs. FC Bayern München, playing what I liked to call soccer, but what all my friends strenuously insisted be called football.

"*Tor!*" yelled the announcer, causing me to jerk my head back up and glance at the screen. The red Bayern players were now running toward a corner of the field in jubilation. "*Arthur Hausser in der 63. Minute!*" continued the announcer.

Max snorted. "Hertha's hopeless," he commented. "They can't play modern football. Look at Bayern! They're playing positionless football. All ten of their players can attack and defend. Just look at the speed at which they play! Hertha's too rooted in the old ways. Only half their team can actually play; the other half is just hopeless when it comes to real attacking football. That's why they're losing by four goals." Robert and Luka grunted in assent.

The barkeep chose that moment to return with my order. The pseudo-beer looked as real as always. It was hard to tell without already knowing beforehand that we were drinking pseudo-beer. Oh, the beer still looked and tasted the same, still contained alcohol, but all beer these days had special compounds that activated upon contact with stomach acid, neutralizing all the alcohol and making it impossible for people to get drunk unless they attempted to brew their own beer, which, naturally, was now illegal. Of course, there were still talented freelance chemists around, but they were slowly but surely dwindling in number, and this bar at least did not have the luxury of keeping one on retainer. Even if it had, Mr. Benton would have realized immediately the next day, an infinitely worse scenario than being deprived of a tenuous high on weeknights.

"So, how was work for everyone today?" asked Robert. "Oh, wait…sorry, how was work for everyone besides Mr. Top Secret?" Max quickly glanced between me and Robert. "Really, Robert," he began, "that's a very leading question. It's not as if our work ever really has any new developments. We all play our roles, going through our same, tired routines. Pierre is on the edge of innovation! And why shouldn't he be? He doesn't *provoke* his superiors."

"Yes, Robert," I added, "I'm sure that with your skill at diplomacy, in no time at all you will become the Europan ambassador to Americana." Robert looked at me, his face falling in a look of mock despair. "O Great One!" he wailed, waving his arms around as he did so. "What have I ever done to deserve such punishment? I only do the best that I can with what I have, just as we all do. Can I help it that some of us are just more *gifted*?"

We all laughed at Robert's charade. Luka turned toward him with a strange expression on his face. "You know, Robert," he began in a conversational tone, "one day, I will finally have developed an AI that will be able to model almost any type of personality. But I am positive there is something that is impossible to replicate: the bundle of contradictions that make up an Englishman, particularly that *irrational confidence* in the face of *stupidity*." All this was said with a straight face. After a few moments of silence, Robert's face changed as he processed the import of Luka's words. Playfully, he threw a punch that Luka ducked, instead connecting with his beer glass.

"Robert," Max hissed, "please don't get us kicked out of here *again*." Grudgingly, Robert stopped, an expression of mock hurt still visible. The bar did not look kindly upon physical destruction of property, and Robert, whose boisterousness at times strayed into the territory of overeager physicality, had already run afoul of this policy several times.

Soon, the evening was drawing to a close, and my friends and I said goodbye to each other. "Don't forget, same time tomorrow!" I yelled over my shoulder. Three voices groaned in unison, and I could almost see the eyerolls that ensued after my last comment. I made my way home in another car, unlocked my door, and fell straight to bed, too drained to even think of taking my clothes off. Everything was as normal as it always had been. All was as it should be.

1

THE DECISION

Rexdael, the Council of Realms, 2073

I chewed nervously at my elongated upper lip. It was all I could do to keep myself from shivering in disgust. The Council had dictated that for this meeting, every member was to appear as some sort of aquatic creature. I had decided that the way to minimize my discomfort was to assume the form of a whale hybrid, a form in which I would be able to walk and generally move without difficulty but would still perceive my surroundings from the viewpoint of a blue whale. I found it hard to understand the real purpose of this "cultural outreach" program of the Council. If anything, it promoted within me only feelings of disgust and hopes that I would never have to journey into the realms of any of my fellow members.

I was already regretting my choice in creature as I felt my newfound craving for krill begin to stir deep within. Such base instincts were beneath me! I was the ruler of Naronig Realm, for crying out loud! I shouldn't have to be subjected to uncontrollable desires that were entirely not of my own making. But it was too late to change. I was already running behind schedule, and I was in no mood to receive yet another tongue-lashing from Yutigo. I waved my left fin, and a red-and-green portal hovered into existence, emitting subtle waves of color and sound. I stepped in, and after a short journey akin to being sucked through a straw, I arrived in the Council room.

It was as colorful as always, the walls shimmering in a full array of colors with no effort at all made to hide the nature of the pocket universe that the room was. Let it never be said that the realm rulers lacked in pride. We reveled in showing off what the common people found unattainable, the skills and abilities that were sewn into the very fabric of our existence, so a part of us that they sustained us and vice versa. A pocket universe was a very ostentatious way of showing off those abilities, even if no one else was around to admire it.

I quietly swore under my breath when I saw the assembled group of aquatic creatures already sitting around the enormous metal monstrosity of a Council table. A voice I didn't recognize suddenly trailed off as all eyes turned to face me. "Rexdael," boomed a deep, melodious voice from the head of the table, "I am so glad that you have found time in your busy schedule to grace us with your presence." Yutigo, naturally, had taken the form of a shark. It fit his personality perfectly, little grubby gold digger. What he lacked in raw ability or natural intelligence, he made up for with his unmatched political acumen. He served as head of the Council of Realms by virtue of the fact that he had been the one to think up the concept of such a council and the political games that it allowed him to play with everyone else. I respected him little, and the council meetings less. The premise was brilliant, but by virtue of the more than five thousand representatives, reaching a consensus on even the tiniest of details, such as the tracings that should go on the armrests of the wood chairs, was impossible. As such, I found Yutigo's sarcasm, interlaced in his voice like the biting nip of a winter wind, to be more entertaining than humiliating. Anything was better than boring deadlock.

I took my seat, two seats down from the head of the table, wordlessly. "Would you care to give an explanation for this unexpected tardiness, Rexdael?" inquired Yutigo, his voice giving the words a mocking edge. It was widely known how much I disdained these meetings, and only a sense of propriety prevented me from skipping them altogether as some other rulers did.

"No," I replied shortly, imbuing the monosyllable with a definitive finality. Wisely, Yutigo knew better than to challenge such surliness, at least publicly, and his gaze shifted from me, coming to rest about halfway down the row.

An audible smacking of lips could be heard as the ruler whom my entrance had interrupted prepared to continue talking. He had chosen to take the form of a pufferfish, and the attention thrust upon him gave him the opportunity to swell up in pride. "As I was saying," he continued (was his name Tinup?), "the dream pod trial in over four hundred test centers located in twenty different realms has provided overwhelming support for the hypothesis that user-manipulated dreaming provides a significant boost to happiness levels."

"By allowing users to select their own dreams, you deprive

them of the need to face adversity," I replied sardonically. "Don't you think that this makes them soft, complacent, and weak, thus decreasing their quality of life even while it increases their happiness?" My entry into this debate belied the utter lack of interest I had in this topic. What use were dream pods when every day creatures starved and choked to death on their own feces, unable to find the means to feed themselves? I was bored enough to play devil's advocate.

The pufferfish began to deflate, looking slightly disheartened. "Bu...bu...but happiness is the most im...im...important thi...thing in life," he said, a severe stutter appearing in his nervousness. "What young Tulin is trying to say," smoothly interjected Yutigo, "is that rulers should strive primarily to ensure the happiness of their subjects in whatever way they can. I, for one, think that these dream pods are a brilliant innovation." The Council broke into hushed conversations, many similarly inexperienced rulers trying to figure out the implications of Yutigo's endorsement. I knew better, however. Yutigo's beady black shark eyes bored straight into mine, and I felt rather than saw the slight disappointment they contained. Yutigo knew why I had tried to crush the pufferfish's confidence, and he did not approve. I stared back impassively, daring Yutigo to do something about it. He looked away first.

"I think the time has come for a vote on the dream pods," Yutigo announced. "All in favor of Phase Two rollout?" Many of the more experienced rulers sent a ball of green light into the air, signifying their approval, along with a smattering of younger ones near the far end of the table. "All against?" Yutigo asked again. The rest of the young rulers sent a ball of red light in the air, apparently fearing the consequences of giving too much power to one of their own, power they potentially still stood to gain.

Pointedly, I had not sent up a ball of light yet. Yutigo's gaze bored into me more insistently, disappointment morphing into traces of annoyance. I remained unperturbed. He knew exactly why I did what I did, and there was almost nothing he could do about it. "All those abstaining?" Yutigo said, his voice losing some of its lustrous qualities. I sent up my singular ball of yellow light, signifying my abstention despite my playing devil's advocate. "The proposal passes with 2,978 votes for to 2,293 votes against, with one abstention." Yutigo's fingertips lit up green and he placed them on the engraved surface of the table in front of him. A line connecting each seat around the table to the engraving Yutigo had touched lit up green, and the details of the passed proposal suddenly appeared in my mind. I dismissed them instantly.

I felt Yutigo staring at me again, but it felt different than it had the last two times in the meeting. Meeting his gaze, I was disturbed to see hints of vindictive glee dancing in the corners of his obsidian orbs. "Moving on to the main topic of discussion for today's meeting," Yutigo said, "the matter of Pierre Hartford's realm." I shot straight up in my chair, banging my head against the headboard of the chair as I did so. Through the sudden pain that pervaded my thoughts, I saw several half-smiles that were quickly hidden. Yutigo did not even go so far as to attempt to hide his smile, revealing row upon row of sharp, glistening teeth in his shark mouth, almost like a predator closing in on its prey. Now I understood why Yutigo had seemed so excited just now.

"I believe that we considered the matter of that particular

realm to be closed. *Forever*," I interjected, a hint of ice entering my voice for the first time all meeting.

Yutigo's smile widened. "Is that *passion* I hear in your voice, Rexdael? Is it possible that you are *interested* in the content of one of these…what did you call them? Oh yes. *Useless meetings.*"

Don't respond, I thought. *Anger will not do you any good. He's just trying to provoke you into reacting.*

"After all, had you decided to attend more meetings or even try to pay more attention," Yutigo added, "you would perhaps have noticed that several changes have been made regarding the status of Hartford's realm. Hartford is a figure imbued with dangerous power, and to let him run wild is akin to us committing suicide. I have recently received confirmation that he has indeed been reneging upon his responsibilities and that his realm has begun expanding into the wider multiverse."

A string of curses flew through my head, though my facial muscles did not twitch in the slightest. Of all the revelations I could have reasonably expected, this one was both the most surprising and the most distressing. An uncontrolled expansion of a realm meant only catastrophe. For every realm that said realm digested, a measure of sentience was gained. A realm that became fully sentient was uncontrollable, a monstrous creation driven entirely by its desire to feed, consume, and murder. The loss of life would be unimaginable. Yet…

"You know, Leader Yutigo, this seems to be an awfully convenient excuse," I replied after a slightly uncomfortable pause. "It is almost as if you are seeking a way to control a being who refuses to be controlled, a being who has never participated fully in the Council and will know nothing of any mandate to preserve order. After all, I remember it was you who so passionately argued against coercing Pierre into this Council after he had assumed power, despite making introductions. I believe you mentioned how ignorance is bliss, or something along those lines. So I ask you now: What proof do you have of this serious allegation, and are you willing to show it?"

Yutigo's teeth seemed to lose some of their pearly luster. "Now, Rexdael, of course I have this proof," he replied, "and you know that I am unable to simply toss around such sensitive information. Isn't it enough to believe that I have this evidence?"

"That would entail putting my faith in your word."

"Have I ever broken it?"

A chill descended across the room. I had my suspicions, but I had no proof to back them up. Yutigo was, if nothing else, scrupulous in covering the tracks leading to his lies and wrongdoing. Yutigo leaned back in his chair, seeming to patiently wait for an answer, though he knew none would be forthcoming. The frequency and severity of the curses in my head grew.

A jellyfish suddenly cleared her throat, tentacles wiggling about in the air. After a moment, I recognized her as Nuarti, another of the elders of the Council. Shockingly, despite my many transgressions with respect to the Council, no one had ever attempted to deprive me of my position as elder. "The Council should also take into consideration that this is not Pierre Hartford's first folly," Nuarti interjected, her even tone sounding as reasonable as always. "When he first fully came into his power, he broke the Fifth Law of the Council, which states that all realm creation must be done from scratch, without any basis in memory."

"He had special circumstances!" I retorted, my voice rising slightly. "None of the rest of us were sprung from a dream, used as a political tool, and forced to assume power in order to defeat their greatest foe! He is a boy of twenty-seven, when the youngest of us here is at least sixteen thousand! You cannot tell me that none of you ever did something that might be considered foolish at the age of twenty-seven!"

Nuarti's bell rippled and undulated, slowly bobbing up and down in an invisible current. "None of the rest of us grew into our power at twenty-seven, either, Rexdael," she replied, slightly apologetically. "He may still be a boy, yet we cannot treat him as such, not with forces he is capable of commanding with a single thought. His retreat into isolation is dangerous and, if Yutigo is correct, multiverse-threatening. We cannot sit here and do nothing. The Council was created to deal with such situations."

Though Nuarti was someone I held in high regard, I sometimes bemoaned her constant levelheadedness. Even the most offensive statements could be made to sound reasonable when spoken by Nuarti, and this only served to aid Yutigo. "Pierre was and still remains traumatized, even if he refuses to acknowledge it at the moment," I said, berating myself for the way my voice cracked on the word "traumatized." "He needs nurture and care, not the chains placed upon irresponsible maniacs! It is only expected that he makes mistakes when he is still so young! Yet all of you would still punish him? When all the evidence we have of a realm encroachment is Leader Yutigo's word? If you punish Pierre, you will snuff out a star shining bright with untapped potential and leave behind a shell filled only with bitter resentment."

"Ah," said Yutigo with a short laugh. "Of course you would step in to defend Hartford. One war criminal speaks in defense of another. You were lucky, but we cannot rely on luck when it comes to Hartford. There is too much at stake now."

"If I survived, then so will he."

"Yes, your process of survival almost involved the tearing in two of three realms. An immensely dangerous act."

"No one did anything to stop it."

"Only because there was no Council to do so. It is because of you, Rexdael, that we are sitting here. You consigned your-self to this 'miserable' chair through murder."

"Yet I still sit here today, whole and in one piece. The mul-tiverse continues to exist. If nothing else, I can help Pierre to overcome this with minimal disruption."

"What, only seven realms will be destroyed?"

"You overestimate his instability."

"His sanity is tied up in that ridiculous 'New Earth' he chooses to reside on as a 'human'! To heal him, that must go, and any predicted further actions are at this point products of ridiculous conjecture, but still on the whole they are likely to be catastrophic."

"You cannot make any ridiculous conjectures about a boy you have never met, either!"

"He is the tainted spawn of the Entity!"

"Don't paint him as a simple caricature!"

"That beast's consciousness is forever intertwined with Hartford's! No matter how far he runs, he cannot escape the past that is carved into his soul."

"He is the next step in the evolution of the Entity! An

empathetic being!"

"Emotions are weakness! Power is everything!"

"And that's what this is all about, isn't it? Despite everything, you feared the Entity, and now you wish to believe that you can still control Pierre, almost as if you hadn't learned your lessons from the first time!"

"You dare—"

"Enough!" interjected Nuarti. "None of us here is willing to tolerate this petty squabbling. Yutigo raises an interesting dilemma, however. Pierre Hartford is indeed a descendant of the Entity. All of you know as well as I do that the Entity, had he not been imprisoned by his own creations, sought a way to control a sentient realm. The Entity reveled in chaos and destruction, as all who have examined the probe-tapes of his final hours can attest to. We all know how close the Entity came to achieving controlled sentience. His assistants and the 'dream-hoppers' they created were the engines of that sentience. Through an incredible stroke of luck, we survived due to an unexpected mutation. Yet even these 'humans' still resort to petty infighting at least half of the time. Their moments of pure, overflowing goodness are few and far between.

"Pierre is obviously capable of immense greatness, as evidenced by his destruction of the Entity and his tainted realm. War criminal though he may be, his actions saved us from a far worse fate. Pierre, however, is also capable of immense foolishness. This shrinking away from the past that he is currently exhibiting is but one example of it. With the invaluable inheritance he has gained from the Entity, that is unacceptable. We all saw him create a new realm before our eyes! Untrained, he is already stronger than most of us put together. When he matures, he will be unstoppable, sentient realm or no. Until then, we cannot put our trust in his mercurial personality. One of his fits of rage could wipe out an entire pocket realm. That is unacceptable. I thereby propose we put limits upon his power until such time as we judge it fit to remove them."

I sank into my chair. My cause was hopeless. The battle was lost. Some might not trust Yutigo for being overtly political, but when Nuarti spoke, other rulers listened. Pierre's doom sounded as reasonable as taking a stroll in a garden for some fresh air. I had survived my ordeal only because I had been able to remain undisturbed throughout the entire process. At this moment in his cycle of depression, Pierre was a powder keg, and the rulers were on the brink of providing the spark to light it, spreading the inevitable shockwaves throughout the multiverse, doing exactly what they were attempting to prevent.

Yutigo no longer even attempted to hide his glee. "Well, I think the issue has been made clear enough," he announced, seemingly recovered from his shouting match with me. "All those in favor of Nuarti's proposal?" A sea of green greeted my eyes. "All those against?" Yutigo continued. My red orb seemed incredibly lonely in that immense Council room. "The proposal passes," Yutigo concluded, "with 5,271 votes for and one vote against. We will discuss at the next meeting what measures should be taken in order to best watch over and control Hartford's actions."

Without waiting for Yutigo to dismiss the rulers, I abruptly stood up, knocking my seat to the floor in the process, and marched over to the portal I conjured in front of me at the same moment. However, no matter what everyone else thought, I was not going home. Pierre had to be warned and helped before the Council could get to him. I was heading to New Earth.

2

FIRST CONTACT

Pierre Hartford, New Berlin, Europa, New Earth

When I woke up the next day, I felt a sense of grim foreboding. For some unfathomable reason, I felt a prickling sensation on the back of my neck, almost as if I were being watched at that very moment. But that was ridiculous! I was alone in my bedroom. The only thing that could possibly be "watching" me was my personal assistant, and I was long since attuned to its presence within this space.

I dismissed the feeling as an offshoot of the paranoia that Mr. Benton had induced in me yesterday. Talk about putting pressure on someone! What did he expect me to do with the new meteorite materials at the moment? Project Wandlung had barely begun initial testing, and project Entdeckung was even further back, still in the early planning stages. Mr. Benton was trusting me with more of his secrets, which was not necessarily a good thing. People close to Mr. Benton had a disturbing propensity to…disappear when things went awry. I feared that this would be my fate if I reported failure as well. Yes, that must be it, I concluded. This feeling was nothing out of the ordinary, merely an outward manifestation of my newest set of fears.

After being told that the weather today would be much nicer, with "sunny skies" expected all day, I began to feel even better. Such days usually signaled that someone working in the government had had a resounding success, resulting in the entire Europan Empire being blessed with beautiful weather, quite unlike the rain we had received the day before. It was a very good omen. When things really did begin to go awry later, though, I regretted having jinxed myself.

After taking my normal route to work, I headed to the secret elevator behind my office. This time, though, instead of heading to Conference Room Seven, I headed up, up to the highest level of the building. I was greeted by a glass wall that slid out of my way when I again pressed my palm against a specific part of it. Instead of being greeted by a relatively non-descript, ordinary conference room (apart, of course, from the fact that Mr. Benton had occupied that space as I had entered the previous day), I was greeted by a hulking mass of humming machinery.

Carefully making my way through the mass of spare parts and tools that littered the floor, I headed toward the control center set over a part of the floor notable for the deep scorch marks that crisscrossed its rough, mottled surface. This was the heart of project Wandlung. Shortly after Mr. Benton had purchased the new headquarters for Energieforschung, he had an incredible stroke of luck when what appeared to be a wormhole sprang into existence on the top floor of his new building. The distinctive energy signatures it left behind definitely indicated that it was beyond anything that human technology could have even created or imagined at that moment. Naturally, Mr. Benton immediately sent a team to study and attempt to replicate the event. I was now the fourteenth lead researcher Mr. Benton had assigned to this project. None of my predecessors had lasted more than three months, yet amazingly, I was now in my seventh month of leading the project, though I had made what I considered to be minimal progress. If this was more than what any of my predecessors had accomplished, I would have been truly shocked. It was a very simple matter to tease out the elements in the energy signature using a spectroscope. The really challenging part? Building a large enough particle accelerator in order to create our own "wormhole."

With that in mind, I headed over to one of the superconducting magnet arrays set in a circle around the room. I was attempting to initiate a proton-antiproton collision in order to generate an energy signature that I could use to compare to our mysterious energy signature, but the task was proving harder than expected. The magnetic field that we were generating with a strength of three teslas was fairly weak, but the proton-antiproton collision was still for some reason generating much less energy than I had predicted. In order to overcome this problem, I had to gradually increase the strength of the magnets in our particle accelerator, but I could only do this in small increments. No one wished to have an event as had occurred in the old CERN complex, where a scientist had atomized the countryside in a five-mile radius when he attempted to generate three simultaneous proton-antiproton collisions. It was frustrating work, and I could easily imagine why Mr. Benton had become impatient. Perhaps, though, the meteorite material that he had recently acquired could be of some use in augmenting the magnet arrays.

I snapped my fingers, and a hologram appeared in front of me. "What is required of me, Mr. Hartford?" inquired the robotic assistant. "I need a sample of the meteorites in Recent Acquisitions," I responded.

"One moment, please," was the only reply that I got. The hologram disappeared. About fifteen seconds later, an unmanned cart appeared in the elevator tube I had come up in, and it slowly trundled toward me after passing through the glass wall. A clear vial containing a baseball bat–sized chunk of metal that was horribly twisted and full of holes sat on top of the cart.

I sighed to myself, having forgotten the need for specificity when dealing with robots that could not completely understand the nuances of the human language yet. "I need a clean sample," I told the robotic assistant, "not this twisted, ruined mess." No response came from the robot as the cart turned around and began heading toward the forging press and lathe adjacent to the control center. A hiss, a few grinding noises, and a multitude of sparks later, the cart returned bearing a shiny tube close in size to a sheet of rolled-up paper. I took it, barely registering the cart disappearing into the elevator tube behind me. Slowly, I picked up a screwdriver and began unscrewing one of the empty magnet casings in the center of the array. When the casing, held in place by magnetic screws, ironically enough, came loose, I picked it up and took the top off. After carefully placing my meteorite sample inside and ensuring that it was securely held in place, I reinserted it into the array.

At that moment, however, a low humming caught my attention. But there should not have been any humming noises yet, for I had not booted up any of the equipment besides the control center and the measuring devices. I turned to the control center and was shocked to see that it was indeed the measuring devices that were making the low humming noise. Even more shockingly, the readings I was getting were off the scale, which indicated that another event was occurring right at this moment, and luckily enough (or not), I was going to be around to witness it. The measuring devices chose that moment to make one last reading and then give out with a spark, the energy levels overwhelming their sensitive apparatuses.

The low prickling that I had felt upon waking this morning returned with a sudden fury, and waves of dread began to wash over me. Something terrible was coming through that gate, something that I could never in a million years face, alone or with friends and allies. A terrible, powerful being was about to arrive, and I sensed that my entire life was going to turn upside down, any semblance of order I had created up to this point disappearing completely. Would I ever see Max, Robert, and Luka again? My parents? Or would I be left here, a shattered, broken body marking the beginning of a path of destruction?

My thoughts were distracted when the control center gave a beep and the particle accelerator somehow began to turn on. Yet another thing that should not have been possible, given that it was not even plugged in. Should I have been surprised at this point, though? I could almost see the energy, thick waves roiling the air around the control center. I could taste it too: a thick, slimy sensation tickling my tongue and leaving a tangy aftertaste. Just in the nick of time, I remembered to engage my personal magnetic field. Glad that I had chosen to wear it just in case I ever did accidentally leave a ferromagnetic object in my office, now I was at least safe from being stuck to one of the magnetic arrays. My personal magnetic field would vary depending upon external magnetic influences to prevent me from being pushed or pulled in one direction or the other.

I felt the magnets engaging, and with a deep groan that I felt through my rib cage, a humongous energy portal opened itself right next to the control center. I wasn't sure if this event was similar to the one we had recorded earlier, but I was positive that it was much, much stronger. It was a relatively small circle but covered in a layer of shimmering energy. Random tendrils of it continuously flared out and then receded into the rest of the circle. With a cascading shower of sparks, the control center blew itself to pieces as the energy portal expanded in size. Luckily, my personal magnetic field protected me from flying metal debris as well, subtly bending the trajectories of the shards that flew toward me in other directions.

To my horror, though, a series of horrifying screeching noises emanated from all corners of the room as the magnet arrays chose that moment to wrench themselves free of their sockets and fly toward the energy portal, their disappearance marked by the portal briefly flaring and expanding in size, before settling down once more. Now, a deep booming noise emanated from the portal, and the entire room vibrated as if struck by a gong. The energy began to flare even more erratically than before, and the entire portal began to shudder. I sensed instinctively that now was when the being I had been expecting would come through.

To my surprise, however, instead of something appearing, the portal chose that moment to blast itself apart, and a wave of energy caught me and threw me backward. Though my magnetic field had not been able to stop the blast of energy from affecting me, it did at least ensure me a soft landing and injuries no worse than bruising. My eyes were suddenly dazzled by waves of color that accompanied the dissipation of the portal, and for a few moments, I saw nothing but some indistinctly blurry shapes. As the room slowly came back into focus, however, I saw that there was indeed something standing where the portal had been.

For an extraterrestrial traveler, the figure that I saw looked remarkably...*ordinary*. If I hadn't known better, I would have mistaken it for a regular human being. There was nothing that marked this figure as out of the ordinary. It was thin and slender, dressed in an all-black suit. Perhaps the attire was somewhat odd, but not unusual for funeralgoers these days. At that moment, the figure raised its head, and I was even more surprised to see a human face staring back. It was a very regal, symmetric face, a pair of green eyes set into a lightly tanned face, framed by a mop of red hair that made the green eyes sparkle like emeralds. It was the disturbingly symmetric face of a king, a leader, reminding me of someone I had seen in the past...but try as I might, I could not remember *who* it had been for the life of me. How odd.

My eyes were suddenly flooded with double images of the

figure, almost as if it were no longer in focus. What was going on? Now it looked as if there were hundreds of the same figure scattered all across the room, some more distinct than others, but all clearly the same figure. As my eyes struggled to focus, they suddenly were drawn to a spot immediately to the left of me. Instantly the figures began to collapse upon themselves and disappear, all merging back into one figure. The figure now stood exactly at the spot my eye had just been drawn to, without showing any indication of having changed its posture or having moved at all. Definitely extraterrestrial, I thought. I had never seen anything like *that* before. I wasn't even sure if I could adequately describe it.

Before I could react, the figure raised its hand and laid a finger against my left temple. At first nothing seemed to happen, but when I tried to pull myself away, I couldn't. It felt as if the finger had in a matter of moments managed to weld itself to my left temple. A wave of pain rushed through my skull as the weight of twenty-three years' worth of memories were suddenly dumped back into my brain.

I found myself in some sort of throne room. How in the world had I managed to come here? I was positive that I hadn't traveled at all, and this definitely wasn't an illusion, or if it were, it was extremely accurate. My senses were all functioning fine, and I could sense nothing out of the ordinary. But I found myself rooted to the spot. Try as I might, I was a dispassionate observer.

When I saw myself running into the throne room, however, looking six years younger, I began to understand. This was one of the memories that I had just recently regained. When I saw Karl, Yuri, my mother, and Dad enter as well and the sounds of a raging battle began to reach me, I realized which memory I was viewing. This was the day that I had defeated the...the...what was his name again? Something pompous and overbearing. Oh yes! *The Entity*. This was the day that I had defeated the Entity. Now the bigger question was: Why had this memory come to the forefront of my mind? Why this memory *specifically*?

I flinched as I saw Karl sacrifice himself and Dad take the Entity's staff in the chest for me. A wave of happiness pulsed through me as the Entity fell to his own hubris and the power of the throne allowed me to defeat him once and for all. However, as I began to destroy the Entity's realm, the memory suddenly shifted. This hadn't been what happened next! What was going on?

Suddenly I found myself back on the streets of Eb Province, where I had first appeared with Karl and Yuri. I was even in the same square where we had been first accosted by our fellow "dream-hoppers." This time, though, instead of insults being hurled at me, or being the center of attention, every creature's attention was fixed on the sky. I looked up, coincidentally in the direction of the palace. I saw quite a spectacle. The sky in the area near the palace was rapidly turning blood-red, and this phenomenon was headed in our direction.

To my horror, as this red sky came ever closer, I began to hear faint crackling and popping sounds, and the smell of burned flesh reached my nose. Was this what I had set in motion? This horror show was what I had subjected these creatures to when I had decided that the best course of action was to destroy this realm? I felt sick to my stomach.

When the red sky was only a few miles away, the sounds

of horrifying screams reached me as well. The sound of death. This was what my decision had created. Knowing that this was a memory, however, and that there was nothing I could do about it, waves of guilt began to wash over me instead. How could I have done this? Was I just as much of a monster as the Entity had been? Who else would cause so much horrifying, tortuous loss of life?

The red sky was now only a few blocks away, and the wave of flame was now within sight. I felt the air around us visibly heat up. The creatures suddenly looked away from the sky, then at each other. Without another word, they began to run as a single coherent mass, their sole goal to get as far away from the flames as possible. Unfortunately for them, it seemed futile. It was quickly apparent to me that this wall of flame moved much faster than these creatures ever could. For a moment, I thought about joining them, but quickly gave that up as I discovered that I remained rooted to the ground.

The flames had reached the square now, licking at the creatures at the back of the mass attempting to flee. Up close and personal, the screams were worse. Many of the wire creatures gave a single piercing screech as their limbs began to droop and fall off, the screech slowly dying away as they turned into small, pitiful-looking puddles of metal. The creatures who looked as if globs of flesh were falling off bodies fared worse. Now their flesh really began to fall off, and they screamed as their bodies became piles of mush. As for the worm creatures? They had no time to even scream. When the flames reached them, they almost instantly became charred and black, falling to the street as flakes of ash.

Then, the flames reached me. The pain felt even worse

than it had looked or sounded. I screamed and screamed and screamed, more than I ever had before as my skin melted away. I continued to scream as I woke up and saw the room where the portal had appeared again. Waves of energy similar to the portal's were radiating off my skin, even stronger than the portal's. The entire room seemed to shake, and I felt tremors beneath my feet. In that moment, the glass wall in front of the elevator tube shattered into millions of tiny fragments.

A hand gripped my shoulder. Instantly, I felt the power disappearing back into me, pulling back into my core. Within moments, the room had stopped shaking and the tremors had stopped. So had my screaming. I took deep, calming breaths and looked to my left. The green eyes of the figure stared back. "Hello, Pierre," he (?) said, his voice a soft tenor that calmed my nerves even more. "My name is Rexdael."

3

NASTY NIGHTMARES

Lili Schwebler, New Berlin, Europa, New Earth, 2069 (four years earlier)

It was the screams that woke me up yet again. Not the tremors, not the air that smelled of thunderstorms, not even the showers of sparks that sporadically appeared around my bedroom. I was long since inured to those. The screams should have lost their potency, for they were as much part of the environment as all the other phenomena. But there was something about those screams that grabbed my attention. Maybe it was their bloodcurdling pitch, the undertones of desperation, hopelessness, and guilt that they carried. Or maybe it was my maternal instincts, unable to bear the sound of my son screaming in such obvious and agonizing pain, roused all the more due to my inability to provide much, if any, help of substance.

An earsplitting crack snapped me out of my thoughts. *That*

was new. I peered over the side of the bed to now see a six-inch gap gouged into the floor where there had once been a smooth surface of cherrywood. What was more, a stream of multicolored lights poured out of this hole. Yuri stirred next to me, presumably woken up by the cracking of the floor. He muttered something under his breath that I didn't catch. "It's worse this time," he uttered simply. I nodded in response, slipping out of the sheets and carefully stepping onto the floor a fair distance away from the crack. "I'll go and see if there's anything at all I can do," I said, failing to completely keep the note of despair out of my voice.

There was a sudden creak of bedsprings as Yuri rolled over to look at me. "I know," he replied, unspoken words hanging in the air, and I knew that had I been able to see his eyes in that moment, I would have seen my pain reflected in them, the pain of being too ignorant and weak to help.

I opened the door and walked out into the hallway. Here, the destructive vortex being caused by Pierre was much more obvious. A small cloud of dust and wood splinters swirled around his bedroom door, and the very air seemed to shimmer and distort. Slowly inching my way closer, taking care to avoid being hit by a stray piece of debris, I realized that, to my horror, Pierre's screams were not the mere cries of anguish I had first taken them for. This time, I could very audibly make out words being spoken. "I DID THE VERY BEST I COULD! DON'T YOU SEE THAT THERE WAS NO OTHER CHOICE?" screamed Pierre. Then, he gasped deeply, and the center of the doorframe visibly buckled. "*Murderer!*" screamed Pierre, but this time, his voice had dropped about two octaves. I stopped in my tracks. I vaguely recognized that voice. But it couldn't be…

"You killed them! You killed the innocent, defenseless victims of the Entity! If that is what I had known you would do with my sacrifice, I would never have taken that damn staff for you! Even that stemmed from your stupidity and incompetence. If only you had been the slightest bit faster, I would still be here!" Pierre continued. A shard of wood whizzed by me, and I was so shocked that I let it graze my cheek. Hissing in pain, I reflexively raised my hand and healed the cut that had opened up. That had been Will's voice, or at least a pale, horribly distorted imitation of it. This had to be a very bad nightmare indeed. Never before had Pierre spoken during these episodes, let alone in the voices of the recently deceased.

Conjuring a repulsive shield in front of me, thankful that I still had my abilities, I entered Pierre's bedroom. The sight of Pierre lying spread-eagled on his bed greeted me. His limbs were stiff, energy pouring out of every extremity and coiling around him and the room in the form of thin, glowing red lines. It was clear that this was the only reason the house, up to this moment, had not blown itself apart. His mouth was open wide, his jaw muscles straining as he screamed, sweat pouring down his neck. I took a step closer, only to once again come to a standstill as Pierre gasped yet again. Even through my shield, I felt a yank on my center, and it took all my willpower to not simply stagger forward. *"I burned myself for you,"* screamed Pierre, this time in a third voice, harsh and grating. *"I committed the ultimate sacrifice for you, giving up the time with my loved ones so that you would win! But this…what do you call this? This is not victory! This is a mere shadow of what could have been, a laughable parody! Those whose lives you so callously snuffed out are the ones who really should be here. If you had had the strength of will to follow my example and sacrifice yourself in the name of purity, your tortured soul would be at peace! You weakling! They trusted their lives to you, and you took that trust, drove it into the ground, and stamped on it for good measure! With some sense, you would have long since done the right thing and died!"*

A tear rolled down my cheek. Karl...oh, how I missed him. Though it had been two years, the pain of his loss had yet to dull. I only held it in check by keeping myself busy enough to not think about it. Hearing something akin to his voice only brought the pain back that much harder. But the words spoken in his voice...they were like nothing I had ever heard him say before. This was most definitely a product of Pierre's imagination, and to see it manifest itself in such a way was disturbing to say the least. I had to pull Pierre out of this before he caused himself and his realm irreparable damage.

I moved until I stood over Pierre's head. Staring into his eyes was an unnerving experience. Though they were wide open, his eyes were black as obsidian, the whites not visible. What was more, flickers of a malevolent-looking flame were visible in the corners of his eyes. Steeling myself, I sent out a mental probe, attempting to interface with Pierre's mind. To my surprise, my probe ran headlong into an impermeable wall of steel. Normally, because of my close familial relationship to Pierre, it should have been a matter of mere seconds for me to enter his mind, invited or not. Now, however, the message was clear. Pierre's mind was in such distress that it had cut off all outside contact.

Focusing on my feelings of love, concern, and pain regarding Pierre, I cautiously sent my mental probe forward again. This time, though I was again met with the same level of resistance, I did not immediately bounce off Pierre's mental defenses. Taking this as a good sign, I focused harder on my emotions. A small chink appeared, and I pressed forward hoping to take advantage. Gradually, the chink widened into a gaping hole, and I sent my probe past Pierre's defenses.

This seemed to be all that he had needed, for Pierre suddenly gasped, his screams abruptly cutting off, and he blinked once, deeply. When his eyes opened again, they once again looked relatively normal. He was still not completely awake though, as his gaze remained unfocused. I gave another push with my probe. With another gasp, Pierre sat up straight, awareness returning to his eyes. The layer of energy that had been coiling around his body and the room discharged in every possible direction. The room and presumably the rest of the house became a cloud of plaster dust and splinters as a red corona of energy arced upward, a beacon probably visible across the globe. Distractedly, I noted Yuri's muffled shout as he presumably had to avoid some falling debris.

Pierre took several deep, calming breaths, his wheezing resembling the sound of a sprinter after running several miles. Looking around, his lips pursed as he took in the scope of the destruction he had caused. He raised his left hand. The cloud of plaster dust that had been swirling around him stopped, individual particles simply hovering in space, and I knew that time had not frozen just in this bedroom, but for every piece of debris and person beyond its walls as well. Pierre jerked his hand in the counterclockwise direction. The wood splinters and plaster debris rapidly reassembled themselves back into the walls, floor, ceiling, and doors they had been in before Pierre's discharge. Yet Pierre was not satisfied. His electric blue eyes were dull, shadowed by the immense guilt he carried. "It seems the only dead I can resurrect are the vengeful spirits of my own past," he muttered under his breath, seemingly forgetting for a moment that I was close enough to hear even his whispers.

"They got worse, didn't they?" I asked. Pierre looked up, seeming to notice me for the first time. He nodded in response, unable to say anything. "What happened?" I continued. "The voices…were they…?"

"Yes," Pierre responded, his voice hoarse and brittle with strain. "The dream started off normally. The throne room battle, the destruction of the realm, being a helpless bystander to my own destruction. But then, Will and Karl showed up. I assume some of what transpired came into the real world then, if you heard voices. It was…horrible. I…I don't want to ever have to see that ag…again." His voice trembled, and his lower lip began to quiver. Then, the tears started falling, and he put his head in his hands, upper body shaking from the force of his sobs.

I took him in my arms and simply held him for a few seconds, shaking slightly from his sobs. "Oh, sweetheart," I sighed gently. "My beautiful, darling son. Your pain…I know it all too well. I have lost loved ones before, killed the innocent, burdened myself with guilt and shame. It takes real strength to be able to pull through and not let yourself wallow in despair. The pain…it never really goes away, but accepting it and keeping yourself busy with other matters will help.

"One thing, however, you must let go of. I knew Will and…Will and Karl for many years, as long as and longer than you did. I knew them well enough to be sure they would never have said the hurtful things which you attributed to them in your nightmare." Pierre shuddered suddenly. "No, they would not have blamed you!" I repeated, stronger than before. "They knew what they were sacrificing for, what the Entity had created. Those creatures, they did not put their lives in your hands. Many of them would not have even known what you were fighting for or what you were about to do! And look at what you have created. A better society, capable if need be of running this and every other world in this realm independently and self-sufficiently. You took Karl's goals, refined them, and pursued them to their idealistic end. Were the people of Earth ever this happy in your dream? Were the dream-hoppers? There was no other way to cleanse the Entity's corruption! Blame yourself for their deaths if you must, but do not let Will and…Karl denigrate you so! You are twenty-three years old, and you have accomplished more in one lifetime than most could in many! You accomplished your task to the best of your ability. I am proud of what you have created, and you should be too."

Pierre suddenly wrenched himself free of my arms. "Proud!" he scoffed venomously. "Yes, I suppose I can be proud of my asylum. This is my self-created prison, my *therapy*, created to ease my *damaged* mind. But have I really done any healing at all? Look at me! Every night, without fail, I blow up at least one room of this house, and no amount of putting it back together can erase the memories from my mind. For two years I've been trapped in this place! I haven't done a single productive thing. I eat, I drink, I sleep, I scream, and I go on the roof to look upon the oblivious people that I created! And tonight…well, let's not even get started. Tonight it was worse!

Dammit, I killed seven people! Seven more deaths. Of all the things the Entity could do, the one he thing he did not possess was power over Life and Death. People's bodies can be healed, but their souls…those are gone forever. This cannot happen again."

"Pierre," came Yuri's voice from the doorway, a low growl. Somehow he had appeared there without either Pierre or me noticing. "Stop blaming yourself for this. Everyone makes mistakes. We learn from them. Look at my…illustrious past. Some things, despite all the power we may or may not possess, cannot be undone. The sooner you accept that, the sooner your mistakes will cease to define your every waking moment."

"BUT DO YOU REALLY KNOW HOW IT FEELS, YURI?" Pierre yelled. "I CAN'T AFFORD TO MAKE A MISTAKE BECAUSE THERE IS TOO MUCH AT STAKE WHEN I DO! I LOSE MY COMPOSURE, AND PEOPLE DIE!" He took another deep, shuddering breath. "For all of your faults, Yuri, you never did commit a genocide." Yuri's face darkened, and his eyes grew misty as he muttered something that sounded like "gypsies" under his breath. Luckily, Pierre didn't seem to notice.

"No," he continued, his voice growing dangerously soft. "This cannot go on. Every night, I see more and more of them die, relive their deaths though I was never present for them. If this goes on, I will go insane or destroy everything I've created, whichever comes first. No, something must be done." He began to pace up and down the room, continuing to mutter to himself as he did so. "I must forget, and in order to forget, I must lose these painful memories and anything associated with them."

Pierre straightened up, looking directly at me. "Please," he said, "I need you and Yuri to leave the room."

"Pierre, what are you thinking of doing?" I asked, slightly alarmed at his change in behavior.

"Just go," he responded, almost pleading in desperation. "I will scream once more, and then never again. Never. I will fix this problem."

"Pierre..." My voice trailed off. "Please, tell us what you're thinking."

Pierre's eyes were still dull, but deep within I could see the spark of determination now. "You said it yourself, didn't you, Mom?" he said in response. "I have created an independent and self-sufficient realm. This realm doesn't need me to run it. My existence will only continue to endanger it. Instead, I will end it. My memories and my powers I will lock away, never to be seen or used again. I will become an ordinary citizen, with an ordinary life, an ordinary job, and ordinary friends. I will become one with my creation."

"Pierre," Yuri said warningly. "Forgetting does not solve the fundamental issue here. You cannot run away from your problems. Face them."

"*That's what I've been doing for two years,*" Pierre hissed, "*and look how well this little experiment has turned out. I've made negative progress in solving my problems. I haven't fixed anything, I've only made them worse. Tonight, it was seven people. Tomorrow, it could be hundreds, thousands, millions! I will **not** have any more lives on my conscience.*"

Yuri opened his mouth, presumably intent on saying more, but I pulled him back, looking at him warningly. "Don't try to stop him," I whispered. "It will only make things worse in the end." Gradually, Yuri relaxed, pulling back. "Fine," was all the response I got.

"Good luck, sweetheart," I said softly. "I hope this is for the best."

Pierre nodded solemnly. "It will be," he said definitively. "I just want...need to *forget*. This is the easiest way." He turned away, and I walked out of his bedroom, Yuri trailing behind me, the door swiftly closing behind us.

As soon as we made it to the kitchen downstairs, a low humming became audible. There was a short, high scream, followed by a deep boom and a shaking of the entire house. Then we heard no more. "It's over," I said, looking at Yuri.

"This is a mistake, Lili," he replied. "This isn't dealing with his problems—it's enchaining them. He'll be better, at least for now. But if they ever escape, they will be worse than ever. And then everything he built will really be at stake."

"Can you deny the truth in his words though, Yuri?" I retorted. "We've tried healing him in the typical way, but Pierre has never been what one would call typical. None of us have. Maybe locking away his memories and powers is for the best. I'm sure that he can construct an impenetrable prison for himself if he really wants it, and he really does seem to. If the situation ever changes...well, then we'll look into having him face these fears again."

"Agreed," replied Yuri. "Though I don't like it, nothing Pierre said wasn't true. We can't rely on his healing the traditional way. But as soon as anything changes, he *will* face this. I refuse to accept it any other way. Now, let's go back to bed and try to catch a few more hours of sleep." Kissing me lightly, he walked toward the stairwell and back to our bedroom. I followed a few steps behind, both of us failing to notice the sudden glowing light that the freezer was giving off.

Lili Schwebler, New Berlin, Europa, New Earth, 2073 (the present day)

I was happily humming to myself, reading the newspaper and eating a late-morning snack of nuts. It had been a normal day in all respects up to this point. It was even sunny out, meaning that there was bound to be good news for everyone. The memory of Pierre and his nightmares had had four years to fade. Everyone was happy and productive.

Suddenly sensing danger, however, I quickly shoved my chair back from the table several inches, and not a moment too soon. A metal ball materialized out of nowhere and fell to the floor with a heavy clang. Yuri stuck his head out of the adjacent room. "What in the world was that?" he asked. "No idea," I replied. Hesitantly, I reached my hand out to touch the ball. Nothing happened at first, but then, the image of a being with the head of a shark filled my head. I gasped in distress.

"Lili?" Yuri asked, concerned. "What is it?"

"Pierre's in trouble."

4

AN UNCANNY GHOST OF THE PAST

Pierre Hartford, New Berlin, Europa, New Earth, 2073

Rexdael (at least, that was what I had heard him introduce himself as) continued standing over me, saying nothing, doing nothing after his introduction. His green eyes stared into mine, not in a hostile manner, but somewhere between mild interest and indifference. Though this was done so calmly, I could not help but feel that Rexdael was searching for something in me, that his seemingly relaxed gaze masked a deeper desire to confirm a suspicion he may have harbored about me. Quite suddenly, Rexdael turned away, looking at a far corner of the room. I thought I caught a haunted look flicker across his eyes before he could turn away.

"Rexdael," I said slowly, swirling the name about in my mouth, particularly the second syllable, attempting to emulate the unfamiliar intonation with which Rexdael had spoken his name. He turned back to look at me, the haunted look I had caught before having disappeared. "I don't suppose you could explain to me why my head feels as if it's been kicked by a galloping horse?" Rexdael laughed slightly at that. "Pierre," he replied in his soft tenor. "Would you believe me if I told you that you yourself had blocked off twenty-one years of your real memories and that this raging headache you so eloquently described is the aftereffect of me punching through your self-imposed mental block?"

I looked at Rexdael in shock. It was not just his words I found disturbing, but something about his mannerisms, his way of speaking, his tone as well. Something was just a bit...*off*. "Why would I ever willingly block off so many of my memories?" I asked Rexdael. "Why would I shy away from the past like that?"

"You just experienced firsthand exactly the type of thing you were trying to prevent in blocking your memories," replied Rexdael calmly. "That realistic nightmare you were experiencing...yes, I do have my ways of knowing what it was," he added in reply to my raised eyebrow. "That realistic nightmare was the most obvious manifestation of your post-traumatic stress. You saw the amount of energy you were giving up when you came to again, didn't you? If I weren't here to help you, that energy would have overloaded you and been released in a humongous high-energy burst, vaporizing this complex and most of Alexanderplatz to boot."

Now that Rexdael had mentioned it...I did remember a lot of nightmares, episodes where only Lili could wake me, where I had many times over reduced the house to plaster and splinters. I had killed people once, and in the short time I had dealt with that before blocking off my memories, I could remember their voices adding themselves to the trillions already present.

There was one voice in my head for every human, creature, or being I had personally killed or for whose deaths I had been primarily responsible. It had started soon after the Entity had been defeated. I had always understood, even from the very beginning, that what I was doing was morally correct, yet simultaneously deeply immoral. The first few hectic weeks after I had created a new realm were filled with logistical issues, setting up the administrative apparatus, allowing my mental creations limited degrees of freedom so that they could self-govern but not to the point where they could think of rebellion, creating proper food delivery, sewage, and job creation systems that could self-propagate. It was only when I finally had a brief reprieve from all the work that my mind turned to the events that had caused the need for me to think about all these logistical aspects of running a realm in the first place. Though I was now functionally immortal, that did not mean I no longer required any relaxation or sleep in order to function properly. My tired mind, given the chance to relax, had, of course, instead of gleefully taking advantage of the opportunity given it, subtly betrayed me, turning to the only issues more troubling than realm logistics.

Thinking of the dead dream-hoppers had done it. The words *dream-hoppers* had barely flitted through my mind when a hissing sounded near my left ear. It was one word, but that word was enough to irrevocably change the trajectory of the next two years. *Murderer*, it hissed, over and over like a broken record, the tone a mixture of derision and schadenfreude. *Butcher*, came a second voice near my right ear, joining the first.

Other voices came to join them, quicker and quicker until I could no longer make out individual words most of the time and was instead treated to a macabre chorus of hisses, susurrations that sounded not only sinister but also malicious. *Devourer of souls*, hissed a voice. *Killer of the innocent and defenseless*, murmured another. Initially, the voices went away when I threw myself with increased vigor into the administrative tasks of my realm, but they returned with a renewed vengeance when I was forced to collapse in exhaustion, unable to even contemplate working a minute more. Soon, the voices were my ubiquitous companion, even during my work. They penetrated my dreams, my most intimate conversations with my mother and Yuri, my ruminations on plans for social improvement of the realm.

I knew deep down, deep in my rational core, that the voices were not real, that they were in my head, and that they were merely the largest and most obvious manifestations of the guilt, anger, and sorrow I felt, the feelings that I had buried so deep in order to continue functioning in a productive manner. But it was not limited to voices either. At least once, while masquerading as an ordinary citizen, I had turned to look at a human on the streets of New Earth only to see a grinning corpse smiling back at me, liquid flesh marring the brilliant white surface of bone, blood dripping to the ground, little splotches of deep red color that sizzled as they made contact with the ground because of the heat. It was a wonder that my screams hadn't roused the whole city block.

"Yes...," I said slowly, knowing that Rexdael clearly saw the weight of traumatic memories behind my eyes. "I do think I understand exactly why I blocked off my memories. Why twenty-one years, though? It seems...excessive."

"Correct me if this seems wrong to you," replied Rexdael, "but I believe the triggers for your trauma encompassed not only the events concerning the Entity but also the deaths and sacrifices of your loved ones, especially your father and Karl von Liebnitz. It was thus necessary for you to remove any memories you had concerning these individuals, down to the point where even your mother or Yuri Klatschnikov mentioning these individuals by accident in your presence would not trigger another episode." Even as Rexdael spoke, my headache was fading, and I realized that it felt as if a great burden was slipping off my brain. The weight of twenty-one years' worth of false memories slipped through my fingers like so many grains of sand even as I tried to grab at them. A hometown here, a grandparent there...only bits and pieces remained coherent enough for me to even make sense of, and they, too, slipped away as I tried to look closer.

"Yes," I mused, "it's all starting to make sense now. I did experience everything you mentioned, and I did what I did for the reasons you have so accurately listed. It's just as if I had forgotten them for the moment...ironic, I know." Rexdael smiled wryly. "Funny, isn't it, how these sorts of things tend to turn out," he said. "Your mind will probably need to take a few hours in order to re-sort the memories you have just had forced upon yourself so violently, but your powers should be available to you now, especially if you're put under duress."

I waved my hand at the glass wall that had shattered earlier. The power, eager as a newborn that had desperately been seeking attention, surged through me, exuberantly welcoming back the master it had thought gone, perhaps forever, for four years.

The shards of the glass wall gathered themselves, sprung back together, but before I could halt the flow of power, the glass wall began to *grow*. A vein of glass snaked along the ceiling and was almost halfway to where Rexdael and I were before I was able to get a handle on my power again and cut off the flow going to the wall. Now unbalanced by the vein stretching prominently in one direction, the glass wall shivered, buckled, and tipped over, promptly shattering once more. "Yes, I should have perhaps mentioned that," said Rexdael offhandedly. "It seems your powers have grown in your absence. Not surprising, given your potential. Try not to do too much too quickly, or your power might just lead you to kill yourself from exhaustion. Enough talk, though. Come, we must go somewhere safer."

"Wait just a moment," I interjected. "Are you not even going to tell me who you are? I'm not in the business of letting myself be carted away by strange men. Who, or perhaps *what* are you? Why are you here? And just what is going on so that I could possibly be in danger?"

Rexdael had begun walking away even before he had finished speaking, but now he turned to look back, an incredulous look coming across his fine features. "*Why?*" he asked, slightly slowly. "I'll be very generous and assume that not all of your most noteworthy memories have returned to the forefront of your mind yet. Four words: Yutigo, Council of Realms. If that doesn't ring a bell for you, then it is quite obvious that I did not restore your memory as well as I believed I had." This last was said somewhat sardonically.

Yutigo...the name was familiar, brushing against the edge of my consciousness. I wasn't sure if I would have made the connection, though, if Rexdael hadn't mentioned the Council of Realms as well. Yes, Yutigo was the head of that…governing body. The few moments I had spent in that room had been some of the most disquieting since I had created my own realm.

It had been a few months before I had decided it was time to block off my memories. I had been mulling over the planetary weather control systems in my head, attempting to come up with an algorithm that would accurately simulate what I deemed a healthy mixture of sunny, cloudy, rainy, snowy, and other days (a surprisingly difficult task, especially when not every planet I wanted to create was amenable to Earth-like conditions), when a metal sphere had appeared out of nowhere in front of me. Without a second thought, my hand shot out to my left, catching the sphere about a foot and a half above the floor. Instantly, my mind's eye was filled with a thoroughly repulsive image. A…creature, or most likely a being masquerading as a creature, with the eyes and ears of a husky, the facial structure of a gorilla, and the snout of a crocodile began to speak to me.

"Pierre Hartford," began a sonorous voice that somehow managed to completely subvert my expectations for what the voice of such a creature should sound like, "your presence is hereby requested at the next meeting of the Council of Realms in order to formally welcome you to the ranks of the realm rulers. This is not an optional request; should you not appear, your realm ruler rights will be repealed effective immediately, and you will be exposed to the wrath of the realm elders. As you have not before attended our meetings, the coordinates of the pocket universe in which we meet have been imprinted upon the memory core of the sphere. Simply press your thumb against the sphere, and the coordinates will be automatically beamed to your head. The pressing of your thumb also signals an implicit oath to not reveal these coordinates, should any of your creations ever be able to interpret and travel to them in the future. This is punishable by death. Naturally, this message will also self-destruct ten seconds after this recording has been viewed by you. The Council looks forward to your imminent arrival, Pierre."

Somewhat dazedly, I pressed my thumb into the sphere, and a set of coordinates flashed directly in front of my pupils, leaving me blinking away spots in their aftermath. True to form, exactly ten seconds after I had finished viewing the message and receiving the coordinates, the sphere suddenly grew much hotter. Reflexively, even though I could easily make myself heat resistant, I dropped the sphere, only to watch its metallic core glow, melting the outer shell and sucking it into something that vaguely resembled a miniature black hole. As the final remnants of the sphere disappeared, I opened a gateway in front of me to the coordinates I had newly learned. Though I had my misgivings concerning the purpose of this Council, I did not doubt that the husky-gorilla-crocodile and his fellow "realm rulers" (I presumed they were beings similar to what I had become) possessed the power to follow through on the threat contained in their message. Both the methods of delivery and destruction had convinced me of the authenticity of these beings. No powers besides those resembling my own could have created something akin to that sphere.

Given that it was my first time traveling to the gathering place of the Council, I was not surprised that, despite the meticulously precise coordinates I had been provided with, the aim of my gateway was slightly off. I stepped out of my gateway and almost immediately had to avoid a near-collision with a heavy wooden chair. Steadying myself, holding onto the high back of that same chair, I looked up toward a chair that was even bigger than the rest of the chairs gathered around a giant table that seemed to be made out of the same metal as the sphere. The husky-gorilla-crocodile I had seen in the message stared back at me. It began to smile, then seemed to think better of it as it considered the rows of razor-sharp teeth in its long snout. "Welcome, Pierre Hartford," it (he?—the voice was most definitely male, and soothing at that) said. "My name is Yutigo. I am the leader of this Council of Realms, and on behalf of the entire Council, I welcome you to our table."

Not a single head in the menagerie of disgusting animal hybrids even turned a single inch to look at me. Except one. The ruler whose chair I had almost stumbled into turned around quite rapidly. The face of a tiger, initially tinted by shock, soon became marred by anger, though I could tell it was not directed at me. Even in feline form, the ruler's eyes were penetrating, calculating, and, as they perhaps always did, carried a slightly haunted look. In retrospect, I knew this to be Rexdael. One of Yutigo's ears twitched slightly, the only sign he gave that he was even aware of Rexdael's movements. Slowly, Rexdael turned back to Yutigo, and the tension, rather than draining out of the room, seemed to ratchet up a bit more. Disconcerted, I prepared to speak.

"Hello," I said cautiously. Yutigo's smile became slightly wooden. "Ah, ah, ah," he replied, somehow managing to click his elongated tongue as he did so. "At Council sessions, rulers do not speak unless they are an elder of the Council or have been given permission to speak by an elder. I will let it slide this time, since you did not learn the rules just yet, but you are now warned for the future." That helped to explain the slightly muggy atmosphere I felt despite the presence of what I estimated were a couple of thousand rulers. I was impressed. I had never thought that so many realms, perhaps even vaster than mine, even existed.

"Anyway," Yutigo continued, "on to business. To confirm that you acknowledge the power of the Council, I'll need you to hold out your hand." I did so hesitantly, wondering how Yutigo would be able to reach my hand from a distance of around ten feet. I suppose I shouldn't have been surprised, however, that when Yutigo raised his arm, it suddenly became quite elongated, his hand almost touching, one long and sharp birdlike talon stretching out to stroke my hand. I felt a sudden sharp pain and winced involuntarily. Yutigo gave a short chuckle. He lifted his talon, and the pain faded away. I saw a small symbol that seemed to resemble a snake coiled in the shape of a circle imprinted on my palm before it became invisible. "Great," Yutigo said. "That's done. Here are the Council rules and decrees," he continued, waving his hand and sending a stack of multicolored lights at my hand, where they were seemingly sucked into the place that Yutigo had marked.

"We'll go over all of the rules and decrees for you at the next meeting, as well as the standard procedures of the Council, should any confusion arise," concluded Yutigo. "You can go now, Pierre. *Goodbye.*" This last word had a particular edge to it, and I hurried to create a gateway and return to New Earth. Nothing about that encounter, given my previous experiences, had been particularly...*odd*, but nonetheless, there was something about the entire tableau that I had found deeply disturbing. Not counting the as-yet-unknown Rexdael's head turning to look at me, not a single ruler besides Yutigo had done a single thing in that short meeting. From start to finish, Yutigo had dominated the proceedings, the conversation, doing his utmost to suck as much oxygen out of the room as he could. The degree of control he seemed to hold over the rest of the rulers, at least in that space, had been disturbing to say the least. Of course, I had forgotten all about it a few months later, but now, the memory returned with renewed fury, and my doubtful sentiments with respect to the Council reemerged.

"But you're one of them!" I shouted at Rexdael. "You're just like all the rest of those, one of Yutigo's minions! Did he send you to fetch me for misbehaving like the poor little boy I am?"

Rexdael laughed. "You're half right, Pierre," he replied. "Yutigo does want to summon you for bad behavior, but I'm not here to bring you in. I'm here to help protect you from him. Because you, in his eyes, have been bad, very bad indeed."

I had heard such words before, but hearing that Yutigo was mad at me sent shivers down my spine. "You still haven't explained why I should trust *you*, though," I continued.

"If you possess a vested interest in not dying a horrible, painful death, you'll come with me."

5

A TALE OF WOE AND DEATH

Rexdael, New Berlin, Europa, New Earth

As I led Pierre away from the midst of his (former) labora-
tory, I couldn't help but notice a general sense of foreboding drape itself over me. Convincing Pierre to follow me had simply been the first step. It was a marriage of convenience, of necessity, a connection we both recognized as being beneficial, though not necessarily one we regarded with trust just yet.

I was reminded by Pierre too strongly of myself at a far younger age. He was impulsive, headstrong, and worst of all, if fully unleashed, too dangerous to be contained. On some level, I did agree with Yutigo: Pierre's decision to wipe the vast majority of his memories was intensely selfish and remarkably shortsighted, for Pierre had given himself no way of restoring those memories on his own. However, I did not deem this sufficient cause for Yutigo to unilaterally decree that intervention in Pierre's realm was required. He needed some guidance, true, but this intervention, if it were carried through, would only drive him further away from the Council and more readily lead to exactly the scenario that the Council feared so greatly: the realm-eater.

At the same time, ironically enough, to not care deeply for Pierre would be to ignore my own distant past. Though my difficulties had played out on a somewhat smaller scale, they resembled Pierre's to such a degree that I was sure I knew exactly how Pierre had felt and would feel as his memories returned to him fully. I silently cursed Pierre for his acts of stupidity, yet simultaneously I was perhaps the only one who truly understood what he was going through. I wanted to both help and berate him, scold him for his self-centeredness but help him so that he could avoid making any more of the mistakes I had made. All that could only be accomplished if I was first able to gain Pierre's trust, though.

Unerringly, I led Pierre back to his office, ignoring the look of shock that passed over his face as I accessed his hidden elevator. He was less surprised when I wordlessly activated his office's security protocols, and he managed to not even flinch when I cast an extra-protective force field and privacy barrier over the office. Quite honestly, he should have stopped being surprised after gaining his memory back and seeing me appear out of nowhere! When one's entire conception of the world shatters within a few moments, is it such a stretch to imagine further heretofore improbable events occurring? Perhaps it was another effect of his memory transplantation, but the six years since his battle with the Entity seemed to have altered Pierre. He somehow seemed less…receptive to sudden change, less willing to accept foreign incursions into his life. Maybe he was tired of having his life pushed around and manipulated by others who thought they knew what was best for him, but the actions he had undertaken in his realm before he had taken his own memory did not indicate a loss of idealism. He had striven to create an egalitarian society, his work only disrupted when he locked away his powers. Despite his outward cynicism, it appeared that a streak of purity still ran through his core.

A twirl of my wrist later, a comfortable armchair appeared near Pierre's desk chair, and I quickly settled myself into its warm contours. It was all for appearances' sake, of course. I had long ago lost my ability to discern comfort from hardship, but unlike the Entity, I wished to conform at least somewhat to the expected human standards. Well, aside from speaking, of course. "Before you say anything, Pierre," I said telepathically, moving my lips as I did so (again to maintain appearances), "I think that you should listen to what I am about to tell you. Afterward, you are free to do as you wish; I will not stop you if you refuse my help and attempt to flee from me. All I ask is that you hear me out." I received a terse nod in reply and took that as a signal to continue.

"I don't know how old I am. Once you've lived as long as I have and control the powers that I do, time ceases to be a fundamental part of yourself. After all, what are a few more years here or there when I can make them fly by with a snap, just like that? And in case you haven't realized yet, your powers make you functionally immortal. Traditional weapons cannot harm you. Until you wholeheartedly desire to die, you will remain alive. Your powers passively encourage your body to self-repair, meaning you will never age naturally, forever remaining in peak condition. I don't think wondering by how much you'll outlive your family and friends should be a top concern right now, so lose the bereaved expression! Anyway, back to the point.

"I was born ordinary. Perhaps more ordinary than you, even, at least initially. My species…we were humanoids, in a sense. Besides the green skin and lack of a nose combined with a strongly enhanced sense of smell, we were not so different from humans. Our society was…authoritarian, to say the least. Our leader, I'm not even sure if he was one of our species anymore. He had outlived five generations…it made it so that unmodified history textbooks depicting our real history prior to his rise were true treasures indeed. Everyone knew him to be benign, the kindest soul there could be, yet it was common knowledge that he spent his evenings bathing in the blood of those who displeased him. We were governed by an ever-growing and ever-more arcane set of edicts, and though day after day, untold thousands disappeared, the total population never seemed to fluctuate.

"Education…what a farce! We possessed advanced technology only as long as our leader wished it, and all we needed to know was 'press this button,' 'flip that switch,' and so on. History, as you may have already guessed, was even more of a joke. Reading and writing? Necessary only to the point of understanding our leader's decrees. There were two jobs: worker and soldier. Being a soldier was a one-way ticket to the upper class, but it guaranteed nothing for your children once they became adults in their own right. It was a very effective way of keeping all of us divided and wary of each other, destroying beyond a point even the very basic structure of a family. By the time I was born, no one could remember a life before our leader, and so no one complained. Freedom had been bred out of us, so to say.

"I believe that I was a child touched by Fate herself, for I can see no other explanation for my childhood. I simply *saw* things no one else could. I remember, one night, someone got shot on our street as I was walking home from school. I was *shocked*, not only by the wanton, almost careless brutality of the act, but even more by the complete lack of reaction from anyone else. No one even flinched a muscle. The instinct to shrink away, to view such acts as extraordinary, as *wrong*—it seemed no one possessed it anymore. *Yet somehow, I did.* What other explanation could there be, if I was not touched by Fate or some other higher power? Once, a soldier slashed my father across the face with a knife for raising his arm more than two wrist-widths from his torso, just one example of an arcane edict. As blood poured out in rivulets, I started to rush forward, only to be held back by the iron grip of my mother, who simultaneously, however, bore absolutely no facial expression whatsoever. Her action was not one of love; it was simply an inbred action that told her this was the status quo, and that it was not to be disturbed at any cost. If my father was in pain, his facial expression or body language would have told you nothing. I was different in that I did not act as if I were part of a subservient class as the rest of my species.

"This propensity for discerning right from wrong got me in trouble all too many times. Never mortal trouble, to be sure, but by the time I was an adolescent, I bore my fair share of scars, each with its own unique signature of pain, yet another way in which I differed from my brethren. Logically, neither our history nor our laws made sense. What point was there to laws such as the one I mentioned before regulating how high we could lift our arms? And how could a leader be brutally benevolent? Though we did not possess such a word for it in our language, I would call that an oxymoron if ever there was one.

"Eventually, our *glorious* leader caught on to my otherness. I had gotten his attention through my many antics, and he had concluded that it was time for me to be taught a lesson, or eliminated. One night, he showed up personally on our doorstep. For all I know, it might have been the first time since he had assumed power that he had even set foot out of wherever it was that he lived. He had dressed for the occasion, wearing thick armor plates made from an insect not found on Earth, and dyed with the blood of my brethren. It seemed that he had just come from a torture session himself, for blood still dripped from his hands. *Pop, pop, pop, pop.* After our door had been blown off its hinges and sent through the opposite wall, this was the only audible sound for some time. I could *feel* the sheer power radiating off him. The whole street had turned out for the occasion, and for the first time, I could make out emotion in the inhabitants' faces: a cautious smile thoroughly ruined by the abject fear plainly present in their eyes.

" 'So, my young Rexdael,' began our leader, 'it seems that you have been *quite* the little troublemaker.' There was no response to this statement. Our leader continued regardless. 'Something must be done about that, you see,' he said, musingly. 'Insubordination is *not* to be tolerated at any cost. Is it true what I've heard, Rexdael, that you can feel pain?' This time, a nod in response. 'Well,' said our leader in chilling tones the likes of which I have not heard before or since, 'I believe it's time you're taught a lesson in emotional pain.'

"Without any other warning, the leader pulled my mother toward him and stuck his upper right arm through her chest. I was close enough to hear her ribs crunch as they were pulverized to dust, and my scream mingled with hers. I felt sorrow, but it was overwhelmed by white-hot anger. I had only the urge to kill. Anything and everything in sight would have worked, but for the moment at least, my anger was focused on the leader.

"As I found out later, our planet had somehow become trapped in a time bubble of sorts. Our leader had taken advantage of this, creating a population that never changed in number, recycled the same jobs and history, and never changed emotional state. Consciousnesses were recycled as he killed them and placed into new bodies. I was different in that my soul had miraculously come into my body from a place outside of this time bubble, which is why I was so different from everyone else. However, the very act of our leader leaving the place where he normally resided fundamentally eroded and destabilized the time bubble, to the point that my hyper-concentrated anger, an emotion the inhabitants of the bubble were never supposed to feel, shattered the bubble, transferring its energy to me and thus giving me my powers.

"I immediately directed my powers at our leader and felt a grim satisfaction as his face, shocked beyond belief, began to contort in extreme pain, and he, too, began to scream. While his flesh melted away, I hoped the smell had overwhelmed his senses and made him at least realize what he had brought upon so many others. When his body finally disintegrated, though, I lost all control over my powers. They had been trapped in the form of a time bubble for so long, and now they exulted at their newfound freedom. They coursed through my body, strengthening me, and fueled by my anger, they did the only thing they knew how to: destroy.

"I heard nothing, saw nothing, smelled nothing as a wave of destruction swept outward from me. I heard no screams, saw no fires spring into existence around me, smelled no burning flesh. My powers simply amplified my anger, and I exulted in it. My new powers were free, and so was I. I don't know how much time passed, but soon enough, it seemed, I had not merely vaporized every single other member of my species but destroyed the structural integrity of my planet, letting its solid iron core erupt and engulf the crust in a wave of burning metal. Soon, even that ended, and I was left floating in the abyss. Almost unwittingly, my anger soon became directed at the next closest planet.

"As I began floating in that direction, however, powers spreading before me and making me look like a glowing harbinger of death, a sound embedded deep in my ear resurfaced: the screams of my mother as she had died. As suddenly as it had blazed into existence, my anger drained, replaced by the sorrow I had initially felt. I stopped in my tracks, and my powers stopped with me. They still flared outward, but they were no longer propelled by that lethal edge, that primal urge to burn, kill, consume everything in sight. My mother...though I was and am unsure whether I really loved her, it was clear in my mind that the way in which she had died was unjust and had affected me deeply. What had I done to avenge it? I had brought a death every bit as painful upon the billions of my species that had once been trapped in that time bubble with me. There was no getting them back, for their souls were well and truly gone by now. I was the last of my species. That is, I would be the last of my species if I were still of the same species, which was not entirely clear, what with my new powers and all.

"It was the epitome of a pitiful revenge story! To avenge one brutal death, I had perpetuated billions. I had become just as bad, perhaps even worse than the leader I had originally deposed. What was more, for the first time I perceived a tear in the very fabric of my soul, the tear through which my powers had entered. Trapped in a miasma of sorrow and guilt, I rashly decided that the best course of action was to use my powers to plug this hole in my soul, to make it so that I could never feel such anger ever again.

"If I thought I had felt pain before, it was nothing compared to what I felt as I turned my powers inward, against myself. Every cell of my body protested, my powers resisting my urge to commit self-harm every step of the way. The hole in my soul through which they had come seemed as natural to them as every single other part of my body, and they did not understand why I would seek to close it. It was like having pure acid run through my veins. My body's cells died, only to be reformed by the very same powers that refused to let me die. Eventually, the hole in my soul was shut, but not before a price had been exacted on my body. My voice, the instrument of my troublesome questions and the catalyst of this series of events, was taken from me forever. I would never speak again. At the time, this seemed a minor price to pay for never having to feel anger again. Yes, this whole time I have been communicating telepathically, Pierre. That is why you may have noticed a disconnect between my 'spoken' words and the movements of my lips.

"From that day onward, I have never again felt anger as I did on that day. My capacity to feel rage is gone, replaced by a heightened sense of deep bitterness regarding the bleak cruelty and hopelessness of this world. Yet again, however, it did not come without a cost. The resulting backlash of power from healing my soul vaporized the two planets nearest to my location at the same time. Two more species wiped forever from the face of the realms. So, you see, Pierre, I, too, have committed genocide. I…I am a…*murderer*, a cold-blooded *murderer*! I killed for the joy of it, without reasonable cause, not out of necessity, but out of a childish fit of rage!"

As my words died away, I felt tears come to my eyes unbidden. Even now, I could not look upon my past but with the utmost regret. Pierre was looking at me with an inscrutable expression. Perhaps I was grasping for straws, but it seemed to me that at least his eyes had softened a tad from the beginning of our conversation. For what seemed like an eternity, neither of us spoke another word. Finally, Pierre spoke, so softly I could barely hear what he was saying: "Do the… Do the dreams… Do the dreams—"

"Do the dreams ever stop?" I said, finishing the question Pierre seemed almost afraid to ask. "No, no, they don't. Eventually, you just learn to live with them, and they become part of the background imagery. The visions don't lose their potency, but they lose much of their shock value."

Pierre nodded, seeming to come to a decision. "All right, Rexdael," he said, his voice firming. "I believe you. I don't think anyone would have the temerity to invent such an intensely personal tale. You probably do know more about me than I think. How do you want to help me?"

Now was not the time for smiling, but all the same, I nodded in recognition, my goal having been achieved. "I must be frank, Pierre," I began. "I have come bearing a warning. Yutigo has decided you are a threat too dangerous to be left alone, especially if you refuse to use your powers and leave your memories buried. Obviously, that much has changed, but Yutigo does not know that yet. He is sending a force to neutralize, at worst eliminate, you. I have come because I want to help you harness your powers to their fullest extent, so that you can defend yourself from whatever Yutigo decides to throw at you. But most of all, I want to help you so that in recovering from your experiences, you do not commit the same fundamental errors in judgment that I did."

Pierre's reply was all business, emotion set aside for the moment.

"Let's get to work, then."

6

FIRST ENCOUNTER

Lili Schwebler, New Berlin, Europa, New Earth

"You have been forewarned. Your powers will be limited and controlled, or you will be...*eliminated.*" The words echoed in my head. I had no idea who that shark-thing was, but the tone of voice left no room for interpretation: submit, or die. Worse, this message wasn't directed at me. It was intended for Pierre, but he was at work. I had to go save him, or at the very least deliver a warning!

"Lili?" Yuri's voice jolted me out of my train of thoughts. "Where are you going?" I blinked, realizing that I was suddenly standing next to the door. "I have to go save Pierre," I muttered distractedly, pulling my drill/screwdriver out of a cabinet. "Lili," Yuri said again, more insistently this time. His voice, though it probably was meant to be placating, only managed to sound harsh and grating to my ears. "How can you save Pierre when you don't even know what it is? If it is strong enough to threaten him, what chance do *you* stand against it?"

"Dammit, Yuri, he's my son!" I yelled, walking through the doorway as I did so, Yuri following closely. "He needs to be warned, and I will do my best to help however I can! I'm not sure you'll ever be able to understand that."

Yuri stopped short, but I could still sense him behind me. "He is my…son too, you know," he said tonelessly. "I know, I know, not by blood, but it's been what, six years? I've come to know him in that time, both with and without powers. Rushing in blindly can only do us more harm than good." I ignored Yuri and continued walking to the door, gasping only when I felt his viselike grip on my arm.

"Lili, I can't let you do this to yourself," Yuri said in a steely tone. "You're not thinking straight. Calm down and let's talk."

Without thinking, I wrenched myself free of his grip, my upturned palm striking Yuri in the face. Blood spurted everywhere. It seemed that I had broken Yuri's nose. Too shocked to do anything else, he simply lay on the floor, his eyes wide with surprise. "You really don't understand, do you?" I remarked, a tremor entering my voice. "I can't lose another one. Not after Will and Karl." As I walked out of the house, I was too caught up in my own emotions to even notice the sky that was gradually turning bloodred.

I had forgotten to call for a car in my distress, but I was quite unworried. There were many empty cars whizzing by on the road. Plenty of potential targets. I pulled a miniature electromagnetic pulse generator out of my pocket. Taking careful aim, I hurled it about three and a half feet in front of my intended target, one of the cars reserved for Autopass+ members: sinuous curves, gleaming surfaces, and a fifteen-hundred-horsepower, fully electric engine to boot. The EMP generator hit the car exactly where I had been aiming: on the hood, just underneath the windshield. A small blast was generated by the device, sending waves of electrical energy surging over the body of the car, jumping from car to car. My target juddered to a halt, all electronics temporarily disabled. Unintentionally, I had created quite the mess. I could count at least twenty car crashes caused by stray bolts of electricity from my EMP generator. Was that really my concern, however? It was a bit of gridlock, yes, but no one was dead and the system could fix it easily. Pierre's life hung in the balance! Any obstacles, no matter how high, had to be surmounted.

Carefully, I reached out to touch the door handle of my target. When nothing occurred as a result, I pulled the door open and clambered over to the driver's seat. Even though the whole Autopass system was, technically speaking, operating as a driverless fleet of cars, there were still more than a few enthusiasts out there who demanded the possibility of being able to drive themselves, a right that they were more than willing to pay a premium for, even if it meant taking their lives into their own hands. Normally, for people like me, the entire front area of the car would have been cordoned off, but this defense, too, had been momentarily disabled. I flexed my fingers experimentally, a few sparks flying out of my fingertips. I hoped that I still remembered a few of my old habits.

I placed two of my fingers on the keyless ignition. Carefully, I let a glowing white spark of electricity jump between my fingers and into the ignition. There was a single sharp buzz. I sent a few more sparks through the ignition. More buzzes. Concentrating, I poured an almost continuous stream of electricity into the ignition for what felt like an eternity, but in reality lasted half a second or less. The car *jumped* in the air, and I felt and saw the electronic systems blink to life, a low hum thrumming through my eardrums. I gave myself a little fist pump. Reaching under the wheel, I found a little nub of material nestled against its underside. I tore it out of its socket. Instantly, the hum doubled, maybe even tripled in volume. That meant I had successfully removed the engine limiter. I could reach Pierre within five minutes now.

Grinning manically, I put my hands on the wheel and slammed my foot down on the accelerator. Even as I devoted my efforts to fully enhancing my reflexes, the world blurred around me. Adrenaline surged through my veins. I had forgotten the exhilarating feeling that came with the tremendous acceleration of a powerful electric car. It was the welcoming back of an old friend.

Offhandedly, I could hear the police warnings coming through the stereo. The sirens began to blare around me as my location was zeroed in on, but I didn't care. At this time, no car could possibly hope to match up with the monstrosity I had created. *"Autodiebstahl...fünf Jahre im Gefängnis...,"* I heard through the blood coursing through my ears. It didn't matter. The police had no way of catching me and, when Pierre was restored to my side, no power over me either.

It was only as I wove my way through traffic, growing bored at the sight of an endless array of seemingly stationary cars, that I noticed the dashboard had a strange red tint to it. I gave it a quick once-over, only growing more confused as

I verified that no emergency lights were blinking or systems coming online. What other thing could possibly be glowing red on the dashboard? Then, I noticed the sky. Finally seeing its change in color shocked me enough that my enhanced reflexes just barely saved me from what would have almost certainly been a fatal collision. A bloodred sky…though I could not remember where I had seen it before, I felt the sense of danger skyrocket. It wasn't simply a matter of knowing. I felt a sudden surge of fear course through my veins, an instinctive reflex to being greeted by that particular shade of sky. Sometimes, ignorance really is bliss.

Though fear further heightened my reflexes, it also made my driving more erratic, serving only to make more tenuous my dance with death. As Alexanderplatz came into sight, I tried pushing down on the brake. I felt the pads shift into place, but the wheels simply kept turning as if there were no hindrance at all. *Now* I understood why all Autopass cars had limiters. Hoping that no one would be idiotic enough to try to stop the car before it met its spectacular end, I kicked out the driver's door and leaped. The momentum of my leap was such that I easily cleared an entire building, so quickly that I momentarily forgot to course-correct in the direction of the Energieforschung building. Hoping against hope that I hadn't miscalculated the force needed to break the door lock, I braced myself for impact. It seemed that today was my lucky day, for the door gave way with nary a shudder. It seemed almost suspiciously too easy. It would be the second sign I ignored against my body's better inclinations. Pierre needed me, and no stupid fear impulse would keep me from helping him.

The lobby was empty, the security checkpoint abandoned,

but this was easily explained by the array of flashing red lights lined up on one wall. The remaining dregs of hope I had still managed to hold onto evaporated. Was I too late? Had what I feared already come to pass? I looked around the lobby, trying but failing to find a way further into the complex that didn't involve the elevators, which were all shown as being occupied. "PIERRE!" My vocalization came out somewhere between a scream and a sob, but nevertheless echoed off the walls.

Almost as if it had been on cue, one of the elevator shafts exploded outward in a mess of glass and metal, all covered in wisps of glowing green smoke. A body as mangled as the remains of the shaft flew out as well, hitting the far wall with a thud. I gasped instinctively, letting out a scream as I realized that it was Pierre. Even as my eyes began to water, however, Pierre began to stand up, with a groan, visibly jerking as his skin whitened and his bones reset.

A cold laugh drew my attention back to the elevator shaft. I would have called him a man, but that would have been a disservice, considering how obvious it was that he was something...*more*, most likely another being. He would have been exquisitely beautiful—with high, arching cheekbones, petite lips, alabaster skin—were it not for the eyes as bloodred as the sky he must have created. The ghost of a smirk played at his lips. "You must be *Lili*, Pierre's *mother*." It was painful to listen to him, to his voice, mellow, rich, and honey-toned as it was, when I knew him for the harbinger of agony he was. Pierre's initial condition flying out of the shaft had been enough to tell me that much. "I knew my message had been misdelivered, but I never imagined it would be to one such as you. So few of the Entity's *specimens* survived his fall, and I am afraid I did not have the time to fully delve into the lovely Pierre's entire familial history."

It was he! The shark-head man! *"Yutigo,"* I hissed from between gritted teeth, enjoying the raised eyebrow my reaction had elicited. "Stay away from MY SON!"

Another cold laugh. "Feisty, aren't we?" replied Yutigo, almost playfully. "Your show of temper almost makes me want to oblige...but it seems the die has already been cast. *Your son* threw away the most marvelous inheritance these realms had ever seen and in doing so unwittingly endangered us all! Just for that, he deserves to be *eliminated*!" All playfulness had left Yutigo's tone by then, replaced by cold, biting cruelty. "And forgive me for being impertinent, but after seeing what I have done to your *darling* boy, what makes you think you could possibly act as his protector, when you are so much weaker than he ever was?"

"Perhaps she is too weak to face you, but I most certainly am not, Yutigo," echoed another voice from inside the shaft. Another being touched down soundlessly. He, too, was beautiful, but his green eyes gave his figure a more humane edge. Perhaps his body had been sculpted by Michelangelo as well, but no sculptor could have imbued those sparkling green eyes with such righteous rage as they were filled with at the moment.

Yutigo's face almost seemed to crack, his mask of supreme confidence falling away to be replaced by outrage, tinged with mere hints of shock and sadness. "I should have known that you would be here, Rexdael," he spat out. "Before you do anything...*unwise*, consider if this is really the way you want your illustrious relationship with the Council to end. Will you really adopt the title of Traitor so readily, all for your new *protégé?*"

Rexdael smiled mirthlessly. "So long have we known each other, Yutigo," he replied slowly, in a voice without inflection, "and yet still you fail to recognize how important my journey was in shaping my priorities. *Pierre* needs companionship, not an extermination squadron. If you would only give me a chance, I guarantee the so-called catastrophe that you fear would never come to pass."

"After what he did, *the boy* does not deserve life!" yelled Yutigo in return. "The realm-eater is the least of my worries. It is the precedent that is truly worth preventing."

"That precedent," replied Rexdael, his calm tone slipping, "is the only reason I stand before you today. If the Council had existed at my inception, I would have been wiped off the face of the realms before I had even drawn in my first breath! Pierre has his powers back, as you can see through his rapid healing. He no longer even possesses the possibility of setting that precedent you are so afraid of. Tell me why you're really here, or leave now and forever hold your peace!"

"So be it," was all Yutigo responded with.

Though I had been watching this interaction with rapt attentiveness the whole time, it was only now that I slowly began to edge backward, unsure if my appearance had really done any good. Perhaps if I grabbed Pierre and got out of here, I could redeem myself.

The very air seemed thick with anticipation. Rexdael gazed evenly at Yutigo, and Yutigo stared back just as evenly. Pierre's raising his hands into a defensive stance was the only indication I got that something bad was about to happen. Finally, Yutigo crooked a finger, and a wall of flame exploded around

Pierre. My shriek was drowned out by the roar of the flames, but both Rexdael's and Pierre's countermeasures prevented any real damage from being done.

With a growl, Yutigo disappeared, followed moments later by Rexdael. It was quite obvious that the two were still present in the room, however. Brief flashes and bangs occurring mere milliseconds apart on opposite sides of the room served to confirm that and also indicated a battle occurring far too fast to be perceived by the naked eye. Even Pierre seemed to have trouble keeping up, his eyes growing slightly glassy and unfocused as he tracked what to me were two sets of invisible movements.

Yutigo and Rexdael suddenly reappeared, two intertwined figures barely visible beneath a cloud of green smoke, interspersed by tongues of flame, more remains of the elevator shaft, and flickers of ethereal energy. Though their bodies almost appeared to be standing still, their extremities continued to be blurs as what I could only assume to be their attacks on each other were continually deflected. If it hadn't seemed so dangerous, I might have even called the balletic display beautiful.

There was a sudden shout of pain as a bolt of electricity lanced toward the pair. Yutigo and Rexdael stilled, long enough for me to notice Rexdael holding a hand up to a shallow cut on his cheek, before Yutigo batted him out of the way, binding him with a conjured set of glowing purple chains. Rexdael's shouts of pain grew more frequent. Completing this tableau was Pierre, still holding his smoking fingers up in shock.

Yutigo turned toward Pierre, a feral smile gracing his face. Pierre raised his other hand, and I felt the air around me warp as an energy shield began to appear around him. Just as quickly, however, Yutigo flicked his right hand and an energy bolt of his own shot out of his fingers, engulfing the shield. Now, Pierre's form blurred as well, and he appeared behind Yutigo, halfway through throwing a punch at Yutigo's neck. I blinked, and Yutigo, apparently having moved even faster than Pierre, was behind Pierre and drove his right hook directly into Pierre's cheekbone. There was sickening crunching sound, and Pierre fell to the floor yet again, battered and bleeding.

"On one thing, at least, Rexdael and I agree," said Yutigo, a slight breathiness the only indication he was any worse for wear, even as Rexdael continued to struggle against his bonds in the background, "so much wasted potential, so much in your technique that could be refined. A pity that you'll never get the chance to learn." Yutigo opened his left hand, and a set of writhing blue wires appeared in it. He then placed this hand against Pierre's neck.

If I thought my scream before had been bad, it was nothing compared to what I was hearing from Pierre now. His face was contorted into a rictus of pain as the blue wires began to creep up his neck, his skin growing pale and waxy as the very life force seemed to be draining out of him. I should have felt the extremes of anguish, the grief of a helpless mother watching her son die before her eyes in what was possibly the most painful way there was, but instead, I only felt an absurd sense of certainty. No matter how dire the situation seemed in the moment, I felt quietly confident that this was not the end. Pierre would survive, and Yutigo would not win today.

Almost as if he had been privy to my mental thought processes, Rexdael conveniently chose this time to break out of

his chains. He lunged toward Yutigo. Yutigo's head turned un-
naturally slowly, a stark contrast to his earlier rapidity, almost
as if the blue wires he was wielding constricted his movement
as well. Rexdael crashed into Yutigo, and with a grunt, the two
beings rolled around on the floor for a moment before disappearing in a flash of purple light. I barely had time to perceive
this disappearance when there was another flash of purple
light, and Rexdael reappeared, bleeding heavily from a head
wound, but alone. He collapsed to the floor, seemingly from
exhaustion. I glanced at Pierre. The blue wires were gone, but
he still looked simply drained and in need of a good night's
rest. I sighed. For once, it seemed I would be playing nurse.

7

RECRUITMENT

Pierre Hartford, New Berlin, Europa, New Earth

Scraps and fragments of the conversation around me penetrated my muddled brain: "...in a coma...draining him... same as being killed...Yutigo...insane...power..." Yutigo... that must have been the name of the fellow who so kindly threw me down an elevator shaft, the same one Rexdael had said would be coming after me for my "crimes." My first impression of him didn't seem to have been that far off the mark, then: controlling and also exceedingly dangerous when crossed. It was just as apparent that I was woefully unprepared to face him on my own. Apparently, I had been in a coma, explaining why my mind felt so disorganized. How had that happened, though? Admittedly, travel via elevator shaft had been painful, but not to the point that my body hadn't been able to fix itself. Obviously, something had happened in the immediate aftermath, yet try as I might, I could not...*remember*.

As I slowly came to my senses, I perceived a certain *heaviness* that appeared to be weighing me down, almost as if weights had been attached to my extremities. Yet I did not seem to have any difficulty in moving my fingers or toes, or even attempting to shift my arms or legs. Obviously, then, it was a sensation more of the mental than physical type. That meant that my powers should be able to in some way dispel this mental block. This heaviness was beginning to make me feel *vulnerable*. But when I reached to where my powers should normally have been residing, I felt...nothing *whatsoever*. What in the world? I reached deeper, flitting through the mental pathways that typically saw the most use. Everywhere was just empty. Nowhere could I find even a trace of the awe-inducing powers I had only so recently been able to regain. It was worse now, however. Now that I knew of my powers, I was acutely aware of my lack thereof at the moment, and it felt as if a chunk of me had simply been ripped away.

I made a turn with the intention of heading into my sub-conscious mind, perhaps hoping to find my powers in some hidden crevasse there. But I was thwarted in this attempt, too, when I ran headlong into a mental barrier of some unknown energy type. As a cavalcade of beeps began to sound around me, presumably from the horde of machines keeping watch over my prone body, a series of blue lines seared themselves into my vision. Pain erupted from deep within me, and I began to scream once more, a mostly silent scream given the strain it seemed my vocal cords had already been through, but no scream could have possibly described how it felt to have my body seemingly waging a war against itself, though I knew that the energy barrier must have been foreign in origin.

Another presence made its way into my mind, ignoring me and the entirety of my conscious mind, making its way to my subconscious with all the subtlety of a battering ram. When it crashed into the same barrier I had encountered, the results, quite logically, were entirely different. The energy barrier was torn into a thousand shreds, more akin to tissue paper than the steel wall I myself had encountered. *Despite* that devastating attack, however, I could perceive the shreds of the barrier already aligning themselves, preparing to fly back into place as if nothing had ever been able to disturb them. My pain had already begun to lessen when the foreign presence in my mind turned to me, and I felt a wave of guilt wash over me, the first half of a question-response module that requested forgiveness. Confused, I consented to offering my forgiveness as my response to the proffered question.

Only then did I understand the purpose of the question. I felt an acute pain behind my eyes as the presence morphed into a sort of pseudo vacuum funnel. The shreds of the energy barrier began to be sucked up by the funnel, but when they disappeared, I simply felt a growing buildup of pressure behind my eyes. *This*, for one, felt not like a mental pressure but instead a physical one. When all the shreds of the barrier had disappeared, so did the funnel, but the pressure behind my eyes was now almost as unbearable as the pain the barrier had been causing me before. With a horrendous rip and a squelch, I felt something burst out from behind my eyes, and I felt slimy specks of particulate matter spatter my upper body. It seemed that the process of removing the barrier from my body had rendered me blind, but already I could feel my power flowing back into me in fits and bursts, enough so that I could regrow my ruined eyeballs.

I blinked as a mild breeze swept over me, collecting the remains of my eyeballs and depositing them elsewhere. The blinding whiteness of what appeared to be the walls of a medical room initially overwhelmed my sensitive, newly grown eyes. When the white dimmed and I began to resolve shapes, I perceived two blurry outlines standing to my left that I assumed were my mother and Yuri, three more to my right (Robert, Max, and Luka?!), and directly over me, staring into my eyes, perhaps even the depths of my soul, for the second time in as many days, the haunting green eyes of Rexdael.

Though he looked somewhat haggard, his eyes still sparked with intensity, and a look of relief crossed his eyes as he noticed me staring back at him. "Well, Pierre," he began, "it seems you've recovered sufficiently from our little endeavor, though I am afraid you will be confined to this bed for just a little while longer. I'm sure you understand that it's just for your own safety." Rexdael's words did make some sense. Even with some of my powers restored, I still felt sluggish and, at the moment, running entirely on fumes.

"Well," I responded, "events have certainly given me a new...*perspective* with which to examine matters." Rexdael's lips twitched, and the upper corners of his mouth bent upward in a semi-smile, before quickly resuming his concerned expression. Robert attempted to repress a snort but failed to do so, though it died upon the withering glare my mother shot at him. "Before we proceed, though," I continued, "what the *heck* did Yutigo do to me that messed me up?"

"To put it succinctly," responded Rexdael, "he attacked you

with an extremely rare *and* forbidden device designed to turn you into a mindless husk." He held up his hand, which contained the glowing, smoldering remains of a mass of tangled wires emitting faint blue sparks every few seconds. "This device's intended purpose was to suck malignant energy sources out of those patients who appeared to be suffering from injuries unexplained by any physical set of symptoms, and which could thus only be cured by delving deep into said patients' minds and removing whatever foreign presence had made its home there. It quickly became clear, however, that the energy sources the device was designed to remove could be considered quite similar in nature to our souls. It was but a matter of days before this device was redesigned to suck 'parasitic' souls out of its 'patients,' leaving them cured…as well as brain-dead."

My mother's right eye twitched, and I saw her bat away a stray tear. Rexdael's lips tightened, though he gave no sign of having seen this. "Pierre," he said grimly, "that Yutigo would sink to such depths as to make use of this device…troubles me in the extreme. It smacks of desperation, yet he has no reason, none at all, to feel that way at present. He has us on the defensive, and for the moment at least, the Council on his side. But that very same Council ordered these devices banned and confiscated and all research about them destroyed because the members of the Council did not wish to brave the danger of a world in which anyone potentially had such a simple way to strip them of their power. If the Council discovers this… Yutigo is done for."

"Where is Yutigo?" interrupted my mother suddenly. "When you returned, you looked battered down, but he was gone." Rexdael nodded slowly. "Yes," he began in reply,

"Yutigo is, shall we say, momentarily trapped in a place from which he will not find it easy to escape. We have maybe a day at best before he manages to break free and return, probably with more reinforcements this time."

"We should press our advantage then!" insisted my mother.

Rexdael held up a finger to stop her from continuing. "If only it were so simple, Lili," he said. "Yutigo is incapacitated, yes, but so is Pierre, and he will not be able to recover without my help before Yutigo returns. I have an...acquaintance who is a Council elder whom I can perhaps count on to grant reinforcements, once she sees what's happening for real and not just through the distorted lens of Yutigo's paranoia. I can also help Pierre so that he is better prepared for this next and hopefully final encounter with Yutigo. In the meantime, I am sure Yutigo has some sort of countermeasures readied for a scenario such as this one in which he may not have been able to lead the battle personally. We need to make use of this planet's defense systems to make sure we can identify and eliminate whatever threats might be coming our way."

"I believe," said Luka quietly from the corner, "that we three can help with that." He indicated himself, Robert, and Max. "I can have the Energieforschung building declared a potential biohazard site and ascertain the exact nature of the energy signatures that accompanied your and Yutigo's arrivals."

"I can use some of the software I've installed on Europan satellites to scan for these energy signatures across the landmass," continued Max.

"And I can contact the Americanian Embassy and see if the embassy would be willing to share satellite data with us," concluded Robert.

"We'll stay here with Pierre while you are off gathering help, Rexdael," added my mother.

"By the way," I began confusedly, "where are we?"

"The secret bunker underneath your house you never told us about," replied Robert with a grin. "You sly bastard."

Yes, I did remember this being one of the last things I had done before wiping my memory, this preparation of my new house, though for what purpose a secure bunker whose existence I could not even remember would have served, I remained unsure.

"Well," said Rexdael, "we are decided then. Chop-chop!" Rexdael waved his hand at the wall directly opposite me, and a door molded itself out of the smooth contours of the wall with a slight pop, silently swinging open. With a sudden flash, a portal appeared that Rexdael stepped into and closed behind him. Upon seeing that, Robert, Max, and Luka all jumped backward a bit but otherwise appeared unmoved. With three waves of acknowledgment, they exited the room as well, the door closing behind them. And thus began the waiting game.

Luka Prosek, Office of the Environmental Counsellor of New Berlin

My, oh my! What an *interesting* day this was turning out to be. To not only discover that an extraterrestrial encounter had taken place just miles from where I lived, but then to learn that this event had occurred because of Pierre, and then to be pulled into a conspiracy whose goal it was to protect him? Even in my wildest dreams, I had never come close to imagining that something like this would happen.

When first ingratiating myself with Pierre, I had hoped for

something like this. I had tried to imagine the most ridiculous statements that could still possibly be applied to Pierre and who he really was. That *had* been my initial reason for deciding to become Pierre's friend. I know, I know, it's self-serving and manipulative, but it was and is a fundamental part of who I am. Every single person is a puzzle composed of hundreds of intricately moving pieces, but each is in its own way solvable. Pierre, on the other hand? The description I came up with that best fit Pierre was *handsome cipher.* Pierre had always been a perfect friend, kind and gracious, always there when you needed him, articulate and knowledgeable on all manner of subjects, with a rarely seen wit to boot. Yet around Pierre, it had always felt as if he was playing a role. He never stayed annoyed for long, he never became angry, he didn't even blink at the worst of our transgressions! I would have even called him a psychopath, were it not for his seeming inability to become violent. Yet the impression I had continually gotten of him was simply that of a perfectly played persona under which lay someone whom Pierre himself may not even have been aware of. By comparison, Max and Robert had been ludicrously easy to read and completely average people (too obsessed with his books and too trusting of others, respectively) but still wonderful conversationalists.

Now, it seems, I had been right. It sounded like a plot straight out of some movie. Pierre had apparently wiped his own memory and locked away the powers which had essentially turned him into a god. Consequently, he was being chased by a bunch of other gods who wanted to either kill him or help him stay alive and come to terms with the post-traumatic stress disorder that had been caused by a massive genocide which had happened before we even came into existence. It was a lot to take in, but I had filed away the information for later and would take some more time to process it then. Now, it was my duty to help Pierre in his hour of perhaps greatest need. Despite what I had said earlier and my completely selfish reasons for wanting to become acquainted with Pierre, I really had grown to appreciate the persona he had constructed and wished to help him should he ever come to terms with his hidden self. Pierre just had some sort of magnetic...*pull* about him, something that attracted capable people to him like flies to honey despite his flaws or lack thereof, and I was not sure it could simply be explained away by his godlike standing among the humans he had created. Not to mention that helping Pierre brought me closer to solving him once and for all.

It was for these reasons I was currently standing in front of my boss's office, hand poised on the bronze knocker (he really was old-fashioned sometimes). My boss, Herbert Kreutzer— or as some people called him, Herbie (not within earshot, of course)—was a kind, generous man, but he was also an environmental fanatic. While this did make him the perfect choice to lead New Berlin's extensive environmental programs, it also rendered him blind to some of the more expedient uses his extensive political capital could be put to. Of course, I cared about the environment as well, or Herbie would have seen through me right away, but I also recognized the potential for unfettered access I could have at any point in the city if I so wanted. I imagined that this current proposal would be somewhat of a hard sell.

I knocked. The door opened immediately, revealing a

short, balding man, glasses askew and a thin metal rod of some sort stuck behind his ear. It was said that Herbie was devoted to nothing but his work, and at times like this, his appearance certainly seemed to bear it out. "Ah, Prosek!" he said after a moment, glancing at me distractedly while he fiddled with his glasses. "*Komm rein, komm rein.*" I sat down in the indicated chair, facing a desk covered with stacks of paper that reached half a meter tall at some point. Herbie bustled around, making sure that he could at least see me from where he sat behind his desk. "What is it you wanted to talk about?" he continued. "This new paper on cloud seeding the office just received? *Wunderbar, nicht wahr?* You know, they are proposing that the most efficient way to distribute the compounds throughout the clouds is with bee-like drones! It's remarkable, the swarm-like patterns they can display—"

"Herbert," I said sharply, cutting him off. Informal, I know, but I found it to be the most effective way of snapping Herbie out of his reveries. He shook his head slightly, refocusing on me. "Yes, I suppose not," he muttered. "You wouldn't disturb me at this time were it not pressing."

"Yes," I responded simply. "You see, we may have a bit of a situation at the Energieforschung headquarters." Herbie looked at me, more intently than before, eyes narrowing slightly. "Energieforschung," he said slowly, tongue rolling over the syllables, "last I remember, they were not dealing with any particularly toxic or environmentally hazardous chemicals, their audits are up to date, safety procedures numerous and effective…what problem could have arisen there?"

Instead of replying, I pulled out my phone and showed Herbie some of the headlines. His eyebrows shot upward.

"Mein Gott!" he muttered to himself. "So much destruction caused by one blast! I still don't quite see..." "It appears the blast has injured or killed quite a number of the security staff," I continued. "And though Energieforschung does not peddle in hazardous chemicals, the company conducts numerous fusion and fission experiments, and I am worried about how secure the containers of radioactive waste are at the moment. It would be disastrous if this waste were to somehow exit the building, which I think is reason enough to have the building declared a biohazard site."

Herbie furrowed his brows. "True, I suppose," he conceded, "but we still have nuclear waste teams ready to—"

"Old and defunct."

"We could lock down—"

"That doesn't solve the problem of disposing with the waste."

"Benton will throw a fit—"

"*I* can deal with *Mr.* Benton, *Herr* Kreutzer."

Herbie threw up his arms, whether in real or mock despair I couldn't tell. "*Ach,* whatever," he sighed. "I suppose you're right, as you always are with these sorts of things, Prosek. You have my full authority to do what you think best, as long as I don't receive an earful from anyone afterward. Now, I really must get back to these cloud papers." Herbie's voice trailed off as he stopped paying attention to me once more and shifted his attention to one of the stacks of paper he had so recently evicted from his desk. As I walked out of the office, I exulted silently. The plan really had managed to work. Herbie was always more pliable after the latest batch of research journals arrived at the office, but even so, he had put up a hard fight, though thankfully without introducing any unexpected arguments. It was time to get boots on the ground and report to Max.

Maximillian Steinhardt, AI Development Center, Siemens

"Max, you're not going to believe these readings."

"Try me," I said after hearing Luka's matter-of-fact statement on the other end of the line.

"Well," he replied, in a breathy sort of tone somewhat masked by static (I sincerely hoped that he was not attempting to be a dramatist at the moment), "besides some trace amounts of iridium, we're getting a whole lot of nothing at the portal site." I frowned. "What do you mean, *nothing?*" I asked. "Obviously, the iridium's the stabilizing agent, but it can't be stabilizing a whole lot of nothing! I'm sure you can see why that wouldn't make any sense. Have you perhaps tried scanning for other forms of matter?"

A long pause greeted that question. "That's...a pretty good idea," finally replied Luka. "I'll look into doing that and get back to you."

I sighed, loudly enough that I hoped Luka could hear it. "You do realize how painfully apparent it is at this moment that you have never run a biohazard site with respect to radioactive waste before, right?"

Luka snorted. "Wow, I'm *so* sorry that we aren't all instantly a genius at whatever strikes our fancy!" he retorted. "Feel free to come run the site if you think you can do it better."

"I wish," I replied, "but we all have our jobs to do, however inadequately some of us may be performing them at the moment." I thought Luka might have growled then, but it may have just been some of the ever-present static on the line.

"You'll get your damned readings, you," he said before ending the call.

I laughed to myself slightly. Luka was so easy to rile up sometimes. He and his mechanistic view of the world. Wherever he went, he saw puzzles, codes to be cracked, and when he ran up against a problem of unknown parameters, the results could sometimes be quite...*dissatisfying* to him. I was that way too, sometimes, but at least I could see the value of knowledge for knowledge's sake. Which, in the end, I believed made me more prepared for whatever type of situation I may have to encounter in the future. Obviously, I was still limited by the finite amount of knowledge I could have imbibed up to that point in my pitifully short lifetime, but what I did know, I did know *extremely* well indeed.

Granted, that was nothing in comparison to Pierre. What a remarkable...what was he even? Man? God? Higher power? Well, whatever he was, he was simply extraordinary. Even when he had essentially lobotomized himself, his knowledge had still far outstripped mine in every single arena in which I had attempted to match him in a battle of wits. While it may not have seemed like it at first glance, Pierre was simply overflowing with raw information, interesting tidbits, and fundamental axioms alike. No matter what I had to muster, he simply had more, both in breadth and depth. It was what had drawn me to him originally. Only a true genius could have been as knowledgeable as Pierre was at such a young age. Yet, in all other respects, he seemed perfectly healthy and normal. Simply being around him made for some truly enlightening moments.

Take today as an example. I did not know *what* exactly I was expecting when I woke up this morning, but the revelation that Pierre was not human was not one of them. Yes, such an event was so far out of the realm of plausibility that when it occurred, it seemed to me as if I was perhaps caught in a dreamlike state. It was only seeing the reactions of the people around me that convinced me I was not alone in my awe. Though it *did* explain many of the things that had made Pierre so extraordinary in the first place.

My phone beeped, probably Luka getting back to me with his updated, more thorough results. It was indeed Luka. "Luka," I said briskly, "got some real readings for me this time?"

"Yes, *Mother*," he grumbled, "I've got your...results." Static had begun obscuring some of Luka's words. "There appears to be...concentrations of what...techies call...and a whole... of positrons."

"Can you repeat that?" I said loudly. "The static's cutting you off." Luka muttered something under his breath. A couple of loud steps later, the static faded away into the background. "Better?" he asked.

"Much," I replied.

"Well, as I was saying, there appear to be abnormally large concentrations of what the techies call WIMPs [weakly interacting massive particles] and a whole lot of positrons. Benton and his stupid security measures...the whole building's wired to white out potentially sensitive topics of conversation over telecommunications devices."

"Remarkable," I said, momentarily awestruck. "The AI

Benton must be using, advanced to the point that it can identify and weed out potentially incriminating words from conversations it legally should be barred from..."

"Max!" yelled Luka over the line. "I'm sending you the
readings now. Work your magic on them while I go clean up
this sham." The line clicked. Once again, Luka had been driv-
en off by the start of one of my many philosophical reveries.
So many interesting discoveries made that way...it truly was
a shame that Luka did not see the value in them. My phone
beeped again and my computer lit up simultaneously. The
readings Luka had sent me had arrived. I glanced them over,
and they did seem to be as he had described. The dark matter levels...off the charts. If that was really what these portals
were powered by, no wonder Energieforschung's equipment
had gone completely haywire. But what were the positrons for,
then? A question best left for after analyzing the data.

Once again, I found myself glad that Germany had been
the dominant player in the old European Union, especially after the Merkels had come into power. It was the only way the
other Europan principalities would have ever agreed to having one conglomerate (Siemens) take over their native factories
and service all of their technological needs. The projects of
multinational scope Siemens was thus able to conduct, and the
unprecedentedly large information streams the company had
access to, both made my job immensely fascinating and useful
for situations such as this one.

Neural networks were my bread and butter and, thanks to
the petabytes of information I was fed daily, could be trained
to remarkable degrees of accuracy for a wide variety of identifi-
cation tasks. This really came in handy when the data set I was

working with was both vanishingly small and likely exceedingly rare in the database as a whole. One of Siemens's most recent projects had been the construction and launching of a satellite network, primarily for weather detection and communications purposes but also equipped with all manner of scientific instruments. There was only one satellite I knew of which had been equipped with a WIMP detector, but luckily it was the central hub satellite, able to cover the entire Europan landmass. Also fortuitous was the fact that at the moment I had easy access to all of these detectors, as I was in the process of debugging the entire satellite network's weather prediction neural networks.

Finding a suitable scientific detection neural network on my hard drive, I entered some rough calibration parameters—the better to ensure that I would not simply be recording random noise the dark matter detector managed to notice—and then fed the readings Luka had given me to the network. After what seemed to me to be mere seconds, the network stated that it had finished processing the data set and was prepared to search for more findings of a similar nature.

"Pierre," I muttered to myself, "if I get thrown in jail for this, you're going to pay for my bail." Technically speaking, what I was doing wasn't illegal in the slightest. I *did* at the moment have full access to the network I was about to basically download a virus onto, but I knew that if my bosses ever found out, it would be frowned upon in the extreme. Following that cheery thought, I quickly uploaded the neural network onto the dark matter detector as well as the positron detector, making sure that the two copies of the network cross-referenced with each other.

This time, it was not mere seconds before I had a result returned to me. As the seconds grew into minutes, I began to grow slightly worried. It couldn't have been that difficult to find a hit. Surely abnormal dark matter concentrations had been recorded at some point in the past four years. As if it had read my thoughts, the network chose that moment to return its results. I looked over at the screen, and my eyes bugged out of my head. Several *million* results?! This wasn't an infiltration; it was an invasion! Though the recorded results stretched back several years, the vast majority had occurred within the past few hours, minutes even. As I watched, the network continued to return more hits. It seemed Pierre's enemies did indeed have effective contingencies in place.

I pulled out my phone, this time calling Robert. "What's up?" he asked immediately. "You found something, Max?"

"More than just something, Robert. It could be a disaster in the making. Look, I'm sending you a file containing a neural network. Tell the Americanians they need to run it on any satellites they have equipped with dark matter and positron detectors. Pull out all the stops if need be."

"*Bugger,*" he muttered under his breath. "I'll get on it, Max." He ended the call.

I held my phone in my hands, staring at it pensively. Would it jeopardize Pierre's recovery if I told him the distressing information I had just found? He needn't concern himself with an invasion when it was really only the main men who posed a threat to him, did he? But perhaps I should tell him after all. I felt it was somewhat my duty to keep him informed of any noteworthy developments...

Um, what had I just been thinking about? Something

involving some files Luka had sent me? Perhaps, but if I couldn't even remember the exact details, was it even worth trying to dredge them up? Probably not. Humming a cheerful ditty under my breath, I returned to my debugging of yet another weather prediction neural network.

Robert Morrison, Americanian Relations

As I ended my call with Max, I felt somewhat concerned. Max hadn't sounded as even-keeled as he normally was over the phone. By his standards, he had sounded positively...*frantic.* I hoped he didn't work himself half to death trying to unravel this latest problem. Hypocritical of me, considering that I was about to do the same for Pierre. Americanian-Europan relations were not sunny at the best of times, but now, they were positively frigid in the aftermath of a recent scandal where the Italian governor had attempted to seduce the president's daughter. Politics! Luckily, I did have some ways of getting around this red tape.

I sighed to myself. Given the sorry state of relations at the moment, official channels were completely blocked off, which meant I had to go through reception. "Americanian Embassy, how can I help you?" answered the cool, female, and entirely robotic voice after I had finished dialing.

"Hi there," I said, out of force of habit more than anything else (I found it impossible to hear a humanlike voice and not treat it as I would any other human being). "I'm looking for a Jane Desner."

"Who should I say is calling?" came the answering query.

"Mr. Mountebank."

"Please hold."

I groaned, putting my head into my hands as some infernal classical music began to play over the line. How Pierre managed to put up with this bunch of noise, I had absolutely no idea.

Speaking of which, Pierre's recent revelations had left me completely flabbergasted and, for once, at a complete loss for words. My dearest friend...not even *human*? A god who had willingly handicapped himself?! How could none of us have seen even a single sign? He had seemed so normal, so mortal, and so utterly conventional that it was hard to imagine a more outlandish outcome.

Pierre had always been a welcome respite from my day job. Diplomacy was just as much a job about recognizing the things left unsaid as it was about interpreting the statements foreign functionaries did in fact say. It was immensely tiring to constantly have to recognize the duplicity of many diplomats, the lack of authenticity with which they went about their jobs, and the utter callousness with which they treated those whom they saw as unimportant to their ultimate ambitions. The diplomatic corps had given me the ability to instantly take the measure of almost any man, and to me, Pierre was a refreshing breath of fresh air. He had simply been so *genuine* about everything. There were no hidden double meanings, rarely if any ambiguity in his language, and a sensitive, caring nature nurtured by his friendships and his thirst for the knowledge to help others. Pierre's purity had brought my most gregarious traits to the fore, and I had trusted him more than even Max or Luka, both of whom had at times taken great pains to hide what they believed were the uglier parts of their natures around Pierre, their selfish reasons for wanting him as a friend. They were not alone in this, though my boisterous mask was a much better cover than the sudden reticence of my friends from time to time.

At times, I envied Pierre. I had perfectly decent intuition when it came to reading people, and I had never had any issues when it came to making friends, but Pierre...he simply made it look effortless. It was so *infuriating* sometimes how he always seemed to know the exact right thing to say in order to make someone see his side of the issue, gain a newfound appreciation of him, and forgive our transgressions, to anyone at all, down to the lowliest barista. Pierre oozed a quiet, confident charisma, but he simply acted as if he wasn't aware of it, or worse, *chose* not to use it.

At that moment, the hold music stopped abruptly, and the voice of the receptionist was back on the line. "I apologize for the inconvenience, Mr. Mountebank," she (?) said. "Ms. Desner is in a very important meeting at the moment, but I'm sure I can schedule an appointment with her, if you'd like."

"Thank you, that will be all," I replied, cutting short the receptionist and ending the call. As expected, then. A few seconds later, my phone beeped again. Incoming call from an unknown number. I grinned. Jane.

"Bobby," came the sweet, dulcet tones of one Jane Desner across the line, Boston accent as apparent as always, "are you *out of your mind?*"

Jane and I had a...let's call it a history. Back when she had been stationed in New Berlin, we both had been couriers for our respective corps. Seeing as we were constantly delivering missives back and forth between the same two battles, we were bound to run into each other at some point. Of all the people I had ever met in diplomacy, Jane was by far the most straightforward. Stubborn as a mule, she never took no for an answer in a negotiation, giving as good as she got. Needless to say, subtlety was not her strong suit. Now she was some special assistant or other to the junior Americanian ambassador, which, sadly, was higher than my own post (I remained a mere envoy and senior negotiator). Our amicable relationship had continued, however, a vital link to the other side in this time of almost total diplomatic silence.

"Hi, Jane!" I said gaily, ignoring her last statement completely. "How are you? I'm fine, thanks for asking."

"Well, I might burst a blood vessel if you keep this crap up," she yelled back snappily. "What on God's green earth inspired you to dial me at the receptionist?! They can *track* your number, even if it's not from your official diplomatic line! And honestly, where in the world do you come up with names as horrendous as Mr. *Mountebank*?"

I laughed heartily. "Oh, Jane, dear," I began, "don't be miffed. I remember you saying that the public line, and I quote here, was 'for emergencies only.' I'm sure you will agree with me on that count by the time we're finished here. And besides, did you really forget the agreed-upon codenames we had come up with in our younger days? After all, you *did* know who was calling."

"Yeah," replied Jane, still somewhat shortly, "only because you're the only *idiot* I know who's stupid enough to use such a corny cover name when trying to get in touch with me! And stop trying to make small talk. Get to the point before we both lose our jobs for talking behind our bosses' backs."

"Fine, fine," I replied in acquiescence, "but you really do take all the fun out of this cloak-and-dagger business, more's the pity."

"Bobby…," Jane began warningly.

"All right, all right! I'll tell you all about my urgent problem. So, as it turns out, my dear friend Pierre—I'm not sure if you met him, exceedingly charming fellow—Pierre, here, has just revealed to his dear friends that he may have been somewhat misleading with respect to his past. He now has some nefarious figures after him, some extremely powerful individuals. Long story short, these individuals aren't acting alone, and according to our satellite data, we may be facing a large-scale invasion."

Jane whistled slowly, audible even over the line. "Your friend and Europa in general really do sound like they're in a pickle, don't they? What I don't quite understand, though, yet, is why you need *Americanian* resources to help you."

"Well, my friends and I would like to analyze the data from your native satellite network," I answered in return. "We think Americana may be in danger as well, and we wish to ascertain if this is the case or not. If it is true, it would help for you to know, wouldn't it?"

Jane remained silent for a while. "You do realize despite all that beautiful fluff you just spouted, Bobby," she said, "that intel will cost you, even more than it would if your Italian governor wasn't a complete dunderhead."

I nodded, even though I knew Jane could not see it. "Fair," I replied, "at the very least, I'm prepared to offer you an information swap."

Jane laughed. "C'mon, Bobby, you joking?" she responded

somewhat derisively. "That's quite literally pennies on the dollar. Give me something I can at least present to my boss without being laughed out of the room, would you?"

I sighed. If I was wrong, my boss would have my head for what I was about to say. "Fine," I said, "if the intel you find turns out to be negative, we'll offer you subsidies to prop up the Brazilian sector. However, if the intel turns out positive, Europa will offer an unconditional offer of military alliance to combat the invasion."

Jane sighed. "I guess it is *something*," she said. "I'm *really* starting to hope your intuition is wrong, though. I don't want to know what the president will do if he finds out that we have suddenly embroiled ourselves in a military alliance. I will talk to my boss and get back to you in a few."

"Wait!" I said suddenly. "Before you go, I'm sending you a file. It contains a program you should give all your satellites equipped with dark matter and positron detectors to scan for the threats I'm talking about."

"Oooh-kay then, Bobby, you just spewed a lot of fancy talk there, and I'm not really sure what you just said, but I'll be sure to pass it on."

The call ended then, and I sat at my desk, staring at my phone's screen, hoping for the best. Sooner than I had expected, I received another call. "Well, Bobby, seems you were right," were Jane's first words. "It appears Americana may be an invasion target as well, based on the words of our techie, the gist of which I'm not able to transmit over official diplomatic channels due to its foul nature."

"All right then," I said grimly, "send the intel over official channels, and I'll start writing up the new treaty." There was a sudden silence, as well as a loud ping on the line. "Jane?" I said cautiously. "You still there?"

"Yeah," she said, though her voice sounded oddly strained, perhaps even higher pitched than before. "Yeah, I got what you just said. See you soon." As the line clicked, I pondered what I had just heard. There had been something...*off* about those past few seconds, but I didn't have the time to look into it now. I'd do it after contacting Pierre and starting my write-ups. Humming a cheerful ditty under my breath, I headed for the ambassador's office.

8

SEEKING OUT LOOSE ENDS

Rexdael

Looks could be quite deceiving sometimes. I was strongly reminded of this every single time I looked at Yutigo, or even just at myself. When we became "human," so to speak, I was reminded how scary perfection really could be. Humans could talk as much as they wanted about ideals of perfection, and perhaps they could pretend that some of them were indeed "perfectionists," but how would they even know what that was? Even when humans perceived something to be perfect, it never really could be for them, simply because there were imperfections their technology could not hope to perceive. What, even, would the purpose of life be for humans if they found themselves in a place where nothing could be improved, where they found themselves staring into the abyss, perhaps at one cliff face or the other, searching in vain for even one crack, the tiniest fissure, the slightest contour change? Humans constantly reached for the stars, but what if the stars reached for them instead? When one could manipulate infinities, imperfection was simply no longer part of the equation. But as a human, I was continually reminded just how strongly life was defined as much by nadirs as it was by zeniths. Humans had a term, the "uncanny valley," for something that seemed realistic enough at first glance but upon closer examination found itself to be...lacking in certain respects. That was *exactly* where Yutigo and I resided. So perfect we could have been sculpted from marble, but yet uncannily robotic. We did not age, our faces did not wrinkle, our skin forever smooth, pores eternally invisible, so...*inhuman*. Luckily enough, we could just as easily compel others to ignore us. Either way, the end result was the same: ostracized.

But if that was the case, then how exactly did Pierre manage to fit in so well with his humans, even though to the best of my knowledge, he did not attempt to hide himself from the gaze of others? In fact, he did the exact opposite of that, if the loyalty of his friends was anything to go by. His friends... yet another paradox that further muddied the picture. Based merely off the few interactions of Pierre I had had the opportunity to observe, he was a very good friend, knowing exactly what other people wanted and exactly how to give it to them, almost like he was the...*perfect*...social butterfly. Perhaps it was simply because Pierre was perfect and yet so imperfect simultaneously. Even without his abilities at his beck and call, he had still possessed charisma enough to create for himself a perfect, impenetrable persona that made him seem as normal as any human, if perhaps a little more affable. At the same time, his human face, his *original* face, possessed the characteristic flaws of any human, unaffected as it were by any of his powers' attempts to attain perfection. Even now, the immense burden of the guilt Pierre carried, the guilt I had once so intimately been familiar with, made him someone less than one of us. This did not mean that none of us had emotions or character flaws. However, our character flaws and emotional burdens did not jeopardize the safety of our entire way of life. Not that I was in a position to judge, of course. Unlike Yutigo, I truly was here to help. Well, to help, but also to uncover the mystery surrounding Pierre.

This desire to help was, however, the primary reason I found myself back on the self-created replica of my home planet, Pong (yes, Pierre and I *really* were alike in quite a lot of ways), my current seat of power. The gambit I was about to carry out required every advantage I could get. Nuarti might be my cordial acquaintance, my frequent ally on the Council, but I would not go so far as to call her my friend. Friendships among all-powerful beings could quickly turn quite...*explosive*. Did I have a choice, though? On my own, I had only been able to trap Yutigo, not immobilize him. The next time, he would merely return stronger, whereas I would be much as I had been before, perhaps with a stronger Pierre at my side, but still...quite horrendous odds in my opinion.

I stood in a central square, the main gathering point of my capital city, usually bustling with life, but today conveniently emptied in preparation for the impending encounter. A few stray beams of sunlight bounced off the shining marble floor of the square, but with a wave of my hand, they disappeared, gone to shine on other parts of the city. Another wave, and a rough-hewn stone rose out of a small niche in the center of the square. As it drew closer, it began to hum and pulsate a dark green color, and a small chill ran down my spine as I assumed my original form. I placed my hand on the stone. A small gasp of pain escaped my lips as the stone drew a fair amount of my blood from my palm without making an incision in my skin. "Nuarti, ruler of the Ekkabad Realm, take this offering of my lifeblood to the Sacred Bloodstone as a sign of my willingness to parley in good faith," I incanted.

A barbaric ritual, perhaps, but one infused with great purpose both symbolic and realized. Though the taking of blood did nothing to weaken us, it represented the loss of a certain amount of control. One drop of my blood, and an enemy would know intimately my physical strengths and weaknesses, my mental powers. Thus, these stones acted as a way to prevent betrayal. Both parties gave their blood willingly, and if one party in some way broke the resulting contract, their blood would be available to the other, a sure path to a quick defeat. Unfortunately, the terms of the contracts were usually quite limited, and Sacred Bloodstones were only used during small meetings between beings, not at full Council meetings or the like. As always, there were limits to the control we possessed over ourselves that we were willing to relinquish to others.

This formality, this relinquishing of control, belonged to our short list of accepted social conventions, meaning it was right up Nuarti's alley. Even if Yutigo managed to force the Council to censure me, Nuarti would still feel obligated to accept my parley offer, especially considering it had been delivered through the proper diplomatic channels.

Nuarti's entire code revolved around rules. Her troubled

childhood (a typical background, at least among the Council elders) had been defined by the ways in which the adults around her had abused their power to perpetrate heinous acts, some of which had benefited her, but many more of which only had served to inflict pain upon her and her family in the end. One of these heinous acts had finally broken her, caused her powers to awaken, but it was the memories of her childhood that had stayed her hand. The ignoring of the rules and the resulting consequences had done more than enough to dissuade her from ever breaking another rule. Instead, Nuarti escaped, then exacted her revenge within the bounds of the law. Nuarti had been a driving force behind the Council as well, a way to place rules and regulations upon those who had seemingly boundless powers, whose actions had no consequences when perpetrated against those too weak to defend themselves (i.e., anyone who was not a fellow being). Why was Yutigo, and not she, the head then? Both because Nuarti did not trust herself with such power, and because she recognized Yutigo as the slick political operator best suited to control the Council. A pity that her faith had been somewhat misplaced. Yutigo was notorious for the abuse of the rules to suit his own purposes, though he was always vigilant enough to mask these abuses from Nuarti.

My task, then? Convince Nuarti that Yutigo had in this case heinously abused the rules, twisted facts to suit his own purposes, that my own violation of Council edicts she had supported was justified by appealing to her sense of morality (unfortunately entangled with her rule-following sensibilities), and that she should join me in combating Yutigo. Simple. I had never personally witnessed Nuarti's fury, but the tales of it were legendary. Irrevocably turn her against something or someone, and chaos would ensue.

My personal history, viewed from afar, should have alienated Nuarti. My coming-of-age had resulted in my rage completely shattering the farce of a government I had lived under, and the "rules" it had created, with the most destructive consequences caused thus far by any being. Yet Nuarti had once privately remarked that my past strongly reminded her of a worse version of her own formative years, and that though she could not bring herself to condone my actions, she could not help but feel sympathy for me. As my absenteeism from the Council grew more pronounced, Nuarti remained my closest ally among the elders, keeping me in the loop. This latest bout of rule-breaking, though? Nuarti was already not sure what to make of Pierre, and my latest actions could definitely be viewed as abetting a potentially dangerous criminal.

"Nuarti, ruler of the Ekkabad Realm, has accepted your offer of parley," came a booming voice directly from the stone, pulling me out of my train of thought. The stone flashed orange for a brief moment before returning to its prior state. There was a deep boom, and a portal opened a few feet in front of me, snapping shut with a loud crack moments later. Facing me now stood a woman. She had pale, white skin, as white as a sheet of ice, complemented by a long sheet of inky black hair falling past her shoulders. Though she had made some concessions to the human form, her eyes remained as ever a pale blue, as pale as the color of ice when it meets water, and with no distinction between her pupils and irises. I would have even called her beautiful, were it not for the lips pressed into an almost imperceptibly thin line and the angry eyebrows.

Nuarti was most definitely *not* happy with me, not one bit.

"Hello there, *Rexdael*," said Nuarti in greeting, my name flying out from between her lips with the speed of a gunshot. "I must say, I am quite surprised that things have to come to this. Not the meeting, of course. That I expected since the Council meeting. What *does* surprise me is that you followed the *rules* to arrange this, an instinct that seems to have deserted you following your newfound infatuation with possible *lunatics*!"

"Nuarti—" I began to interject, but she cut me off with one wave of her hand. "I respect you enough to come to this meeting and hear you out," she continued, "to perhaps find some logic in your likely twisted reasoning, but I won't have you groveling or making excuses. I *might* even consider giving you my support, but at this point in time, that appears quite implausible, given the rumors that have been swirling around concerning the events occurring on that charming little world, New Earth. So speak then. I'm listening." She folded her arms, fixing me with her characteristically piercing but now also cold stare, waiting.

"Nuarti, I don't know what you've heard," I began somewhat uncertainly. Nuarti raised one eyebrow fractionally. "What I do know, however, is that whatever you've already heard about events concerning Yutigo, Pierre, and me paints an incomplete picture. What I hope to do here is to provide my perspective of these same events as well as hopefully dispel some crucial mistruths that will at the very least help you understand why I have done what I have done and why I will continue to act in that matter until this crisis is resolved.

"The first thing you must understand is that Yutigo has

been lying to you all of these years. While you did recognize his potential to expertly take control of the Council, you failed to see all of the attendant consequences. All those 'incidents' that came to the attention of the elders, only to remarkably resolve themselves before you could call for an investigation? Yutigo's doing, cleaning up for his dishonest messes. The only thing he has ever cared about while carrying out his little games is whether news of his actions reaches your ears or not, since he *truly* does fear you and what you could do to him if he really enraged you."

Nuarti affixed me with another piercing look. "Really, Rexdael? Are you sure that *Yutigo* is the one who at this moment should be fearing my wrath? Do you have any evidence for your potentially grave accusations?"

I laughed, a short bark of sarcasm. "Nuarti, Yutigo is not *that* incompetent," I replied. "He would not simply leave evidence lying around like that! But please, I encourage you, after this meeting, look up some of the closed incident reports, and I assure you that a certain trend will become apparent. The incident of the nine rings? The bubble cage fiasco? The issue of the green fish? Everywhere you look, there will be retracted witness statements as well as dubious and late-appearing circumstantial evidence conveniently convicting the most logical culprit. Investigations that run like clockwork! Bureaucratic competence! Is there anything more suspicious than that?"

Nuarti continued to stare at me. "Efficient bureaucracy," she began slowly, "shouldn't that be a given? I don't see how inefficiencies would appear in a system where rules really could be followed to the letter, where perfection is a reality."

I scoffed. "Nuarti, perfection will never be reality as long as emotions remain in play," I replied. "After all, we are not psychopaths."

Nuarti grimaced. "Fine," she said after a while, "I will look into the discrepancies you have brought up here. Though I don't expect to find anything, I will say that you have never led me astray before, Rexdael." I smiled slightly, and Nuarti held up a finger in warning: "However, these discrepancies pale in comparison to the situation of the Hartford boy, whom I notice you now so *lovingly* call Pierre. Care to elaborate?"

"He is now my protégé," I said simply. Nuarti laughed, revealing a gleaming set of incisors as white as her skin. "Your *protégé*?" she asked after she had recovered. "Rexdael, are you quite mad? I know where you could see some similarities to your own situation, darling little boy driven past the point of insanity by an abusive ruler, blah, blah, blah, but you never showed the characteristic signs of being a realm-eater!"

I stared at Nuarti in shock. "But you understand!" I yelled back at her. "You know what I went through, what you had to endure, and you can see the similarities yourself! You expressed sympathy for my past—"

"Sympathy, Rexdael, not approval. You were a complete idiot who destroyed three planets, even if I do understand where you were coming from. You were stupid and reckless, but Pierre has *completely* thrown the rule book out the window. Yes, perhaps he had no choice but to commit genocide in order to fully destroy the Entity, but that does not give him the right to relinquish his birthright and threaten our entire way of life because he had a little tantrum!"

"It was not a little tantrum! He was racked by the spirits, imagined or not, of the billions he killed! A little break could

THE REWRITING OF TIME • 101

have helped him, had he done it correctly."

"Exactly! He rejected us! We could have helped him after that first meeting had he really come clean to us!"

"Why would he have done that? Because Yutigo was *so* friendly and welcoming?"

"He acts that way to everyone!"

"Well, twenty-three-year-old broken boys are not Yutigo's typical clientele!"

"So what? If he had just followed the rules, we wouldn't be here right now!"

"He's young! He needs to forge his own path, not become mired in our dated traditions intended to deal with unexceptional cases!"

"Not when that path could lead to a realm-eater!"

"But that problem is solved! I gave him back his memories and powers, and thus I gave him control back over the realm!"

"And who's to say he won't do it again after all this is over? Don't you see why Yutigo wants to add some safeguards to prevent that situation from arising once more?"

"Yes, except Yutigo, he didn't even try to subdue him; he went straight for the killing blow!"

I threw the tangled mass of wires still emitting blue sparks at Nuarti's feet. Her mouth snapped shut, whatever retort she had been preparing dying on her lips. "Where did you get this, Rexdael?" she asked softly, but with a deadly edge to her words. "From Yutigo's hands as I beat him away from Pierre's defenseless body," I responded. "Yutigo is not the only one with access to the Forbidden Archive," Nuarti retorted. "All elders have methods of accessing the devices stored within. Who's to say you didn't intentionally break one and aren't trying to plant evidence on Yutigo, now that you had your little spat on New Earth? Incidentally, *that* fiasco was also caused by your seeming inability to follow rules!"

I exploded. "Come off it, Nuarti!" I yelled, purple sparks flying out of my fingertips. "Since when have I been so deserving of your suspicion?! Have I ever attempted such underhanded tactics as planting evidence, even if it were against Yutigo? This is becoming ridiculous now, and your attempted explanations are collapsing under the weight of the assumptions they must uphold!"

Nuarti's eyes flashed with true rage for the first time in this conversation. "I'm being ridiculous?!" she screamed back at me. "You're insane, Rexdael! In all the time I've known you, the only thing you've ever done is show apathy for almost everything related to the Council, going so far as to skip required meetings on important issues to ensure our safety! And then, from time to time, you suddenly begin to take interest in a seemingly obscure topic that turns out to be near and dear to your heart because it's related to something from your *oh-so-tortured* past, which you never fail to invoke when it suits your own twisted purposes. You intentionally antagonize Yutigo and often the rest of the Council, simply because you are a big baby and need to get your way whenever you seem to think it matters! If you were an alcoholic, you would be drinking yourself to death, except that wouldn't work because it's impossible for you to kill yourself that way! So instead, you gum up the gears of the bureaucracy I have worked so hard to maintain, and now you turn around and say that that very cleanliness I have been striving for is the very *sign* of the graft and corruption I have been trying to avoid. How dare you?! I do feel bad for you. I really do, Rexdael! I feel pity! Because I can see what you could do if you simply woke up and stopped pretending to be living in the nightmare of your past! Instead, what do you do?! Up pops Pierre Hartford, and your heart melts because he's well on his way to following the same doomed life path that you are! You take up yet another doomed cause, except this time, you really might end up killing us all!"

"SHUT UP!" I roared back, and Nuarti shrank back for a second. I knew how I must have looked, purple sparks spewing out of my fingers, green eyes flashing. "Just shut up and listen for a moment!" I said, slightly more calmly, taking deep, shuddering breaths. "How many lives has your efficient bureaucracy wasted? How many innocents have you killed? All in the name of the rules! A state of security where murders, abuse of power, and criminal activity are viewed as bugs in the program that must be ironed out. Sometimes, it's even done through experimentation! Oh look, more people died because of something I changed? Guess that was a bad idea! No looking back, though! It's all in the name of progress! You know why I stopped caring about the Council?! Because nothing we did changed anything! Yutigo could get his way anytime he wanted, and you were his blind lapdog because you thought he could be your champion, your shining paragon of light! This is exactly how he could hide his flaws from you! You refused to see the corruption growing right in the center of your intricate, efficient web! I spoke up only when I reached my limits, when I felt something had to be done to keep the Council from going over the cliff of sanity and killing lesser creatures for no good reason at all. And what happened every time? I lost because the stupid *rules* always had to win! So I spoke up less and less, started skipping meetings, and stopped caring, since nothing I could do would effect real change! But here, Pierre?! Yet another innocent life, but one with far greater importance. We don't need to subdue him when we could help him! I *swear*, if you lay one finger on him, I will not hesitate to kill you with my bare hands!"

I whipped my right hand up, and a pale blue shield instantly formed around Nuarti. But I was not aiming at her. The Bloodstone flew into my hand, glowing green as it nestled into my palm. "I swear upon the Bloodstone that the memory I am about to deliver is the truth, and only the truth, untainted by any bias, emotional or otherwise." The Bloodstone flashed an even brighter green, and a metal sphere appeared in my other hand. Concentrating, I sent the memories of my conversations with Pierre, the battle with Yutigo, and the ensuing scene into it. I hurled the metal sphere at Nuarti. Only her lightning-fast reflexes prevented a sudden six-inch gaping hole from appearing in her chest. "Watch the memories before making any judgment about me or Pierre!" I growled. Nuarti took one look at my face, and any words she may have been planning to say died on the tip of her tongue. She nodded mutely. "Well, what are you waiting for?" I asked. "GET OUT!"

Nuarti finally took the hint, and with a deep boom, she was gone. I screamed, so loudly that I shattered the surrounding windows, and listened to the echo bouncing off the walls. I drove my fist into the floor, and hairline cracks appeared throughout the marble, all the way to the edge of the square. That entire encounter had been confusing to me. Everything seemed to have been going if not well, at least decently, and then Nuarti and I had almost come to blows. Both of us were usually more even-keeled than that. One thing, however, was crystal clear to me: no one, and I meant *no one*, was going to take Pierre away from me or keep him away from his destiny.

9

A Shifting of States

Pierre Hartford, his dream scape

"Pierre, wake up."

I blinked, and *yet again*, green eyes filled my vision. I twitched, slightly startled. "You have got to stop doing that, Rexdael," I muttered under my breath. The corners of his mouth twitched upward. "My apologies, Pierre," he said in reply. "It was the only way that I could easily use to initiate the next step of your training."

"What do you mean, next step of my...training..."

My voice trailed off. I suppose it should have been apparent from the very beginning. I had no recollection at all of having nodded off or lain down while waiting for Rexdael to return, yet now he stood over me as I lay on a soft surface which I then realized was *not* in fact my hospital bed. The walls of the room were a deep blue, rich as the ocean. Thin streamers of white light traveled along the walls, sometimes forming mesmerizing swirls and eddies as they went. When I stood up, I could not help but feel a sensation of weightlessness, though I was positive that I was standing on solid ground.

"Rexdael, where are we?" I asked, a slight edge creeping into my voice. "Where are my mother and Yuri?"

"This, Pierre?" Rexdael replied, waving his arm to indicate the space around us. "This is your dream space." Despite my best efforts, a small snort escaped me. "Oh, please tell me this is all one big joke," I said.

Rexdael simply smiled wryly. "The irony of the situation is not lost on me, but it is the only way that we can safely focus on enhancing your old powers and training the ones you were not aware of before."

I nodded slowly. "You're talking about the way you and Yutigo could move so fast, for example." Rexdael tilted his head in assent. "OK," I said slowly, "and you're in *my* dream space because…?"

"Because I established a psychic link with you," Rexdael replied. "The reason for the staring which you have so come to enjoy."

"You *induced* a dream state in me?" I said, somewhat taken aback. "With your assent, of course," Rexdael said reassuringly. "Everything might be a bit fuzzy at first, but I assure you, the memories are all there. They're simply a bit hard to access, since, well, this is taking place in a different region of your brain than the hippocampus, and your mental energies haven't yet completely acclimated to the effort of maintaining this physical manifestation of your dream space."

It seemed Rexdael was correct. With some effort, a few

blurry images of Rexdael talking to me about dreams flitted before my eyes before vanishing. "Fair enough," I said. "So what are we supposed to do now? It doesn't appear that this space is an *ideal* location for training. A bit too amorphous, one could almost say dreamlike. *Oh,* wait…"

Rexdael gave a short bark of laughter. "*Very* funny, Pierre," he said, attempting to sound humorous but utterly failing. "I want you to imagine a typical training space."

Doing as he requested, I immediately noticed the walls of the room wavering. Suddenly and noiselessly, a series of dark red panels burst through the blue walls of the dream space, forming part of one wall and the ceiling. More and more panels flooded through this gap, rapidly expanding to cover every available surface and create a spare, rectangular room. The rich burgundy color proved to be quite a contrast to the ocean blue I had already grown used to, but my mind, it seemed, was not done creating yet. A series of weapon racks containing a large variety of knives, swords, and guns popped up in one corner. In another, two sets of protective gear appeared. Finally, a dark green circle emblazoned itself upon the floor, denoting what I assumed was supposed to be a sparring area of some sort.

So caught up was I in wondering at my subconscious creation (for the only specification I had thought of had been "training area") that I barely stopped myself from plunging headfirst into a rack of katanas as artificial gravity asserted itself. My muscles began to tremble from the effort of keeping upright, and the details of the room began to flicker in and out of view. A surprisingly cool hand caught my right shoulder in a firm grip, and some of my exhaustion disappeared.

"Impressive, Pierre," said Rexdael, almost idly. "I've stabilized the projection using myself as the anchor, but an impressive creation nonetheless, especially for a first attempt. It can, of course, only grow easier with repeated use. But now, we proceed to the matter at hand."

Upon saying that, Rexdael did indeed lift his hand off my shoulder. I looked up, only to see that Rexdael was currently standing in front of me. But his *hand* had grabbed my shoulder from behind. So how…? I realized then that Rexdael's right hand did not at the moment look very much like a *hand* but instead more akin to an amorphous blob. Ghostly imprints of Rexdael's hand and wrist were seemingly scattered throughout the room: there one gripped a longsword, there one loaded a hunting rifle, there one examined the shuritanium breastplate of an armor set…but even as I saw this, these afterimages blurred and rippled, forming a series of particles streaking toward Rexdael's arm and forming his hand in its proper position.

I realized that my jaw hung slightly agape. Rexdael raised an eyebrow. "Why so surprised, Pierre?" he asked without any inflection. "You *have* seen something like this before. You know, when you were busy regaining your memories." Now that he mentioned it, I did indeed have a vague recollection of Rexdael seemingly phasing across the room to meet me at our first encounter. "Is that supposed to mean I know what you did, though?" I replied, a challenging tone in my voice.

"No, but this is your first lesson with me," Rexdael retorted. "When you were human, I know you were among the smartest. So, given the clues I have dropped for you in our conversation so far and what you have observed on your own, what do you infer I just did?"

The answer became embarrassingly obvious within just a few moments. "You...hijacked your wave function. But that doesn't explain how your hand can physically be in a place quite separate from your body or how you're managing it in any form in the first place." Rexdael gave one short clap. I might have construed it to be a sarcastic gesture, but given the circumstances and Rexdael's mannerisms up to this point, I thought it perhaps to be the closest thing to a gesture of appreciation that Rexdael was capable of at the moment. His reactions had been...oddly emotionally stunted, somewhat in contrast to the faint aura of depression he had carried before he had left to seek whatever it was that he sought. "Good," he said simply. "I myself would not have used the term 'hijacked,' but I think it applies well to the technique I will be teaching you. As for what I just did? An advanced technique that is difficult to maintain over long distances if you don't want to permanently lose a limb.

"Now, as to how it works? Well, in essence, you are 'cloaking' yourself so that you cannot be directly observed. Thanks to quantum physics, we know there is a chance, quite small but nonzero, that we are not in the place one would expect us to be in. The wave function tells us exactly what the probability is that we find ourselves in a given spot and with a given posture. To make yourself unobservable, you simply vibrate the air molecules surrounding you." Rexdael lifted his hand, and a patch of air in front of it became quite fuzzy all of a sudden, rendering it impossible to make out distinct shapes behind it. "This creates a semiopaque barrier," he continued, "which for our purposes is more than enough to access our own wave function.

"Once you have accessed your wave function, you'll be able to see every possible potential position you could be occupying at that moment, which you may have picked up on as an infinite series of figures superimposed on each other. The 'hijacking' takes the form of you *warping* your probability density function so that your most probable position is the new position that you have chosen. You then allow yourself to be observed, collapsing your wave function and depositing yourself in your new chosen position.

"It's easier to move if you decide to keep your bodily posture constant, but it is of course entirely possible to simultaneously change your posture as well as your position. Fair warning: the movement is extremely disorienting, in the sense that you don't feel as if you are moving at all. You simply disappear from one place and reappear in another with, for all intents and purposes, no time passing at all. As a result, your sensory perceptions are thrown completely off-balance. It took a lot of practice before I was able to seamlessly integrate this technique into my movements, not to mention combat."

"What about other objects?" I asked.

"Those are extremely hard to influence this way," replied Rexdael. "The reason this technique is even remotely effective for us is that our powers allow us to be far more attuned to our bodies than any mere mortal could ever hope to be. It is this concentration that allows us to move all of our body's atoms as one seamless, cohesive unit. This intimate familiarity, however, does not extend to foreign objects. Only objects that one has handled extensively can be transported in this way. Hence, the preferred method of combat using this technique is to generate bursts of energy to stun, disorient, or otherwise incacitate foes."

I nodded. "And what about the dismembered limb thing you were displaying earlier?"

"Just a matter of concentration," replied Rexdael. "You simply have to subdivide your body's atoms into distinct units and transport only certain subunits of your body at a time while still maintaining the level of concentration necessary to make yourself believe that these subunits still are parts of your body, even though they may not be connected to you at that exact moment in time. The limiting factor in most cases is then line of sight.

"Now," he continued, "is there anything else you would like to know in order to fully sate your curiosity?"

"There is one thing you could explain for me," I replied. "If this is a technique that you use quite often, especially, it seems, in combat situations, why do you use wormholes to travel around instead of this technique, which, from what you tell me, is an even faster method of transportation than said wormholes?" Rexdael's eyes suddenly regained their typical faintly haunted look.

"When we don't travel through wormholes, Pierre, the speed of our movements is, like that of all other creatures, limited by the speed of light. Thus, the volume of our possible movements within a second is confined to a sphere with a radius of one light-second. Equally important, the probability of us being in a given location that we could travel to within one second remains quite high. This means that, relatively speaking, it is quite easy to use this technique in the confines of a battlefield that may at most span only a few tens of miles. It grows slightly harder on a thousand-mile battlefield, harder still on a hundred-thousand-mile battlefield. If this theoretical battlefield were to span light-*years*, however? A light-year is many orders of magnitude larger than a light-second, and as anyone who knows what a probability curve is can tell you, the probability of traveling instantaneously to a point a light-year away from your current position is correspondingly smaller. Say there is a fifty-fifty chance you could travel to a point between 0.99 and 1.01 light-seconds away from here. To warp the wave function to accept this new reality is not so difficult. But assuming this, the probability of traveling to a point between 0.99 and 1.01 light-years away is perhaps one-*millionth* of a percent. And the distances we must travel in our journeys across the universe often number in the millions of light-years! What do you think the probability of reaching a point *millions* of light-years away is?!

"I had a…friend once on the Council. Well, perhaps protégé is a better term. He was yet another being whose powers had been awakened under troubled circumstances. He was quite interested in probing the limits of these techniques, a researcher to the very core. One day, he decided to conduct an experiment very much along the lines of what you were describing—attempt to travel a few million light-years—but by warping his wave function, not using a wormhole. Now, it must be noted that he *had* successfully done jumps of several light-years before this, though he almost killed himself in the process. I did not hear anything from him after he attempted his initial jump, but this was not unexpected, as something similar had occurred after his previous jumps, and the energy expenditure temporarily exhausted his mental circuits, rendering telepathy impossible in the short term. The next day,

however, it was found that a supernova-like explosion had occurred a hundred thousand light-years along his intended path.
His body had decohered, and the resulting outburst of energy
had ripped apart a star cluster. It turns out that it is far easier to
fold space and cross the resulting crease than it is to attempt to
move your atoms across that same space in its unfolded state.
The lesson? *Do not gamble with Fate.*"

This last was said in the barest of whispers, in a tone so unlike any Rexdael had used up to this point that I found myself
slightly taken aback. The traces of gravitas I had been noticing
up to this point emerged in full force, and it was quite clear
that, if nothing else, this one *sentence* I should sear into my
memory. I wasn't sure if I'd imagined it, but I also thought that
perhaps a gust of cold air, or whatever took the place of air in
this dream land, had whooshed past my face for the merest of
moments.

"Well, Pierre, are you *satisfied* now?" Rexdael's stony expression had disappeared, but every syllable he spoke was tinged
in bitterness. "I suppose I am," I replied, somewhat meekly.
However, this only seemed to make Rexdael angrier, and he
turned away from me, muttering under his breath. "What are
you waiting for?" he called over his shoulder. "Get to work!
I've told you the theory; now put it into practice, clever *boy!*"
There was an insult somewhere in that statement, though I
was unsure of its purpose.

Creating the air barrier was simple enough, a matter of
repurposing well-known and well-explored abilities. The barrier was indeed semiopaque; I found it as difficult to peer out
from within its confines as I was sure Rexdael would find it to
peer in had he actually been looking in my direction. Focusing

inward, I attempted to pinpoint the location of every atom in my body, to visualize myself as a collection of nodes, connected through the transmission of electrons and other subatomic particles. A shimmering net of red-black dots appeared before me, connected by gossamer-thin golden threads. This was what I had intended, but it simply was not *deep* enough. This foundation would not allow me to visualize my body as simultaneously being there and not there in many places at once.

I shifted my focus to the electrons, and the red-black dots disappeared in a mass of golden ones. These, I presumed, were the electron clouds and their respective orbitals. I attempted to locate a single electron. This was no easy task, and my eyes began to ache as the electron I was tracking disappeared into a fuzz of particle trails. A bright yellow spot was occasionally visible but disappeared almost immediately as the electron moved in a seemingly erratic pattern. As my eyes refocused, however, the yellow spot became visible for longer and longer, even as it was moving (seconds for me, femtoseconds perhaps in real time). Even though I still could not predict the electron's movements, I could track the beginning and end of each of its sudden motions, though I still could not see what occurred in between. Then, just for a moment, I saw the electron seemingly wink out of existence...only for a *ghostly afterimage* to continue traveling across the orbital, before it reappeared in its new position.

Maintaining my current mind-set, I pulled out of my mind the visual I had created of my body's atoms. A bolt of pain surged through my head, making me feel as if it were splitting in two, and when I opened my eyes, my left eye *saw something different* from my right eye: one gazing at Rexdael's back, while one regarded his face, heavy with interwoven melancholy and anger. I could feel, too, a plethora of microscopic pricks on my consciousness, views of the same scene from an infinity of varied viewpoints,as well as views of other, less well-developed parts of my dream space that I had not even been aware of.

I decided that I did indeed want to go from where I was/ wasn't standing behind Rexdael and materialize directly in front of him. There was a sudden wrench on every single atom of my body, and the atomic map I had visualized earlier flared bright gold in front of my eyes. When it cleared, I found myself standing in front of Rexdael, in the exact same position I had assumed before creating my air barrier. Rexdael had raised one eyebrow, a look of mild surprise visible. I myself was so surprised that I promptly toppled into a heap at his feet, noticing that, if anything, I had definitely given myself the mother of all headaches.

"Well, I must say, I *am* impressed…for a first attempt."

10

MORAL MEANDERINGS

Rexdael, Pierre's dream scape

I was supposed to be angry with Pierre, yet I could not help but feel a swell of pride as I looked over at him. He and his absolutely *infuriating*, *stupid* questions about the techniques I was so generously teaching him (though a little voice in my head sagely pointed out that they had been perfectly reasonable questions, not tools of torture designed to home in on my weak points)...but simultaneously, here he was, several hours later (only in the dream scape, of course), well on his way to complete mastery of quantum travel. One moment he stood beside me; the next he leaped up and over me, only to land on the opposite side of the room. One moment he stood on the ceiling; the next he prepared to brandish a throwing star. All this he did so quickly that I even had difficulty following the path of his movements, slivers of his ghostly silhouette flashing across my vision the only traces I could even hope to follow. My job had been simple: to sit and brood, occasionally shouting out a new set of instructions. But *why*? Why were old wounds choosing these moments, more crucial than ever, to rear their heads? *Why* and *when* had I suddenly become so *prickly* (not just with Pierre, but also with Nuarti)?

These questions I could not answer immediately, however, for Pierre suddenly appeared in front of me again, looking winded (a rarity for us beings). Through his pain, moreover, he glared daggers at me; whether it was out of anger directed at me or simply a byproduct of his pain, I was unsure (I *had* been perhaps a tad too harsh earlier). "I finished...another set," panted Pierre through a series of harsh, stuttering breaths. "Good," I replied. "Your speed is definitely improving to the point that even I couldn't see each of your jumps clearly, but you're still telegraphing your jump direction because you hesitate for a moment too long coming out of every single one of them. I can't predict *exactly* where or *when* you'll jump, but as you're choosing your next destination, your head tilts slightly. Such a weakness could prove lethal against Yutigo."

I stood up, barely noticing Pierre's eyes tracking my every movement. My joints popped as I stretched out my body, a chorus of bones grinding against each other, ligaments extending and retracting, tendons and muscles expanding and contracting. My skin began to crackle with energy as I conjured a basic shield.

"Rexdael," Pierre began uncertainly, "...what are you doing?"

I smiled slightly, not pleasantly, yet not angrily either. "Well, Pierre, there is only one way I can teach you to rectify your ways," I replied. "Now, we fight."

Pierre's eyebrows shot up his forehead, and he winced involuntarily. "Like *this*?" he asked, his voice laced with repressed anger. "Hardly seems fair, does it?"

I smirked. "Since when does Yutigo play—" I began, sending a bolt of lightning at Pierre's head while doing so, immediately afterward jumping behind him and sending a lance of ice at the small of his back, "—*fair*?" Pierre's eyes widened as a ball of rubber, materializing out of nowhere, shot out to absorb the lightning bolt, and a gout of flame shot out of his fingertips to melt my ice lance. Suddenly, I found myself again face-to-face with Pierre. "Headache or no," I continued, jumping to the other side of the room, ripping a shuritanium blade off a drone and sending it just to the right of Pierre's current position (the corners of his eyes peered that way), "Yutigo will fight regardless."

As predicted, Pierre jumped directly into the path of my blade, but I felt an iron will suddenly wrestling with me for control of the blade, and I watched as the blade *bent*, cracked in two, and had both its pieces reverse directions. "Shut up and *fight* then!" yelled Pierre, and for the first time, I sensed true anger coming from him. The floor beneath me cracked, and a three-foot-wide abyss appeared where I had been standing. Unfortunately for Pierre, I had already leaped into the air, flipping backward as I went. Halfway through my flip, I reappeared behind Pierre, landing nimbly on my feet. A ghostly white blade of energy that had been heading forward suddenly curved in an arc, seeking me out once more, but I warped around it, reappearing inches from Pierre's side. Pierre had already turned to meet me, however, one hand lashing out at my face while the other conjured a forest green energy barrier. It was for naught, though, as my arm, newly separated from the rest of my body, phased right through Pierre's shield and held a glowing orange dagger to his neck. Pierre's motions stilled in an instant, and the room went silent, the only audible sound the snap and crackle of Pierre's useless and now rapidly fading energy barrier.

"Again," I said softly.

Pierre snarled, batting my hand away and dispelling my dagger, in the meantime letting his energy barrier fall, all the while standing stock-still. The reason for this became clear in a moment, as Pierre's hands disappeared in a hail of ethereal afterimages. Each of his finger joints, it seemed, had separated from each other, every one of them throwing a punch from a dizzying variety of arm angles, directions, and speeds. At the same time, waves of energy flared out from Pierre, so strong that they were visible to the naked eye, forming winglike protuberances sprouting from his back. These energy flares, too, joined the assault on me. The first joint I blocked left me gasping for air. Somewhat foolishly, I had tried to deflect it directly with my palm. The joint went through my energy shield as if it weren't there, and the line it scored into my palm burned on contact as if I had dipped it into a vat of boiling acid. Not trusting myself to split my body into as many parts as Pierre had (*truly remarkable*, the degree of controlled focus he was displaying), I instead conjured small transparent shields of clerium in front of my hands every time I went to block a punch. Yet every time I made to deflect a joint, it simply ghosted out of existence, and somewhere else, one joint became two or simply assumed a new position. I knew it couldn't be true, but it certainly seemed as if for every punch I went to redirect, two more appeared, and it took every last bit of my strength to phase my hands around fast enough to keep up with Pierre's barrage.

One blow grazed the edge of a clerium shield that I had not positioned precisely enough, and it simply ate right through it. Before I could react, around half the punches being thrown at me seemed to disappear, and a full, acid-wielding fist smashed right into my left eye socket. There was a loud crunching noise, and a blinding burst of pain coursed through me. Half-blind, blinking a combination of blood and acid out of my eye while also trying to shield it, I desperately phased to a spot behind Pierre, haphazardly sending a beam of ions at his back. But even before Pierre had phased to face me, he had allowed some of his energy flares to roam free, and they swirled around to swallow my relatively feeble attack. Already the hail of punches had begun to surround me again. I tried phasing as fast as I could to somewhere, anywhere in the room that could possibly be far away from Pierre, but it was useless. He was simply too fast, and moreover, he was *tailing* my movements *exactly*. Not just approximately, as I had been doing before by observing Pierre's tells, but *exactly*. I was sure he couldn't know where I was going before I phased, which could only mean he was somehow tracking me *as* I was phasing. Supposedly impossible, but apparently the rule book was simply meant to be thrown out when it came to fighting Pierre.

I suddenly tripped over a stone protrusion where there had been none before I had decided to phase to that location, and I began to fall. In slow motion seemingly, Pierre's left fist and arm coalesced into one as he swung at my jaw. Seized by a sudden blast of inspiration, I ripped two pillars of stone out of the floor—one where Pierre's fist had been, and one where he had phased his fist *to* (yet again, his eyes had betrayed him, particularly lethal at short range). There was a horrific-sounding crunch as every bone in Pierre's left hand and forearm was pulverized, and I phased forward, landing on Pierre as he was forced to join his body into one again and driving him into the floor. "Again," I managed to rasp out, another glowing orange dagger held at his throat.

I caught a glimpse of a gaze that could potentially have signified wonderment (perhaps Pierre wondering what kind of a crazy devil he had made a bargain with this time) before the stone pillar around Pierre's arm shattered and he phased to the other side of the room. His left arm hung limply and uselessly at his side, but then again, my right palm still felt as if it were melting away. My depth perception was somewhat affected by the peculiar angle my eye had been shoved into upon the breaking of what I assumed was an orbital bone, and it also stung like crazy.

For fifteen minutes, things ground to a standstill as Pierre and I battled it out. My movements were slower and my attacks not as powerful, but this was more than compensated for by the fact that Pierre's rate of fire had plummeted by more than half, his punches rendered somewhat useless by the fact that he could effectively only pin in half my body at any one time. Tripping or otherwise sending each other off-balance was no longer effective now that it had already been successfully implemented once, but nevertheless every surface of the room was covered with cracks, dust, and a score of dents as well as scorch marks, tears, and bulges.

Phasing once more to a point near the center of the room, I ducked under Pierre's disembodied fist and sent several arcs of molten metal at the places where Pierre initially was and where I thought he might go next (his tells were still visible, though they had become more difficult to read over the course of the battle). I prepared to phase again as an energy flare hurtled toward me, only for it to *fail*. Conjuring a red shield to capture the flare, barely sidestepping in time when the flare sliced right through the shield, I attempted to phase again… and *failed again*. What in the world?

I heard a laugh and saw Pierre smiling, standing in front of me, silhouetted by the energy flares stretching around his body. The third time I tried to phase, I realized. As I tried to vibrate the air around me to render myself unobserved, I perceived a countervibration occurring simultaneously. Pierre was canceling out my attempts to become unobserved, and thus I could not phase out of my current location.

I *could* still move normally, but even as I stepped forward, a golden dome sprang into existence, ominously crackling with energy, and I caught glimpses of Pierre's fist phasing around me, maintaining the dome, and, to someone currently limited to nonrelativistic speeds, impossible to escape. The dome slowly began to shrink in on itself, and I caught glimpses of Pierre striding forward. Another energy flare headed toward me, completely unaffected by the dome surrounding me, and I perceived Pierre suddenly appearing behind me, inside the dome…yet *still* I found myself unable to phase. Desperately, I lashed out, falling backward at the same time to attempt to avoid the flare, but the dome was too small, Pierre was too close, and my feeble attempt was easily dodged. A hand closed around my throat, Pierre's newly healed left one. The energy flare tickled my face, its tendrils coming millimeters away from truly harming me yet remaining in place nonetheless, and the dome continued to flare bright gold around us.

"*Well done,*" I breathed out as warmly as I could. "Truly, I find myself deeply impressed. I believe we can conclude this part of your training now." Focusing beyond my currently broken body, I located the full mental presence of my physical self. Using that as an anchor, I snapped the stabilization still holding Pierre's dream scape together. There was a huge shudder, and all of Pierre's attacks against me disappeared as he fell to the floor next to me, clutching at his head while patches of the environment flickered in and out of existence around us. Holding tightly to Pierre, I wrenched myself and him into states of wakefulness.

Calmly, I opened my eyes, finding myself sitting in the chair next to the head of Pierre's bed that I had been sitting in before establishing our psychic connection. Surprisingly, though, I also discovered that I was now nursing quite the pounding headache. Pierre had certainly proven to be quite the handful...and knowing him, this next part was likely to be just as painful. *I could not afford to become angry again at any cost.*

Pierre sat up with a gasp, looking around wildly for a moment before he seemed to realize where he was. Tentatively, he reached out and felt his left arm as if to ensure that it really was whole again. "As I said, Pierre," I continued, speaking as if our conversation hadn't just been interrupted by a transition between dreaming and wakefulness, "the dream scape makes an *excellent* practice area. Now you know why." Pierre gave me a sidelong glance, but he also stopped grasping at his arm. "There is one last thing that I feel you must be taught," I added.

Pierre looked up at me again, a grim sense of foreboding clouding his blue eyes. "Don't try to sugarcoat it, Rexdael," he said quietly. "Just get it out and over with, if you're so sure that I won't like it."

I dipped my head in acknowledgment. "Have it your way, then. I'm not sure if you've been made aware of this, but the fact that you are standing on ground that you yourself have created lends you certain privileges. You are far more in tune with this land, this air, this water than any other being could possibly be, to the point that you could theoretically prevent them from using it in any way whatsoever if you focused enough. Call it, if you will, a 'home field advantage.' This attunement, however, goes far beyond material resources. It extends to the sentient creatures inhabiting this planet as well."

I could see the light slowly being extinguished in Pierre's eyes. "In other words?" he prompted, voice menacingly, silkily soft.

I swallowed. "In other words, you could, if you so chose, control your people."

One of the lightbulbs in the room popped and shattered, throwing half of Pierre's face into shadows. "*No*," he answered, even quieter than before, as harsh as a nail scraping across a chalkboard.

"Pierre, Yutigo is not just going to lie down in front of you because of a pretty light show. You need every last advantage—"

"*No.*"

"They won't even have to remember—"

"*No.*"

"If you don't, someone else—"

"*No.*"

"It's for your own—"

"*No.*"

"Dammit, Pierre," I growled through gritted teeth. "Principles have never—"

"NO!" he roared, and the ceiling cracked, raining a fine sprinkling of plaster dust down onto us. He got up and paced about the room, waving his hands as he did so. "No, no, no, no, no, no! *I* don't think you *understand* what the *real* problem *is* here. You see, *control* is perhaps my only buzzword. You start doing it, and you just *never* know when to *stop.* It's *addicting,* since it feels so *good* to bend another person to your will! It *enables* power fantasies! What has the point of my entire life been, if not to *break free* of *control?*! My entire life story is based around a saga of breaking barriers, of destroying inhibiting ties, of promoting freedom and equality for all. And I'm just supposed to *throw that all away* because I might die? Heck, I *was* ready to die before wiping my own memories! So don't try to *lecture* me on using control, Rexdael!"

Not for the first time, I realized, something felt wrong with a conversation that I was currently partaking in. Pierre was being…*different,* even if it was in defense of his principles. But this thought was soon overwhelmed by the roar of blood I heard pumping through my ears, drowning out all other sounds. "Oh, shut up and stop being all high and mighty!" I yelled back. "You think you're so perfect? You think what you've created is so perfect?! Because when I look, I see something, and I'm pretty sure it's not called communism! You and your pretty little ideals, you can't even be bothered to put them into practice in your pristine little corner of the universe! So forgive me if I don't really believe you when you try to peddle your code of ethics across the galaxies. Our purpose as beings, as leaders of our realms, is to deal with the universe as it *is*, not as we *wish* it were. If that means we have to dirty our hands a little, that is a fair price to pay if in the future, we can breathe easy without having to worry about a further defense of our ideals. You know what I call what you're doing? *Cowardice.* You said it yourself: you're afraid of what would happen if you handed yourself the keys to that power. You think you'd become the monster that you hate so dearly. Well, if you're the saint you make yourself out to be, you shouldn't be corrupted! So stop dithering and just do it already!"

Pierre just stared at me for a few seconds, mouth slightly agape. When he continued, he sounded no less angry, but perhaps even icier than before. "I really, truly, honestly thought that you were *nice*," he whispered. "I believed, or at least I wanted to, that you were my ally, maybe even my *friend* or *mentor.* You *understood* what I had gone through, what I could possibly still undergo, and your sympathy warmed my heart to its very core. But then, you up and disappeared, supposedly 'looking for more help,' but when you came back, *you were changed.* What happened?! I feel it now, all the time; even when you think you're feeling something else, I can feel it. So tell me, Rexdael: *Why are you so angry?*"

Out of habit, I opened my mouth to reply, only to realize that I had nothing to say. My mouth opened and closed, flapping about uselessly like a fish gasping for air. "I…I don't know," I replied haltingly, the fire gone from my tone. "I guess that I've just been losing...*losing control.*" I sat down with a thump (when had I decided to stand up?) and rested my head in my hands. Pierre stared at me with an unreadable expression, his eyes still dim, but not dark with icy rage (it would be quite the testament to his character if he found it within himself at this moment to feel sympathy for me). "Oh my word," I said softly. *"I've been losing control of myself."* Unbidden, the words flowed through my head.

Do not gamble with Fate...and expect a world undisturbed.

11

THE POWER PLAY

Yutigo

I should not exist.

Call it my mantra, if you will. I should have died at birth a scrawny runt. I should have died when my brother's punch cracked my skull open like an egg. I should have died when my newly awakened powers tried to consume my frail, broken body. I should have died when an older, far wilier and more powerful being tried to annex my little corner of the universe. I should have died many times over during my tenure as head of the Council of Realms. I should have died when I *dared* to incite Rexdael's ire, and yet...here I was, in a precarious but not impossible position.

My brethren lived and breathed in a culture that prized physical strength above all else. Dominance battles decided anything and everything of importance, and more often than not, the vanquished did not live to see the consequences of their failures. You are familiar, I'm sure, with the "fantastical" creature known as the Minotaur? Well, if you can picture that, then you already have a fairly good idea of the physical appearance of an average specimen of my species. Unlike the cows you are undoubtedly familiar with, however, both male and female "Minotaurs" sported sets of horns protruding from their heads. Moreover, our culture was savage, but we were not mindless beasts.

Knowing all this, then, allow me to present you with a not-so-hypothetical scenario: How do you think this culture would deal with one of their own who was born so weak that he needed to be nursed for two whole years before he was strong enough to stand and survive on his own, where the typical nursing period is two weeks, who, even at the still tender age of sixteen, showed not even a single trace of having horns grow, where even the latest of late bloomers can expect the first signs of growth by twelve or thirteen (a year on my home planet translates to approximately 1.5 Earth years), but who also spoke his first words at three months, who could read even before he was weaned from his mother, where the typical ages for these events to occur are, respectively, three and seven years? What does a culture do when faced with a genetic anomaly, vastly superior in so many ways, and yet so vastly inferior in all the ways that supposedly matter?

I'm sure that by now you've become aware of the fact that I am, in giving this description, of course referring to myself. I was so weak, in fact, that I was told later that my heart had stopped beating for a few moments before my mother soundly slapped me back to life. My precociousness did nothing to impress my peers and everything to alienate them. Within earshot, I even heard whispers of the "demon child," the "freak," and, worst of all, the "coward." They saw it as cowardice, but to me, it was staying alive. I quickly learned which situations I could and couldn't get out of using my wits, and those that I couldn't...those were the times I ran. For no matter how much I ate, my body stubbornly refused to grow beyond a certain point, and I remained a sickly yet frighteningly intelligent (to my culture, at least) waif.

It was worst within my own family. If there was one thing my culture prized even more than raw physical strength, it was *family*. And thus, my kinsmen were put in an untenable situation. Kill me, and all of them would be immediately exiled, their fellows no longer able to trust them wholeheartedly. Keep me, and all of them would be shunned for possibly carrying tainted blood in their veins. Not outwardly, of course, for all in our culture treated each other with dignity. But behind the sweet words, the kind gestures, would lie an impassable abyss, a gulf that would limit the stature of my family members, derail friendships, poison marriages, slowly, insidiously, but inevitably. My parents still bore this burden to a certain degree. My father was kind, if distant, never one to punish, but also never one to reward. My mother came closest to loving me, a certain affection clinging to her heart for the babe she had suckled for two years. She never lacked in kindness, in extra portions, hidden sweets, even gifts to foster my true interest in science (my own way, perhaps, of gaining strength one day). And yet, every time passersby spat on her, every time her husband was denied a promotion, her sons and daughters friends and lovers, a small spark of affection was extinguished, and the seeds of bitterness sprouted further. For my mother was proud, as strong as her husband, and no amount of motherly affection would ever allow her to love me as she did her other, normal children.

The other members of my family did not even attempt to mask their hatred. My brothers and sisters, my uncles and aunts, my cousins, they spoke to me with derision, stole my food, drink, anything they wanted, sparing my books only because they had no desire or need for them. At least within my family, violence was not wielded against me. Until, of course, it was.

My oldest brother had always hated me most of all. He was the pride of the family, stocky, well-built, with a set of beautiful, curling horns. He was fifteen years my elder, and before I was born, he had been expected, even groomed, to be the next leader of our clan. He had never lost a fight, but the stigma of my birth was one fight he could not hope to win, one driven by the collective stupidity of my species, his included. And so, in a few short years, my brother went from clutching the reins of power to clutching the bottle instead. Every year he grew drunker, more depressed, and more brutal, yet still none could hope to best him in combat. For him, the last straw came when his wife (who, surprisingly, allowed herself to be exiled from her family to stay with my brother) decided she could no longer stand the "Minotaur" she had once loved and left him for good. In my brother's decidedly one-track mind, the cause of this latest, perhaps final betrayal was quite clear: I. And thus, dealing with this problem much as he always did, he came to my room one night, swung a meaty fist, and nearly cleaved my head in two. My vague recollections involve only the words "killing the devil." At the time, I was fifteen. My bones had the strength of a six-year-old's.

In yet another quirk of Fate, my brother's punch managed to completely spare all the parts of my brain I truly considered important, while irreparably (at least for the moment) damaging my chances to ever become physically strong. From the neck down, I lost all motor function. I was in a coma for months. For my family, at least, this was temporarily a good thing. They were spared from having to deal with the even bigger humiliation I had become at the hands of one of their own and from having to determine the fate of my brother. Indeed, when I woke up, the first thing I did was to kill my brother. Figuratively speaking, of course. While my brother's "lawyer" (our judicial system was just a tad too simple for lawyer to really be a respectable profession) successfully argued that my brother shouldn't be charged with attempted murder, having only unintentionally driven me into a coma, I countered by pointing out that what my brother had done instead was further shame the family. Cripples were traditionally killed at birth, but I was no helpless babe anymore. Instead, my brother, for being the one who had created a cripple, was put to death. In that same moment, I forged a measure of grudging respect. Even if I was a cripple, none could reasonably call me helpless. This, at least, exhibited a strength of will my culture recognized, and I realized for the first time how my mind could be not just a tool to further myself but also a weapon with which I could strike down my enemies.

Sadly, this realization I was never able to put to good use. Days before I was to be released from the hospital (it speaks to the crudeness of our judicial system that my brother's trial could be conducted in my hospital room), I fell into another coma. My brain, having been forced to extensively rewire itself to circumvent the areas which had been rendered unusable, found the new configuration it had adopted to be far more efficient, now that it was no longer forced to devote precious energy attempting to sustain my feeble body. This, in turn, unlocked the latent potential I had always possessed for gaining special powers. Before this, it had been a slow but continuous process of awakening, but my injury had destroyed my body's natural equilibrium, and now, in turn, my newly manifested powers threatened to consume me.

The battle itself I no longer remember, a chaotic affair of pretty lights and loud explosions. All I can remember is... something less than a presence, a single-minded force, perhaps, its sole intent to wallow in its newfound freedom, even if that meant my ultimate destruction. What finally won the day for me was recognition of the fact that now, at last, I had within my grasp real, tangible strength, powered still by my brain, but extending beyond the mental realm and into the physical one. My hatred, sharpened over the years into a blade of devastating cutting force, rose from the depths in which I had imprisoned it and sliced apart the force that dared to rise against me. It rose up, and I embraced it, in so doing becoming the finest version of myself.

Armed with this newfound physical strength—the strength my culture lived and breathed so easily—more strength even than my brother, who had always been the strongest among us, even when drunk, what do you think was the first thing I did? I killed my family members, of course. Their mocking had always hurt worse than mere physical blows could have.

They had hated me not for my personality traits but rather as an abstract object of revulsion. I had never even been *afforded* the opportunity to show myself in the best light, and nothing I could have possibly done short of sprouting muscles could have saved me in their eyes. The treatment of my family members naturally precluded any hope of me ever gaining a single friend. And so I paid them back in kind. My condescending aunts and uncles, my cruel cousins, my malicious siblings, my absentee father, even my mother, whose so-called affection had never extended far enough to shield me from the psychological torture of my own family. Of them all, she was the one who had the audacity to beg. Supposedly she had been strong, and yet, in the moments before her death, she was reduced to nothing. Utterly disgusting.

To take revenge against all who had ever mistreated me would have meant killing my entire species, something I could as of yet not bear to think of. They were, despite their numerous faults, in many ways still quite respectable. Now that I, too, could flaunt my own physical strength, I fully understood the subliminal appeal of the fighting my culture prized. In this way, I positioned myself as the leader my brother had once hoped to be. The fate of my family instilled fear, and anyone who dared defy me only granted me an opportunity to further my political acumen (which mainly consisted of finding creative methods to destroy my newly inferior opponents) and test my new strength and new powers. Every day, I thought I grew stronger, more invulnerable. And within my culture, that was indeed true. I never came close to losing a fight. But then, after all, I had never been introduced to the wider world.

His name I never learned. He called himself the Devourer,

and my world was simply the next morsel on his dish. His power was great and terrible, greater even than mine, and moreover, wielded with a brutal efficiency that only years of experience could have yielded. I was woefully underprepared, arrogant, and complacent. It sounds like a certain death, yes? It would have been, had my wannabe conqueror not been as stupid as any average member of my species.

The first step of his plan was clever enough. But then, after all, this was the first step of a plan that had been meticulously honed to perfection, which at this point the Devourer could have carried out in his sleep, unthinkingly, blindly. That is to say, while the plan as an abstract concept lay on perfectly solid foundations, it contained no room for adjustment, no mechanism for troubleshooting. The first thing the Devourer did was to turn my own species against me. This proved an easy enough task, as the balance of power was at this time firmly on his side, and my method of ruling had garnered me no friends (and really, is it such a surprise that my species never bothered to consider the possible implications of exchanging one dictator for another?). The catch: while the Devourer had temporarily left me isolated, his conquest would only truly be complete when he had bested me in ritual single combat. Of course, this was a step within a step of the conquest, and so the Devourer accepted this condition without hesitation, perhaps even with some measure of arrogance.

I mentioned earlier that I had never lost a fight. What I did not mention was that no opponent had even come close to touching me in any of these battles. Not only did I possess bountiful physical strength at this point, but the tender treatment of my childhood had rendered me quite proficient at all manner of dodging. All the Devourer's overwhelming numbers (for he did not merely conquer for himself, but also for the good of his *own* species) were rendered moot if only he alone was allowed to face me, and the danger of his power was greatly diminished if he could not effectively use it.

The fifteen minutes I spent in that arena were the most nerve-racking minutes of my life up to that point, the battle the most taxing I had ever fought. So taxing, in fact, that I was even hit once, a glancing blow. The sound of my left leg snapping like a brittle stick reminded me of just how stark the power imbalance was, similar to the one I had already faced once before, before I had known strength at all. It was like dodging an anvil, a burst of concentrated raw power, lethal if successful, but ponderous to aim and wield. The blow that finally killed the Devourer was somewhat of a lucky one. Two columns of fire had swirled about, aiming to snap shut around me, when the Devourer tripped over, of all things, a stray pebble. His concentration thrown off and his attack disrupted, my fist flew straight and true through his neck, taking his head off in a shower of blood and gore.

Unfortunately, I had to kill off the majority of the rest of my species at that point. Betrayal was one of the things I found myself least able to tolerate. Death as an ultimate end, however, was a bit too cruel for my taste. So, instead, I left two families alive (though I first considered killing only half, it did not ultimately suit my intended purpose). I allowed them to live much as they wished, but it had to be done in each other's company. As successive generations went by, they would naturally have to breed with each other to sustain the species, and as their genetic lineages became more and more intertwined with each other, their breeding would eventually amount to little more than incest, with all of its attendant benefits. And thus, a species once proud and strong would be reduced to a pack of gibbering, puny idiots.

Until the Council of Realms was created, I allowed myself to become a new, smarter version of my would-be conqueror. A Devourer 2.0, if you will. Using the remnants of his own empire as my base, I reseeded my home planet and beat the drum of conquest in an ever-expanding circle. Some of my opponents remained stronger than I, some of them, I am ashamed to say, smarter even than I, but none possessed that optimum blend of intelligence and strength that I now had.

Rexdael derisively calls me a slick political operator, an oily con man bereft of morals. He posits this as the reason that I was made head of the Council. To an extent, it is true. What is equally true is that I was owner of the most resource-rich parcels across multiple realms. And indeed, I am and never will be as powerful as Rexdael, perhaps unable to beat him in single combat, either (for all his faults, he is not lacking in intelligence). But I am unencumbered by morals, by petty emotional ties, by venal mortal desires. Those who have never known my power, who joined the Council long after its conception, respect me. Those who have dared to cross me, even those who may have thought they possessed an overwhelming abundance of brains and brawn, have all learned to fear me.

All except, to a certain degree, Rexdael. That was still indeterminate. Our struggle was ongoing, though it should have already been over. Rexdael had attempted to trap me within a black hole, which was where I still found myself. However, he had been uncharacteristically slow (I refused to believe

that I had been able to seriously weaken him in our little sparring bout), and moments before I crossed the event horizon
(beyond which even quantum phasing could not help me), I
had encased the black hole in a time bubble. Rexdael, in fact,
had seen this occurrence, but unless he, too, wished to get
trapped in a black hole, he could do nothing about it. And so,
by desynchronizing my body's internal clock and that of the
black hole's, it was a simple matter of fighting with just enough
strength to resist the black hole's gravitational pull for a long
enough period so that the black hole could evaporate within
the bounds of its accelerated time frame. This still took a fair
while, though, which gave me some time to think on my next
move.

Pierre was a softhearted romantic, and given time, I could
have destroyed him on my own, were it not for Rexdael. Pierre's
code of ethics, however, opened a wide variety of attacks. For
one, I highly doubted (though, again, it was perhaps possible
that Rexdael managed to convince him otherwise) that Pierre
would bother to take control of his populace. There was one
man who had caught my eye during my preliminary research
of Pierre: a man by the name of Aloysius Benton. A man of my
inclinations, so to speak.

With a sad little popping noise, the black hole chose this
moment to give up the ghost. Within seconds, I was already
in motion. One wormhole later, I found myself on the fring-
es of the star system where Pierre's "New Earth" resided (it
wouldn't do to be overly conspicuous, after all). Setting my
sights on my target, I found him, surprisingly, sitting in his
office within the remains of his once-secure building. Turning
myself invisible, I landed on the outskirts of New Berlin and

strolled through the streets on the way to Benton's office.

Though I had not detectably triggered a security system or made any noise that I could hear, at least, Benton's eyes focused on me the moment I stepped into his office. "Show yourself, intruder," he said in his best attempt at a menacing tone (perhaps it worked on his fellow "humans"). Nevertheless, I was impressed that he had managed to see through my invisibility.

I let it drop, remembering in the nick of time to put on my human face, and greeted Benton with an upturned eyebrow. "You are Aloysius Benton, are you not?" I replied in a drawl. Benton inclined his head, the only indication that he resented my tone the slight crinkling under his eye. "I have a business proposition to discuss with you. But first, I must say that I find myself quite impressed. How ever did you know I was here?"

Benton scoffed, a small whoosh of air escaping from between his lips. "Your research was obviously not extensive enough, my good fellow," he answered. "You think that once I had decided to build my company on the site of a wormhole, I wouldn't find a way to detect the distinctive negative energy signatures of anyone who had ever used such a method of travel? You can't possibly be human, for you positively *reek* of it." I, too, inclined my head. "I have no business with you then," Benton spat. "I do not consort with *aliens*."

I laughed. "Quite narrow-minded, don't you think? Let me show you what an *alien* can do."

Even before I could prepare my first attack, however, I sensed an energy net homing in on my right hand as Benton's eye flicked away from a retinal scanner hidden in a niche on the wall above me. I nimbly danced out of the way, sending bolts of lightning at Benton, only for an energy shield to flicker to life around him and absorb my attack. A piercing noise drilled into my ears, and pain exploded in my brain. Benton stared at me, unaffected. Snarling slightly, I batted away the telepathic probe and conjured a knife that I sent hurtling at Benton's carotid artery…only to stop short when a hissing sound indicated tiny vents opening on the walls. Benton's right index finger was poised on a trigger that had not been there when I had entered the room. "It's quite interesting," he remarked, "what exotic poisons one can create simply by investigating methods of energy generation. Even I'm not sure what the effects are, but I'm sure you'd make a lovely test subject…*alien.*"

I smirked. "You're grasping for straws, Benton," I replied calmly. "Would you really use a poison for which you have no antivenom? Perhaps it would kill me, perhaps it wouldn't, but I'm sure you'd die either way. *Painfully.* And besides, do you really think there is anyone clever enough to stalemate an *alien* as you have?"

Benton hesitated for a fraction of a second. It was a fraction too long, for it gave me enough time to phase my hands over to Benton's side of the room. My fingernails shredded through Benton's forearms like confetti, and Benton's index finger remained firmly rooted on the trigger even as blood spurted everywhere and he gave a yell of surprise.

I raised an eyebrow. "My, my," I mused teasingly. "That *does* appear to be checkmate to me." Benton shot me a baleful glare. "What do you want from me?" he muttered. "The answer to a question, dear Aloysius," I answered. "I may call you Aloysius, of course?" Without waiting for a reply, I continued. "Tell me, Aloysius, have you been suffering from any sudden headaches, memory loss, or strange physical sensations lately?"

Benton shook his head. I clapped my hands together and a broad smile stretched on my face (most would call it creepy, perhaps, but why should I care?). "Wonderful news, Aloysius," I said gaily. "I look forward to a long and fruitful partnership then."

Benton looked as if he were going to be ill. "Partnership?" he repeated slowly, disbelievingly. "Yes!" I replied. "I'm your new business partner. And believe me, I do intend to pick up the slack around here. How many bodies have graced the walls of these rooms, my dear Aloysius?"

"Twenty-four," he muttered in reply.

I tutted. "Such a low number," I murmured. "You can be quite sure, that will change soon enough."

I turned to leave, intentionally stopping at the door. "I almost forgot," I said, striding back over to where Benton still sat, attempting and failing to be stone-faced. "There's one last thing I need from you. Don't worry, it won't hurt a bit." A lie, of course. My fingers pressed against Benton's temples. Whatever mental defenses he may have had were presumably shot to pieces by the obvious discomfiture of having his arms chopped off. My mental presence strangled his like a vine, and I completed a task Pierre should have accomplished long ago. My newest puppet screamed, and I cackled.

12

SHADOWS OF A DOUBT

Nuarti

I was well and truly incensed. How *dare* Rexdael speak that way to me! How could *he*, of all beings, sink so low as to target the very core of my personality?! More than anyone else, he himself should know how much it hurts to have one's sense of morality questioned. He lived in the shadow of his greatest mistake, and it never strayed far from his thoughts. This much I knew. But, more troublingly, when had he become so angry? I had made some perfectly reasonable assumptions and objections, and Rexdael had exploded! He had acted more like a madman than I had ever known him to be, and something did not fit.

But…then again, so had I. Could I have perhaps used words less harsh when initially confronting Rexdael? Probably. Had my rejection been completely unwarranted and cruel? No, but that did not mean the things I had said were very nice, either. Had it been tit for tat? Was it the right thing to do, or simply a petty case of schoolyard cruelty?

These questions swirled through my head as I returned to my home planet, Pik. I knew that I had been quite...flexible concerning Yutigo's methods over the eons, that I had turned a blind eye to the offenses I had noticed and deemed to be fairly minor and insignificant. A necessary evil, I had always told myself. A stepping stone to a world where such a thing was impossible. But was it possible, in fact, that Rexdael was right? That Yutigo had willfully, knowingly, shielded me, only me, while doing his best to shamelessly manipulate the Council, twist it to his own purposes? Perhaps Rexdael had overstated things by quite a bit (the memories he had given me would suggest otherwise; conversely, they represented perhaps only a single, isolated event), but my niggling suspicions refused to let me leave things be. Perhaps a (minor) investigation was indeed warranted.

If there was only ever one thing another being needed to know about me to fundamentally understand who I was, it was my acute sense of right and wrong. My code of ethics is *my* everything, just as Rexdael's past is *his* everything. Technically speaking, my code of ethics is rooted in my past as well, but I view it more as an amorphous, ever-changing thing, the beautiful capstone of my personality. I would only truly be happy when injustice was wiped from the world for good, as clean as my soul now was.

My people always called themselves "protohumans," a term implicitly accepted but never truly understood. I did only when I met true humans and saw for myself the subtle but important distinctions. Our only distinguishing traits were our cold-bloodedness and our long, almost reptilian tongues. We were lucky, then, in the fact that we lived on a sunbaked planet, warm but never uncomfortably so, with long days and shorter years. It was a happy, prosperous society, unfamiliar with the wonders of space but comfortably self-sufficient.

Ironic, then, that what I now see to be the fatal flaw of our society is the fact that we were *too* happy. Anger was something completely foreign to our society. Forgiveness was the watchword of the day. A neighbor accidently stepped on your foot? Profuse apologies were sure to follow, accompanied by a juicy harvest of whatever seasonal fruit happened to be growing in his or her garden at the time. Of course, a gift of equivalent value must then be reciprocated, coupled with an acknowledgment of the initial apology. This is a minor example, however. How about something such as, say, theft? In the grand scheme of things, still relatively minor, but believe me, on my planet, theft was treated as something akin to high treason, for even it was a rarity in and of itself.

Theft was punished through…community service. This consisted of giving back the stolen items, working for the owner of said items for a period of time equivalent to the monetary value of the stolen items, and signing a written contract swearing not to steal again. The problem becomes clear when the letter of the law also implies that it is possible to substitute community service, a fair if lenient form of punishment, with simple monetary compensation. This, then, begins to sound to me suspiciously like a *bribe*. Have you ever heard of an *ethical bribe*? Neither have I. What an oxymoron! Nevertheless, that is what my people called it! This was an implicitly accepted part of our society, just as much as the term "protohumans" was! And now we come to the real crux of this system of falsehoods. People were so happy and forgiveness flowed in such abundance because it was so easy for money to be exchanged, palms to be greased. It may have worked, but it was also exceedingly fragile. Lies built atop lies!

I first learned about this reality in an exceedingly uncomfortable way. My father had, for as long as I'd known him, been the gentlest soul in the world and, even in a world of happy people, positively effervescent. Well, one afternoon, I learned exactly why this was the case when I walked in on my father... *kissing another woman*. Remember how I said that theft was considered high treason? That was because the other, more serious crimes, like adultery, for example, were simply not reported. I must have shrieked, for the couple jumped apart immediately. My mouth hung agape, and my father seemed to be attempting to string together a sentence, but he quickly gave up and (wisely) decided to exit the room with his mystery woman. That night, my father brought home two fruit baskets instead of one. My mother accepted hers without complaint, a broad smile on her face, as if this were an everyday occurrence. I was too shocked to truly comprehend what was going on and rejected my fruit basket out of hand, which was good in the moment, for I'm not sure how much *community service* I would have been required to perform had I actually decided to throw my fruit back in my father's face. I became truly disgusted, however, only when I heard the bedsprings in my parents' bedroom creak that night.

Once I noticed it, I could not help but observe it everywhere I looked. An extra can of paint here, a stolen car there.

Fortunately, because of the system of barter our whole society used, we had no formal economy to completely ruin. If anything, fruit was our main currency. On no terms, however, did I allow myself to become part of this *abomination*. A boy once offered me two ripe peaches for a stolen kiss, and I was so disgusted that I slapped him (incidentally, worth three bananas *and* a peach). While everyone around me retained a jolly good cheer, I grew more and more depressed. I could not bear the pure venality of my people. It felt to me simply as if justice was being sorely misappropriated, a whole host of injustices swept under the rug daily. Sadly, natural selection one day bequeathed the perfect set of traits to undermine our system to one of us.

He started off small, stealing pieces of fruit at a time, practically worthless. And so he was amply able to compensate his victims. If that had been the end, everything would have been completely fine. Sadly, it was most definitely not. Petty theft soon turned to beatings, arson, kidnappings. This was crime of a scale and magnitude my society was unused to, and yet this man, this hard-core criminal, this corrupted individual, remained a beloved public figure, though the cause of his publicity was the sheer unprecedented scale of his crime. He shocked and wooed in equal measure. This spiral of crime finally reached its logical conclusion when this individual carried out his first murders. This was *completely* uncharted territory. How was the worth of a life to be determined, particularly so when the units of measurement were *practically worthless fruit baskets*?! And through this worth-determining question, this murderer became a mercenary for hire. Because what is worth a person's life, if not the life of another in its stead? To clear the debts with one family, this mercenary would kill a person of that family's choosing, and then he would kill a person that the family of the person whom he had just killed chose, et cetera, et cetera. Other families had the same bright idea, and the homicide rate shot from zero to a hundred within a few days. It did not stop at homicides, either. It was quickly recognized that live people obviously have more value than dead, rotting corpses, so mercenaries, instead of being hired killers, became slavers. That was truly the day the battle for survival started.

Indeed, the day my powers awoke was the day I was to be sold into slavery. By that time, the corruption had spread far and wide, leaving only a few pristine pockets of goodness here and there. Ironically enough, my slaver was in fact the murderer who had started this entire destructive cycle. The moment he touched my skin, my entire body began to flare up, and I felt as if I were being consumed by a raging fire coming from somewhere deep inside me. But instead of destroying me, it burst out of my skin and set the surrounding room on fire. The murderer's skin burned so hot that large chunks of it simply melted off his face and dripped to the floor, leaving me to stare at his grinning, bone-white skull, flames for eyes, nose already blackening from the heat. I was so incensed by what was about to happen to me that day that my internal raging fire burst out of me and went to consume every single sinner it could find on my planet. Yes, even the slaves were sinners, for at this point there were very few truly *free* people, only many slaves of slaves of slaves of slaves...you get what I mean. When I was done, there were perhaps no more than two hundred of my species left.

Instead of gratefulness, however, I was greeted with

horror. The pure, uncorrupted souls looked at me, and they saw a mass murderer far worse than any of the ones who had come before me, a devil to end all devils. They ran as far as they could, aiming to escape the planet as soon as possible. With the right incentive, it was amazing how quickly the space "ark" could be built. I'm sure that somewhere in the realms, my people still cling to survival and have hopefully begun to increase their numbers again, all while retaining that pure innocence I so prized. The day my people left, I cried as I never had before and never would again. I had committed an act of almost-genocide, and I could barely bring myself to accept it, but I had to, since it was the *right* thing to do. I sat among the ruins of my burned-out planet, fat droplets leaking out of my eyes, and I swore a vow to myself that from that day onward, I would become a paragon of justice, a defender of the weak, a tireless worker striving for the ideal of complete harmony. I would not, *could not* stand by and watch corruption unfold before my eyes anymore.

The fact-finding investigation I was about to undertake, then, was of crucial importance. I sincerely hoped Yutigo had not been abusing his powers (well, at least not more than I already knew about), for I could not bear to imagine the alternative. If he had…uncountable billions would have been ravaged by the scourges of corruption, brutality, and other injustices, and my rage would be immeasurable. I was quite unaware of my own strength, but I was also quite sure Yutigo would not be able to stand against it, whatever its true extent was. Moreover, if Rexdael were indeed correct, then I owed him quite the spectacular apology.

Entering the pocket universe—the typical meeting place

of the Council of Realms—and striding atop the giant metal table that was the centerpiece of the great Council room, I placed my hand down on the indentation in the middle. "Nuarti, Council elder, Records," I barked out. "Access granted," replied Yutigo's voice, having been the one who encoded the biometric detectors of the Council table. Razor-thin green lines spread like a spiderweb out to the edges, then enlarged themselves to form cracks, segmenting the table. These segments folded themselves up against the walls of the room, revealing a spiral staircase under the spot where the indentation in the table had been. *That* was quite the nifty little enchantment. When the Council table was in place, the area of the staircase was held in a constant superposition. However, when a Council member gave the correct credentials and stated which room of the Council he or she would like to access, this superposition collapsed in on itself to select the desired wormhole to access the even tinier pocket universe that held the desired room. Moreover, this wormhole's entire length was traversed by said spiral staircase, a clever method of travel, especially compared to the typical void of nothingness wormholes contained.

The Records room, in quite antiquated fashion, contained row upon row of spartan steel bookshelves, each filled to bursting with what looked to be a collection of rare and valuable books. Records extended in both directions, farther even than the limits of the extended eyesight that those with powers possessed. The books were purely a gesture of artistic license, another suggestion of Yutigo's. Each book contained the record of a Council decision as well as all the transcripts and documents pertaining to that particular decision, all beamed directly to the mind of the viewer upon opening.

I strolled idly among the shelves for a while, eventually deciding that I wished to look at one of the new laws concerning realm jurisdiction. There had been a sudden influx of rulers, I remembered, five or six entering the Council at once, all hailing from the same patch of space. The resulting border dispute had been long, loud, and contentious. In the end, Yutigo had proposed giving one of these rulers the entire parcel of space, a valuable star nursery, and the Council had agreed unanimously. Merely upon my thinking this, the shelves around me began to warp and contort as my desired record emerged from the bowels of this cavernous room. The record sped to a stop inches from my outstretched hand, emitting a faint glow. Grabbing it, I flipped it open at random (the enchantment was such that the page selected to access the record did not matter). I was greeted by two dialog boxes: PUBLIC and SEALED. That was...curious to say the least. All records should have been public, particularly to me; I was in fact the Council elder responsible for making sure new records were filed properly.

The public portion of the record was much as I remembered it. It consisted of several loud and contentious arguments, followed by Yutigo's extensive geopolitical argument for giving the parcel of space to his chosen champion, followed by said Council member giving a speech of his own expounding his personal virtues. Thereafter, the vote was quick and simple, and the Council session of the vote came to a quick close. The conflict had been wildly contentious at first, and a messy resolution had seemed inevitable, but within the span of two Council sessions, the Council had gone from raucous discord to a coalescing of opinion around one seemingly particularly suitable candidate. It had all been resolved quite neatly. At the time, I had chalked it up to the components of the system working as they should, a smooth whirring of the wheels of justice. But what if it had instead been the specter of corruption greasing those very same wheels? A bribe-like action? I could not bring myself to believe that just yet, but I knew that I had to investigate the SEALED file before coming to any definitive conclusions.

"Who has sealed off access to this part of the file?" I demanded. "You did, Elder Nuarti," replied Yutigo's voice. I raised my eyebrows. "I most certainly did not," I replied. "Show me the date of sealing." The computer did so, and I found that I had indeed sealed the file, just not in the way I had been expecting. "This file has been sealed by order of Leader Yutigo, using the authority granted to him by the Recordkeeper Nuarti." I was beginning to regret the decision I had made early in the life of the Council to grant Yutigo equal authority to mine over the Records room, for it meant that he could open and seal files at will, even if he could not remove them from the Records room altogether. My suspicions continued to grow.

"Override seal order," I commanded, "using the authority granted to me as recordkeeper."

"Granted," replied Yutigo's voice calmly. A series of video files popped up. Opening the first one, I saw Yutigo and one of the five or six claimants for the valuable piece of space in Yutigo's office. "My dear Metixalos," began Yutigo, addressing the young ruler. "I hear that you have a family of sorts." Metixalos nodded. "I do indeed, Leader Yutigo," he replied. "Before I came into my power, I was able to get married and sire several children."

"Yes," Yutigo mused. "Your children are quite beautiful, if I daresay so myself. I wonder how your oldest daughter would feel if I planted a brood of spider eggs in her abdomen, allowing the spiders to feed on her internal fluids and then burst out of her, and repeating this process for all eternity, bringing her always to the point of death but never beyond it?"

Metixalos paled instantly (his species had evolved from a species of insect whose mortal enemy was just such a spider that planted its eggs in said insect's body so that its young could consume that body from the inside out). "Leader Yutigo," he stammered, "I'm afraid I don't quite grasp your meaning."

Yutigo chuckled, a nasty chuckle he had never employed within earshot. "Oh, Metixalos," he simpered, "I'm quite sure you do. Unless you wish for your oldest daughter to suffer much in the manner I've described, you will do as I say."

"What do you want from me?"

"Simple," replied Yutigo. "All I want you to do is renounce your claim to star nursery 223B-04-C and throw your support behind Siboto at the next Council meeting."

Metixalos glared at Yutigo with undisguised hatred. "*Damn you*," he replied thickly. He sighed. "You have my support."

Yutigo smiled. "As always, a pleasure doing business, Metixalos." He extended his hand to Metixalos, who looked at it in disgust and instead chose to stalk out the office door, whereupon the clip ended.

I was barely fast enough to conjure a bucket for myself to retch into. *This* was what Yutigo had been hiding from me all those eons?! That...that utter brutality and casual cruelty? *What was wrong with him?!?!* I had enabled a monster, putting him in the position from which he was best poised to inflict maximum casualties. With a horrified sort of fascination, I scrolled through the rest of the video clips. Similar scenes played out in each one. And in the ones where Yutigo was defied, clips of the punishment were also included. I retched several more times before reaching the end of the series of videos. If those records were fake, or at the very least *incomplete*, what did that mean with respect to Yutigo's claims about Pierre being a realm-eater? When I attempted to search for *this* record, however, I was told simply that the requested record did not exist. Another lie, then. Realizing only now the severity of my blunders, I felt tears pricking the edges of my eyes. I had failed again when I had been so hopeful that I was close to achieving ultimate success! All for naught!

I stomped out of the Records room—locking it securely behind me, ensuring that no one, not even Yutigo, could enter without my permission—before going to seek out Rexdael. He was owed an apology *big-time*, though I expected one in return as well. One thing, though, was abundantly clear to me: I was on the warpath now.

13

THE BIG THREE

Nuarti

It so happened, however, that Rexdael had slightly complicated things by sort of...*disappearing* since we had argued. When I returned to his home planet, outside the purview of a Bloodstone parley, the planet felt exceedingly on edge, as if it were watching me, just waiting for something dangerous and catastrophic to happen. For the moment, then, that meant that Rexdael's feelings toward me were still somewhat hostile, or at least unresolved, if his planet was behaving this way. I noted the addition of a large crack running along the center of the square where we had met, and I paused for a moment to ponder where Rexdael had conceivably gone after this. Unless he had spontaneously discovered more friends (acquaintances, perhaps) whom he wished to canvass for support, he had probably returned to Pierre, to New Earth. Therein lay the problem:

the lack of an existing up-to-date map done in sufficient detail and the paucity of information Yutigo had presented to us at the Council made it so that I personally did not know where New Earth was. Rexdael knew, obviously, because of his infatuation with damaged, psychologically wounded souls, but before Yutigo had mentioned him at the Council meeting, I had not even *remembered* who Pierre Hartford was. He had seemed rather a sideshow to the "important" work I was doing at the Council ("important," and moreover, useless!). Well, of course it was apparent now that Pierre never had been and probably never would be a shadow, what with his having burst onto the scene with a stunning defeat of the Entity. It was just that... he had simply faded from the public consciousness, as was his wont to do, struggling mentally but betraying none of this to the outside world.

I saw two plausible possibilities for definitively determining New Earth's location. One of these was returning to the Council room and doing a deep search of the planetary database. The logistical obstacles that would have to be surmounted in that case, however, were quite high. The barrier I had placed severely restricting access to the Records room also severely disturbed the superposition of all the rooms that lay in the bowels of the Council room. Without my approval, walking down that staircase, no matter which room had been requested to be accessed, would lead simply to an empty pocket universe, a sign of the "lockdown" protocol I had initiated. The complicated bit of the matter was that the originator of the "lockdown" protocol could not under any circumstances grant him or herself permission to access the desired rooms unless the protocol itself was lifted again. But doing so would leave an opening, one Yutigo would be sure to pounce on.

The second option was, while logistically simpler, not without its own set of problems, however. It involved taking a sample of Rexdael's blood from my Bloodstone and using that to track him down. Technically speaking, this went against the spirit of the agreement both parties parleying under the protection of the Bloodstone agreed to, but was it really unethical if it was part of a codified set of unethical laws? Perhaps, but I was willing to call the distinction subtle enough to be splitting hairs, and it would not impede any sleep I may or may not have in the future. The Bloodstone had been yet another one of Yutigo's ideas (barbaric, but whom was I kidding if I didn't call it somewhat expected at this point?). However, having grudgingly agreed to help in its creation meant that I knew the secret back door through the Bloodstone's typical protections (supposedly to quickly probe and eliminate points of failure within each stone but likely used simply for nefarious purposes). Once both parties infused their respective Bloodstones with their blood, the two samples were tied together through quantum entanglement. In essence, both samples simultaneously existed in the Bloodstones of both parties. Typically, one could only access one's own blood sample from one's personal Bloodstone, but the mechanism existed to manipulate and flip the quantum states of the blood samples such that the samples switched Bloodstones. Typically, this mechanism was only activated when a pact made with Bloodstones was broken, but one of the functions of the backdoor was to manually activate this mechanism. Using Rexdael's blood to track him was a matter of extracting his energy signature from the blood sample once I extracted it from my Bloodstone and tracking that across the universe.

I returned to my home planet (still ruined and still abandoned; I thought it a good way to remember my self-proclaimed purpose). I thrust out my hand, and my Bloodstone immediately whizzed into it, soaring upward and then down like a rocket from the mountaintop above. Pressing the palm of my left hand onto the stone, I preempted the taking of blood by muttering the password that opened up the back door ("liquid gold"). There was a blinding flash of green light, and when I looked again, the stone had divided itself into two halves. Hanging in the air in front of me, rotating slightly, was a viscous red liquid, glowing slightly and pulsing periodically. I reached out a hand, careful to only brush a fingertip along Rexdael's blood (believe me, the stories of what happens when the blood of two beings interacts for too long are exceedingly disgusting and gory). A momentary brush was all I needed though, for Rexdael's energy signature now pulsed quite clearly in my mind. Focusing on this signature, I endeavored to track where the greatest concentration of that energy signature might be found. It took what felt like hours to me, but what I knew to be only moments in the real world (the universe may be a large place, but no one had ever said that time compression couldn't be used to speed up many of its most grueling processes). Eventually a set of coordinates popped into my head. Banishing the blood back into the Bloodstone, I opened a wormhole and stepped through.

I was greeted by twin looks of surprise as I emerged in a sterile white room that seemed to be connected to a hospital of sorts. Well, more accurately, perhaps, one look of pure, unadulterated shock from Hartford, and one sidelong glance of recognition from Rexdael that soon melted into an odd combination of anger and despair as he seemed to be holding his head in his hands.

"Who are you and what are you doing here?" asked Hartford brusquely, if somewhat confusedly. "Her name's Nuarti," groaned Rexdael from his hunched position. "She's the help that I was hoping to convince to our side earlier, but instead we had a…falling-out of sorts. Which leads me to wonder what she's doing here." Rexdael fixed me with a look, one eyebrow raised. His piercing green eyes were wearied, but I saw as of yet no trace of sympathy in them.

"Well, if you must know," I began haltingly, "I went and checked the Council records. Within, I found a disturbingly large number of irregularities in the form of a large contingent of sealed files that I had never ordered sealed, had not even known existed. What I found within…it appears you were right, Rexdael. I believe I owe you an apology, then."

"Nuarti," began Rexdael, exhibiting far more warmth than he had just a few moments earlier.

"Before you say anything, I'd like to say my piece. What I said to you before was way out of line…"

"Nuarti."

"…I should never have insulted your past or taken it for a sort of joke…"

"Nuarti."

"…I probably could and should have addressed you a bit less scathingly even before you asked me for help…"

"Nuarti."

"…I said and did all those horrible things, and even earlier when I thought I was doing the right thing, I was just being used as a pawn..."

"Nuarti."

"...I'm here to help in whatever way I can that makes me feel less like an idiot and complete failure."

"*Nuarti.*"

Rexdael's voice had a strange edge to it. He looked at me with an inscrutable expression, some mix, I thought, of perhaps joy, sorrow, regret, pity, and affection. "What?" I asked. "I think you should sit down," he replied. "It seems that the enemy we're facing is one far more sophisticated and powerful than Yutigo. In fact, he's probably being used as a pawn too, even if he doesn't know it."

Now it was my turn to look confused. "Rexdael," I said slowly, "care to explain what exactly you're talking about?"

Rexdael simply looked at me, and all I could see now was sadness. "Nuarti," he said softly, "I think Fate has become involved."

The chair Rexdael conjured under me smashed into a pile of kindling as I crashed to the floor. "I don't believe you," I gasped out. "You must be joking. *You have to be.* This cannot be *true.*" By the end I was almost pleading, begging in fact.

Rexdael continued to regard me, still melancholic. "You think I'm not despondent?" He laughed bitterly, a harsh sound that cut off like the snap of a whip. "I am beyond mad with sadness," he continued, "but being that way doesn't change the hard, cold facts. How else do you explain the way our argument got far out of hand?"

"I...," I began, only to stop short as words refused to fill my brain. "I...I..."

"You don't know, do you?" replied Rexdael. "The solution

becomes elegantly simple when you factor Fate into the equation. Our sudden bouts of anger, wild mood swings, inability to control our words or actions in the moment...they all speak to subtle manipulation of the most insidious sort, don't you think?"

Damn him, I thought, but it didn't help that he was infuriatingly correct. It was the simplest possible explanation that still fit all of the known facts. But if it were indeed the case...what good would my warpath be against Fate?

Fate is the moniker we beings give to the higher-up who we believe is in charge of us. We may seem powerful—and relatively speaking, we are—but we also know that we must be puny ants compared to the one who created us. Yes, *created* us. How else do you explain the fact that, without exception, every single ruler I had ever met had had his or her powers awakened at some critical turning point in his or her life? Not a single ruler had come into his or her powers naturally or by birth. It could not be written off as a series of increasingly advantageous genetic mutations that all happened to coalesce in a single being at the same time to form something...greater. No, it was always a set of environmental triggers that initiated a cascading series of genetic mutations (not even latent ones; a quick study of our genomes revealed that much) that ended in us having these wondrous, godlike powers. But the fact that these powers came about in such an unnatural way indicated that it must have been a higher power of some sort who had decided to grant us these powers, for whatever inscrutable reason.

One might hope to have a benevolent god of gods, but sadly, in our case, this quite obviously did not seem to be so. Fate, for all intents and purposes, appeared to be a cruel, whimsical, godlike figure. It rather appeared sometimes as if decisions were truly made at the throw of a dice. There was the case of a being who *willingly* walked off a cliff and refused to use his powers to save himself, the being who stepped into a room of carbon dioxide when his lungs were only able to adequately process oxygen, the being who drank herself to death, the being who hanged himself, the being who set his own skin on fire "just to see what it felt like," the being who cut off his own limbs in perpetuity...you get the idea. Among us beings, there are a wide range and significant number of head cases. Not only that, but the pattern of who was afflicted appeared to be completely random as well. None of the beings could figure out any discernible pattern, so any being who was suddenly afflicted with an odd phobia or desire for self-harm was simply put out to pasture and allowed to die. What point was there in helping those who could not be helped?

These cases paled in comparison to some of the truly scary occurrences, though. There was the time one of Rexdael's earlier protégés had attempted to quantum phase across a distance of a few million light-years, both as an experiment and as a way to thumb his nose at the limits of what Fate allowed to be possible, and turned into a supernova in the center of a star nursery. There was the time one of the old Council elders had firmly stated that he didn't "believe in all this hogwash about Fate," only for his mouth to start turning to ash even as he spoke that last, the rest of his body joining his mouth soon after. None who had been present in the Council room at the time would easily forget the look of utter horror in his eyes as they had melted and his skin had flaked away. There had been a time that a chronic gambler among us had tossed his dice, only for them to shatter upon impact and the shards to spell out the following message, now drummed into each of our brains hundreds of times over: *Do not gamble with Fate…and expect a world undisturbed.*

That was truly the moment that the last vestiges of grudging respect we had had disappeared to be replaced instead by complete, unthinking fear of Fate. Fate had proven quite clearly what the consequences for defiance would be and given us more than fair warning that none of us was ever safe if one were to go by the number of head cases in our ranks. If Fate was involved here…something dire was afoot.

"Why?" I finally managed to whisper. "Why here? Why now? Why *us*?" Rexdael simply directed his glance at Hartford. "*Him*?" I whispered. "How and why?"

"He is a boy of uncommon talents," Rexdael replied. "Of raw power, I am quite sure he possesses more than any of us. His skills are equally unparalleled. He picked up quantum phasing quicker than I've ever seen anyone do it, and he does it far faster as well. We had a mock battle, and Pierre beat me once using techniques I've never even seen before. He is special, and special people naturally attract special interest."

"So, what exactly does this…*Fate* character want from me?" Pierre asked, sounding the words out slowly. Rexdael and I shuddered simultaneously.

"Don't say that name," I hissed. "Don't even think it if you can help it. If you really need to, just think of the Boss Upstairs."

Pierre looked perturbed. "I don't understand. What's so bad about Fa—the Boss Upstairs? And again, what could the

Boss want from *me*, of all people?"

"Pierre," Rexdael said harshly. "You're uncommonly talented and powerful, even for someone who *willingly* locked away his powers for a few years. The Boss wants you for one reason and one reason only: to control you. The Council has learned that lesson far too many times. You act scared, or bad things will happen."

Pierre's expression darkened. *"Control, control, always control,"* he muttered. "I don't care who the Boss Upstairs is—no way will I allow myself to be *controlled* ever again!" This last he shouted out. I looked questioningly at Rexdael, eyebrows raised, but he simply gave me a look that said not to push it. "So, what's the plan?" continued Pierre. "How are we going to fight?"

Rexdael and I exchanged another look. "Pierre," he replied slowly. "You don't *fight* your creator. That's an unwinnable, untenable fight from the very start."

It was Pierre's turn to raise his eyebrows now. "I'm sure you two realize you're talking to the man who destroyed his original creator in pitched battle, right?"

"That may be true, Hartford," I interjected, "but we don't have the numbers for that sort of conflict. There are three of us here. Seven of you faced the Entity. Only three survived. And wasn't there a substantial amount of luck involved as well?" Pierre's face fell slightly as he acknowledged the validity of my points, but it did not stop him from looking positively mutinous. Just as he opened his mouth to respond to me, however, the door to the room flew open, and five more humans burst in. I shot Rexdael a confused look. *His mother, her husband, and three friends,* he mouthed back at me.

"I'm sorry, are we interrupting something?" said one of Hartford's friends, a male with a sly smile on his face. I'm sure the sight must have been at least somewhat amusing. We three made quite the incongruous trio. The blue-eyed hothead, the green-eyed brooder, and the lawmaker who could have been carved out of a block of ice.

"That depends, Prosek," replied Rexdael coolly. "Do you have news for us? We were just discussing the latest updates we had to share with each other."

"I think we've discovered the energy signatures behind the way you lot travel," said the ruddy-faced male. "Sounded to me like a whole bunch of gibberish, but apparently WIMPs and positrons are all the rage when it comes to all of you and wormholes."

"And?" Rexdael prompted.

"Well, aside from the few obvious hits that we've been able to verify," said the last male, "there appears to be little to no activity in the data set that we collected."

Rexdael raised an eyebrow. "Do pray tell, Steinhardt, why you deemed this information important enough to interrupt our little meeting."

"There's more!" blurted out Hartford's mother suddenly. "We picked up a huge spike in WIMPs and positrons a few hours within the solar system, and trace amounts of these particles show a path headed straight for New Berlin. We have our reasons to believe that Yutigo has returned."

I looked at Rexdael. "Don't worry about me," I said calmly. "I'm staying. That prick is going down for the falsehoods he forced me to help him perpetrate."

Rexdael agreed. "Ready?" Pierre nodded. "The rest of you

stay here," Rexdael continued. "You have no chance of helping us to fight Yutigo on even terms." Hartford's mother opened her mouth to protest, only to snap it shut when her husband stomped on her foot. "Fine," she said sullenly.

"Do you have an approximate location?" I asked Pierre's mother. She nodded, tossing a tablet to Pierre. "Well, come on then," I said impatiently. "I'm itching to get the first punch in."

14

THIS MEANS WAR

Yutigo, New Berlin, Europa, New Earth

I made a big show of checking a nonexistent watch when Rexdael, the Hartford boy, and…*Nuarti* walked into Benton's (my) newly refurbished office building after what felt like an eternity. I tutted. "I must say," I began, "I really did expect more from the…three of you. I'm disappointed, especially in you, Nuarti. How does it feel to be betraying your precious ethics, knowing that you're consorting with outlaws?" The absolutely withering look Nuarti gave me would have, under other circumstances, perhaps sent a tremor of fear down my spine, but now, did it really matter whether I tested my new weapons against two or three beings? Not particularly, I would think.

"You dirty, lying, backstabbing, double-dealing piece of *scum*!" snarled Nuarti. "How *dare* you talk about ethics when, for all these eons, all you did was to use me as the front being for your disgusting, sadistic political dealings! I'm here to put an end to all that, and to you in the process as well."

So Nuarti had found my "sealed files" then. That was to be expected. Any real digging on her part should have almost immediately revealed that my hands, and hers by extension, were by no means as pristine as she believed they were. I gave Nuarti this much credit: she was powerful, and the devotion she had toward her ideals was like none other I'd ever seen, but I just *knew* that she had to have been willfully blinding herself with respect to some of my particularly crass actions. If she had been even the slightest bit more politically aware, she would have surely taken ample advantage of any number of opportunities that had been thrown at her feet to strike at me. It was stupefying, and to strike now was quite the miscalculation (though somewhat excusable; it wasn't as if I had laid all my cards on the table yet).

"Well, I suppose there's no point in trying to deny these allegations you levy against me," I responded, "but truly, can you honestly look at me and say that you don't find your ethical qualms to be constricting in the slightest?" My gaze flicked from Nuarti over to Hartford, the boy whose bumbling hesitations had, as he was soon to see, cost him much.

Hartford stared back at me unblinkingly, not showing even a trace of fear. "Our ethics may constrain us," he said calmly, though with undercurrents of boiling rage, "but at least they prevent psychopaths like you, Yutigo. I'm sure you don't need to be reminded of how my last encounter with a leader of dubious moral standing ended."

I raised my eyebrows. "Oh, my dear Pierre," I said, letting

tones of wistfulness creep into my voice, "you seem to be quite misguided at the moment. I, a psychopath? Please, don't take me for a crackpot or anything along those lines! I am far more than that. I have become something you could never hope to achieve, reached a state of enlightenment that has *truly* broadened my horizons. And yet, here you are, trying to make this out to be some sort of personal conflict! I know the elevator shaft must have been quite painful, but it was just another calculated maneuver, a way of incapacitating you, not a personal insult of any kind."

Hartford's eyes flashed at the mention of our previous encounter. "Forgive me if I find that hard to believe," he said, "but you seem awfully hell-bent on destroying me, and for a being supposedly unencumbered by ponderous ideals, you've displayed quite the expansive emotional range. You may not feel that much for me quite yet, but can *you* honestly look at Rexdael and feel nothing for a longtime rival, or at…Nuarti and feel no regret for being obligated to face her on the battlefield when you have been working partners for so long?"

Without even allowing Hartford's words to fully die away, I threw my head back and laughed. "I'm most certainly not here for *you*, Pierre," I scoffed. "I'm here for that extraordinary wellspring of power that you possess and have shown yourself quite incapable of wielding properly. Really, it doesn't matter to me who you are or what you've done, Pierre. Anyone who possesses as much power as you do and exhibits a similar emotional profile would receive the same treatment from me. You're just someone who can be boiled down to a series of behavior-determining numbers, as are Rexdael and Nuarti. Why should I feel anything toward them as a result of familiarity? Their numbers are simply that much more refined, their actions that much more predictable. Who's to say that I don't simply plug your numbers into an equation, study the result, and tailor my emotional responses accordingly? This is how power politics is played and *won*. Emotional responses interfere with reasoning, but well-practiced facsimiles can simply be shuffled around as needed without taking up valuable thinking capacity."

Rexdael looked at me with revulsion, as if he were seeing me for the first time. "You're so...*sick*," he spat out. "I had my suspicions before, but I've never truly been your opponent, and so I've never really had the opportunity to deeply scrutinize you. You definitely feel genuine emotion, but that is confined to a narrow range: exultant happiness. You get off on winning these sorts of conflicts. *This* is your high, this thrilling chess match, these face-to-face encounters with opponents, and especially your victories. You're addicted to power. I'm *appalled* that you could give less of a damn about Pierre, his background, his personal struggles. This is just a typical day at work for you."

"Though I agree with what Rexdael said," added Nuarti, "I think you're peddling a load of crap, Yutigo." A raised eyebrow. "There is no *enlightened* state. You're simply a disgusting but clever excuse for a being. What you've done is learn to harness your emotions and carefully regulate them, making sure none of them flicker out but also ensuring that you cannot be struck with sudden bouts of whimsy that cripple you at the most inopportune of times. Yet here you are, blabbering and boasting like an arrogant sot, and like the idiots we are, we've just been standing around and letting you talk instead of throwing punches!"

Nuarti quickly realized what a bunch of idiots she, Rexdael, and Hartford had been when she attempted to lunge toward me upon finishing her statement, only to find that she quite simply could not. Hartford and Rexdael found themselves similarly immobilized. I laughed. "I must say," I remarked, "despite everything, I do find this situation somewhat ironic. I believe there is an Earth saying that applies quite well here: something about being hoisted by your own petard. You scoff at me and my ways, and yet here you are, having just proven them correct. My words, designed to provoke and to anger, kept you talking long after you should have stopped and attacked without giving me ample time to prepare. My supposed arrogance and self-centeredness encouraged you to rage at me, to want to refute and retort my shocking and appalling statements. It only helps that what I said about myself was not in any way untrue. Finally, had you gotten rid of your moral sensibilities, you would in all likelihood still be able to move at this moment regardless of what I had been saying to you up to this point. And you know why?" I paused, purely for dramatic effect at this point (OK, that was perhaps a tad self-indulgent). "It's because I've been making the rounds and become acquainted with some of Pierre's dear old friends!" I concluded with a flourish.

An invisible opaque barrier suddenly disappeared, revealing the fact that my puppet Benton had been standing at my side this entire time. In his newly regenerated hands he held the remote controlling the force fields surrounding the three. Nuarti simply looked slightly bewildered as she glanced at Benton without a hint of recognition in her ice-blue eyes, while Rexdael looked resigned, giving Hartford a sidelong glance, and the person being glanced at gaped like an idiot. I should have refrained from doing so (really, though, what was stopping me at this point?), but I was feeling a little self-indulgent (which kind of proved Nuarti's point, too, but I had won, which I thought preserved the integrity of my overarching point).

"Oh, my dear Pierre," I sighed mockingly. "Is something wrong? You look so distraught! And here…here I thought you were so *smart*, so *intelligent*. Yet you stand before me, stuck when faced with quite the simple conundrum. Oxymoronic, yes, but for a *conundrum*, I think this tends toward the simpler end of the spectrum." Hartford's mouth snapped shut, and fire flared in his blue eyes. Next to him, Rexdael coughed quite loudly, and I could have sworn that he mumbled, "Morals!" I saw when the puzzle pieces finally connected in Pierre's head, and, if anything, his rage increased.

"Mr. Benton's not your *ally*, is he, Yutigo?" Pierre said stiffly and coldly. "You took advantage of the ability I was unwilling to exploit, and you took control of him and his various inventions."

I clapped my hands together in a pantomime of appreciation. "Oh, *very good*, Pierre! I'm disappointed it took so long to figure out, though. Are my actions really so—"

"*I'm not done*," hissed Hartford, cutting me off mid-gloat. "I *know* what you're using on us here. I worked on an early prototype. This is just a skin-level restraining force field that exerts a force exactly equal and opposite to what we attempt to exert *physically*." He smirked, mad glee dancing in his eyes. "There is absolutely nothing physical about what I'm going to do next."

I fervently wished that I could have blinded myself to the

irony of the moment because I knew that it was my mocking that had cost me the advantage here. The "war" could have been over, but for an uncharacteristic moment of weakness costing me a step in this dance.

A battering ram smashed into the mental connection tying me to Benton's mind, and for a fraction of a second, I foolishly attempted to resist Hartford's incursion. It was a fraction of a second too long, however. I felt the mental connection break, as I had known it would. Benton screamed, dropping the remote and rolling around on the floor clutching his head. Disoriented, I made to activate the poison vents (except this time, of course, unlike Benton, I had dosed myself with the antivenom beforehand). But before I could release the poison, my jaw snapped shut with a jarring force, and the coppery taste of "human" blood flooded my mouth as my teeth bit through my tongue. I flew backward, idly taking note of the fact that Nuarti was a far better puncher than I had ever given her credit for.

Spitting a gob of blood out, I attempted to release the poison, only to realize that every single vent in the room had been covered in a thin, gelatinous substance. Hartford smiled without a trace of warmth. "Did you forget, Yutigo, that I *worked* here for three years?" he asked. "I am quite familiar with the security systems in place."

I bowed my head, acknowledging the point. "Only the shystems you're familiar with," I slurred out, activating Benton's energy barrier around myself and deploying the newly constructed energy-restraint guns. As they began to spit out circular, glowing purple bands far faster than any human-constructed gun would have been able to, Hartford put up an energy barrier of his own…which my bands went through as if it weren't there. Hartford's eyes widened, and his gaze flicked to his left. Even as he phased, though (when had he learned to do *that*?), another gun had already shifted its focus and scored a direct hit on Hartford's left wrist as he reappeared. Instantly, his arm went stiff, and Hartford's face turned purple with strain as he tried and failed to remove the band from his wrist. I smirked and raised my eyebrows. Hartford sighed in frustration and *closed his eyes* (was he insane?!). He continued moving, however, occasionally sending bolts of lightning, gouts of flame, and shards of ice at me, which all fizzled harmlessly against my barrier. Rexdael and Nuarti found themselves otherwise occupied simply trying to dodge my guns. It was not the speed at which the projectiles were being fired but rather their sheer volume that made it so difficult to continually phase out of the way of their trajectories.

A slight groan was all the warning I got before the floor beneath my feet *rippled* and shards of metal began to shoot toward me. With the floor paneling in disarray, my energy barrier was disrupted and disappeared with a pop. Maintaining the concentration to float and phase at the same time was giving me one heck of a headache. Now it was not just shards of metal but also the elemental attacks I had been able to ignore earlier that assailed me from all sides.

I began to assess the situation between dodges. Hartford was angrier than I was at the moment and simply more powerful as well. The environment was no longer my friend, and presumably the battlefield I had so meticulously prepared would soon be destroyed as well. Even were it not apparent that each of these three beings probably could have taken me on individually and won comfortably in a fair fight, a three-on-one skirmish was suicidal under the best of circumstances.

Right on cue, my energy-restraint guns were torn out of their sockets, accompanied by a cacophony of screeches. The very air around me seemed to chill as I sensed what appeared to be a tornado form around the entire building. Hartford's eyes remained tightly shut, but he was positively *glowing* with power now. He raised his right arm high, his left still stubbornly stiff at his side, and the sound of rending, twisting, and snapping metal overwhelmed all other noises. It almost seemed as if the very foundations of the building were being consumed in this maelstrom as tons and tons of debris floated out of the floor and turned into a hail of deadly shrapnel at Hartford's back.

His right arm slowly moved down until it pointed directly at my face. Hartford's eyes snapped open suddenly. They, too, were glowing, the electric blue really bringing out his cheekbones and giving his face an eerie tint. Hartford smiled, and all hell broke loose. The force field I conjured in front of me barely held as Hartford sent what could have been, for all I knew, the entire building at me. So focused was I on maintaining the force field that I barely noticed in time when Rexdael and Nuarti had phased into existence on either side of me and were advancing rapidly. Desperately fixing the force field in place with my eyes, I decohered my arms and sent one to each of the two. I knew from the start, however, that it was likely a hopeless effort. I faced a one-on-two situation to either side of me, unable even in the best-case scenario to move twice as fast as either Nuarti or Rexdael, and that was without taking into account the tornado being hurled at me from the front.

A burning, searing pain ran down the center of my chest. Rexdael's and Nuarti's punches had simply come too fast, but instead of hitting me, they had grabbed hold of one of my arms each, and now, my body was trying and failing to be in two places at once. I knew that if I didn't yield soon and accept that I was going to lose at least one of my arms, my body would be ripped apart. At this proximity, the resulting energy explosion would mean certain death for Rexdael and Nuarti, perhaps even for Hartford.

Just as I decided on this course of action, the searing pain in my chest disappeared, and I felt my arms reattach themselves to my body. The tornado of force hitting me from the front receded as well. And finally, there was…a hunk of metal *sticking out of my stomach*. Blood welled up around the wound, and I fell to the floor with a crash, noticing now that I had been skewered from the back. It seemed the elevator car I had just repaired had been driven through my rib cage in pieces. This time, I was quite sure the irony was intentional. I tried to laugh, but only blood came up, dribbling out of the corners of my mouth and flowing down onto my chin. Idly, I noted it dripping down onto the metal sticking out of my chest.

My arms were pulled back sharply as Rexdael and Nuarti restrained them again. Hartford's right hand grasped my chin and jerked it up sharply, forcing me to look in his eyes, no longer angry, but simply disinterested. "This is the end of the line, Yutigo," he murmured softly. "Your manipulation, your double-dealing, your corruption, your moral flexibility. It all ends here. No more tricks. No more escapes. No more *slimy* words."

I attempted to spit on Hartford, but my throat was too

weak, and the glob of blood and sputum I hawked up simply dropped onto my chest. *Is this really it?* I had cheated death so many times, faced seemingly insurmountable odds, been encumbered by potentially fatal weaknesses, that yet another escape simply seemed like second nature. And yet…here I was, stronger than ever, all out of cards to play, brought down by the need to gloat.

"Well," Hartford continued, "if that's all you have to say, Yutigo, I do think it's time for a long overdue farewell." He flicked his hand, and an orange blade appeared (appropriately, Rexdael's execution weapon of choice, I knew). He raised his hand above his head.

"*Wait.*" Nuarti's harried plea cut through my muddled final thoughts like a hot knife through butter. I laughed, rasping, wheezing, coughing up blood as I slipped into unconsciousness.

I should be dead.

And yet here I was.

15

THE DICE ARE TOSSED

Yuri Klatschnikov, New Berlin, Europa, New Earth

Hours must have passed since the series of events that had culminated in my wife running out on me, but my nose *still* smarted. She had actually managed to break it, which hadn't been painful so much as shocking. I suppose I should have expected as much (never, ever, *ever* stand between a determined mother and her endangered child), but personal experience was really needed to reinforce that particular lesson. I had, with the limited abilities that remained to me, managed to heal my nose, but I periodically felt the inclination to scratch the spot of the fracture. Lili certainly packed one hell of a punch.

I sat next to her now, in the room Pierre and his two similarly powered companions had just recently exited. His three friends sat across from us, sometimes talking quietly among themselves, other times simply staring at the ceiling, the floors, the walls, or their hands. A strangely muggy atmosphere hung over the entire room. Though there was no particularly bad piece of news to be despondent about, nobody seemed to be in a very talkative mood. It was worst of all with my wife. Though we had barely left each other's sides since Pierre had been brought to his room, we could not have exchanged more than twenty words. Our prior conversation hung heavy between us, since each unresolved issue had evoked another obstacle to be surmounted.

I suppose I shouldn't have been surprised, not just with respect to that particular hornet's nest but also with respect to the general discomfort I felt just by sitting in the presence of the other four. I had never been and would never be one of Pierre's…acolytes. I say that disparagingly only because I cannot ever imagine giving myself over completely—mind, body, and soul—to another person to be used. Technically I had been that way with Karl, before we had been released from the dream, but that had been different. That had been unwilling. This behavior that the other four exhibited…it was almost doglike. I could not ever imagine willingly behaving in that manner. This was not to say that I did not have the utmost respect for the other four. I most surely did. I respected the degree of their devotion, just not the ideas it was based on. I found it too degrading, particularly for someone like Pierre.

I like to call myself a realist when it comes to Pierre. For all his skills and accomplishments, which were storied and numerous, *he was not a god*. It was easy to forget when he was in the midst of performing breathtaking feats and bending the laws of nature I had been taught growing up, but outside of that arena, he was quite ordinary. He had, like any human, emotions and flaws, both small and big. He was not perfect, he was not omniscient or even omnipotent, and *he was not infallible*. His emotions made him vulnerable, but it was his power that made him dangerous, wielded without the fine emotional control I assumed other beings like him had managed to build up over thousands, perhaps even millions of years. What would a temper tantrum look like? What would it do to ordinary humans like me?

I already had some experience in this department, having lived under the same roof as a Pierre who had clearly been suffering from post-traumatic stress disorder, whose nightmares had broken the house more times than I could count, whose spells of depression had almost flooded the house with rain, whose bouts of anger had come close to killing passersby with stray shards of masonry too many times to count, miraculously missing each time but the last. I had been an advocate of Pierre's idea to shut away his memories and powers in order to make himself ordinary and happy. To me, at least, it appeared as if Pierre had won everything he had aimed to attain, achieved everything worth doing. What point, then, was there in him retaining these hazardous powers and endangering the livelihoods of everyone around him? It was time for him to return to an ordinary life, to being an ordinary citizen with no special rights, no extraordinary characteristics.

Of course, I had underestimated the complexities of the situation, the universal ramifications of Pierre's actions, and the resulting backlash. I most certainly wouldn't have predicted the existence of other beings, or even of other universes.

Now, of course, it did make more sense for Pierre to have his powers and memories back (which he did, thankfully), but it did not change my underlying concerns. Pierre still possessed the same emotional makeup and fragility of spirit he had possessed four years ago, which made another breakdown entirely possible, though I suppose the risks were somewhat mitigated by the fact that we appeared to now have two other beings on our side as well, and presumably they could control Pierre in some way if he ever did lose control.

No, more concerning to me were the ways in which Pierre had twisted the behavior of so many of the people who were closest to him. My wife had always possessed a very acute sense of motherly affection toward Pierre, and she was immensely fond and protective of him. After having lived and interacted with Pierre for six years, both with and without his worst memories, I could not deny that I felt the same way. But particularly in the four years after Pierre had effectively handicapped himself, my wife's affection had gradually morphed into obsession. Her whole being had become warped by her desire to continuously remain close to Pierre, to watch over him, to protect him. All of this had been abundantly clear in the aftermath of my broken nose and her frantic escape from our home to chase down Pierre, even if it was obvious that she could not really protect him in this scenario. I loved my wife, and I had grown used to her in the six years since Karl and Will had died, but it had only recently become abundantly clear that I was the third wheel, the front for the real relationship that existed between my wife and her son.

And his friends...these three were the only friends Pierre had been able to make and retain in the span of four years, and it was an uncommonly close friendship. Not many would risk their jobs or their lives for friends. Not many friends would have remained at Pierre's side after the magnitude of the lies he had been feeding them became clear. But I was unsure if these friends even knew that much about each other besides what they could glean through the lens of conversations with Pierre and, by extension, each other, or if they were connected solely through their connections to Pierre, like planets orbiting a sun. Even now I would wager their conversations concerned only Pierre, which was perhaps more excusable under the circumstances than it would be otherwise, but still! Did they not have the presence to reflect on what effects the changes they were witnessing could have on them and humanity as a whole?

These questions, though, I set aside for the moment as I leaned over and tapped my wife on the shoulder. She glanced at me, not unkindly, but with a look devoid of emotion. Obviously, I was not and had not been at the forefront of her thoughts (I *wonder* who *was*). "What do you want, Yuri?" she asked tonelessly. "We need to talk," I answered earnestly. "Have we *not* been doing that recently?" she retorted. "Because it doesn't appear to me as if we've been ignoring each other. Our conversations have been perfectly fine."

I snorted. "Yes, Lili, because the exchange of twenty or so words now constitutes a conversation. You've spoken more to me in the past minute than you have in the past five *hours*."

My wife turned to regard me fully, but my words did not appear to have angered her, merely made her...annoyed, as if I were some bothersome little fly that needed to be brushed off now. "Oh, *I'm sorry*, Yuri," she half simpered, half spat. "I wasn't aware that the nature of our relationship necessarily required us to conduct sappy conversations with each other in which we bared the hidden depths of our souls and talked *feelings*. As I'm sure you're well aware, there are far more important things afoot than the nature of this...*marriage*."

I had always, to some degree, been aware of the true way in which my wife regarded this marriage, but knowing that and hearing it spewed at me so callously were two very different things. "You know, sometimes, *dear*, these things tend to overlap," I replied stiffly. "For once, open your ears and listen when I say that we need to talk. We *need* to talk about the events of earlier today, which I at least think do have some wider ramifications when it comes to Pierre." As I had known they would, my wife's eyes filled with tenderness for a brief moment (an aspect of her temperament I had desperately yearned for, yet never received). Her lips parted slightly, and her entire body hunched forward, bringing her closer to me. *Just like a dog*, I thought, disgusted.

"Talk, then," she said, a tremor of excitement running through her voice. "That is, if this really has something to do with Pierre and not just your petty insecurities."

Swallowing my disgust, I looked at my wife again. "Fine, then. Tell me, what did you think you could accomplish by running out to try to help Pierre this morning?"

My wife stared at me, confused. "What do you mean, Yuri? Pierre needed my help. The message I received indicated that he was in great danger! What if he hadn't known about that? What if he had been caught by surprise because I hadn't delivered that message to him? What if I could have protected him? You can't have expected me to stand idly by and let my son face an unknown danger!"

"Fine," I replied. "Did you ever consider, however, what I told you this morning? Did you even think about it at all while you were in the process of running out of the house and toward Pierre? Realistically, what could you hope to do against a threat to Pierre? Pierre, who is so much more powerful than you and accordingly possesses commensurately powerful enemies?"

My wife's cheeks began to flush bright red. "You can't *definitively* prove that Pierre might not have needed my help," she replied. "Of course it's possible that the enemies I run into far outstrip me in power and skill, but that doesn't preclude me from contributing in some way, no matter how small! Every little bit helps!" She nodded to herself. "Also, Pierre was in danger, and I couldn't bear to stand around while he possibly risked life and limb for us," she concluded stubbornly.

"And if you had died for Pierre?"

"That's a mother's duty, isn't it? To protect her children?"

I sighed internally. *Like talking to a brick wall.* "Yes, but what do you think your *death* would have done to Pierre?" I asked. "Don't you think it would have shattered him completely, made him less able to protect himself and others?"

"Perhaps, but what if I had stayed back and he had died instead? I wouldn't be able to live with myself either! I could have been that final edge, that slight difference between life and death. My life could have saved my son for the benefit and glory of everyone else, including you." She looked at me beseechingly, her eyes beginning to fill with tears. "Can't you understand that, Yuri? Can't you understand what I feel when I look at my son?"

"I think I understand perfectly well what you feel when you look at Pierre," I replied derisively. "I simply can't bring myself to feel that same way or even to halfway agree with your sentiments. For goodness's sake!" I said, raising my voice at those last few words. "Can't you see that Pierre makes you a danger to yourself and those around you? I don't know what he's done to you…" I waved my hand to indicate not only my wife, but also Pierre's friends, who had broken off their separate conversations to stare at me, wide-eyed. "…but the level of devotion you exhibit toward him is quite frankly unhealthy. Lili, you broke my nose earlier today when I tried to reason with you in order to prevent you from potentially doing something suicidal, but I imagine you could have just as easily killed me. This…this…this…this *cult of personality* that's being created here is just disturbing. I doubt Pierre even sees it, even knows what's going on, and moreover, I don't think he would condone it if he knew. The three of you…" I pointed at Pierre's friends. "…if you had any sort of self-preservation instinct at all, you would be running for your lives just about now. When Pierre returns, dragging his battles with him through the door, the three of you will be ground up to a paste, scattered into pieces so small that nobody will ever be able to positively identify a corpse or even a limb! What more information could you provide Pierre with? Anything more is simply derivative, something Pierre could just as easily find on his own and without your help!"

I only realized after I had finished speaking that I had stood up in the process. I looked around the room, breathing hard. The other four looked at me with varying degrees of shock, pity, and indignation. *They think I'm the crazy one*, I realized. I had just been lecturing them about what I saw as the dangers of Pierre, ranting, even, and I could quite clearly see how *I* could be the one considered mad when faced with an audience of madmen. A moment of silence passed before all four of them began speaking at once, loudly, frantically, their voices blending together and overlapping so that I could only catch snatches and fragments of their various retorts.

"Look here, Klatschnikov—"

"—you're his stepfather, you should understand this—"

"—of course we can protect him, knowledge is power—"

"—I'm *sorry* for accidentally breaking your nose—"

"—he's the best friend any of us could have ever asked for—"

"—would we really be safer running than staying—"

"ALL OF YOU SHUT UP!" I roared, and the four of them jumped all at once, now looking at me with more than a little fear in their eyes as well. "I can't hear what any of you are saying, and it's making my head hurt," I said a bit more quietly. "I'm sure I wouldn't agree with it anyway, but your pointless shouting is definitely not making it any better! So if you have something to say, could you at least have the decency to say it one at a time?" Now Pierre's friends looked slightly abashed, while my wife regarded me as if she were only truly seeing me now for the first time, even after six years of marriage.

Finally, the Czech boy spoke up. "Did you consider, Klatschnikov, that the three of us here may possess a fine sense of camaraderie and a distinct desire to experience the adventure of our lives, beyond the simple fact that we're here to help out Pierre?"

I gave a sarcastic little laugh. "Must be quite the desire for adventure, then, that you're still here when faced with almost certain death. Surely if you're so smart, you must have done the math and come up with a near-zero number when determining your odds of survival?" I stared intently at the Czech boy (was his name Luka?). He gazed back at me evenly. "Ignoring that for the moment, however," I continued, "let us investigate this camaraderie of yours." With a moment of hesitation, "Tell me…Luka, if the three of you are such good friends, what is your friend's birthday?" I asked, pointing at the German sitting next to him.

Luka gazed back at me, letting the silence stretch for many moments. After a minute or so, he opened his mouth to reply. "I don't know," he said evenly.

I raised an eyebrow. "Four years you've known each other, I assume. Are you telling me that the three of you, in four years, have *never* found opportunities to celebrate each other's *birthdays*? Yes, I can see now what great friends the three of you really are."

Now the third friend, the Englishman, spoke up. "See here, Mr. Klatschnikov," he said in a placating tone, "birthdays really aren't that big of a deal. We always celebrated them, but we never turned them into big-ticket events or anything like that. Just last cycle, we had a small get-together for Pierre's birthday—"

"So you *do* celebrate birthdays," I interrupted triumphantly. "Yes, you celebrate *Pierre's* birthday. I do think you're proving my point for me quite wonderfully. Let's try again, shall we? What's Luka's favorite color?" The Englishman's neck, already a pale shade of red, began to darken in color. "No?" I asked mockingly. "What's Pierre's favorite color?"

"Green," answered four voices in unison, including that

of my wife, who had tried and failed to clap a hand over her mouth.

But just as I was looking to further capitalize on this moment, my train of thought was interrupted by a veritable orchestra of beeps. The German's personal communications device was the source of most of these beeps, but the Englishman's had begun to ring as well. Luka tore his gaze away from mine to look at his two friends in confusion.

"Jane?" the Englishman spoke into his device. "What's so important that you're up...every single screen? Yes, yes, he's a close friend. Danger? Believe me, around him that's old news at this point. Send me the details and I'll be sure to pass on the message. Good luck." He looked up at us again. "That was my contact in the Americanian Embassy. They've just had a message go up on all their screens simultaneously. Here, I can show you."

"There's no need for that, Robert," interjected Luka. "Look." Indeed, a patch of nondescript wall had slid to the side to reveal a hidden security camera, which was now projecting a message onto the opposing wall:

To the Most Honorable Pierre Hartford:
If answers be what you most sorely need,
Then, perhaps, within my grasp, I have what you seek.

Come and find me ere it's too late.
Flip a coin and determine your Fate.

We were torn away from the contemplation of the message and its accompanying coordinates when the German spoke up. "There's also been a huge spike in dark matter readings," he said into the silence. "Much larger than when that other being came back to Earth."

"So we have a message, and we've been given a location," murmured my wife. "But for what purpose?"

I almost gagged on the next words I forced out of my throat, but they had to be said. "If you possess even a scrap of true affection for Pierre, not merely devotion, you won't show this message to him." Now the other four really gave me long, searching looks, not even bothering to hide that they thought I was crazy now.

"This is a message for *Pierre*," said the German insistently. "The least we could do is deliver it to him."

I scoffed. "If the message were for him, it would have been delivered directly to him. No, there is something very wrong with this. We receive this message, and then we're also conveniently given a set of coordinates. Someone or something is toying with us. Do you really want to leave Pierre's life in the hands of Fate?" At this last word, the temperature notably dropped for the fraction of a second, and a cold breeze ruffled my hair. I could have sworn I had heard a woman's laughter as well. The others looked as discomfited as I felt.

"Perhaps you're right," conceded the German. "Pierre has so many things to worry about. We shouldn't bother him with petty trivialities."

If only the words had matched his expression, however. For the first time, I was positive no one in this room held thoughts of Pierre at the forefront of his or her mind. I saw my fear reflected in everyone else's eyes. This external stimulus had shown them what I had been trying to explain to them all along. So why did I feel so profoundly unhappy about it?

16

CONTROL, OR A LACK THEREOF

Pierre Hartford, New Berlin, Europa, New Earth

For the second time that day, I found myself in a hospital-like room. But this time I was not the one who was occupying the bed, for I was not the injured party. Far from it, in fact. I *was* the primary reason that Rexdael, Nuarti, and I were in this room, for none other than Yutigo himself occupied the bed.

I was torn between my guilt and my anger at the moment: guilt for having come so close to killing Yutigo and anger for not having finished the deed, for having had the presence of mind to hear Nuarti moments before delivering the killing blow. As soon as I had seen Yutigo's smile, I had known as well as he had that he was not going to die in that instance. Nuarti's voice made me hesitate, but my arm had nevertheless continued on its downward trajectory. Nuarti had then proceeded to release Yutigo's arm in order to bat the blade out of my hand. She had taken a long slash wound along the space between her middle and ring fingers in the process, but the moment it had no longer touched my skin, the blade had disappeared, and the hand that would have killed merely had rendered him unconscious instead. I had been too shocked to shout, so Rexdael had picked up the slack instead. "What are you doing, Nuarti?" he had roared. "We were going to end this once and for all, here and now! Instead, we get another heap of problems dumped upon us! You would have us consider whether to end him or not? Even now that you know what he really has been doing all this time?!"

Nuarti had been close to tears, her face caught in a profoundly pained expression. "I have no doubt in my mind that he has done any number of horrible things," she had replied, "but he at least *deserves to know.*"

"Know what?!" Rexdael had retorted, exasperated. "Know about *the Boss*," Nuarti had responded insistently. That, of course, had shut everyone right up.

It was quite difficult to not feel paranoid. I had been given knowledge, knowledge that I desperately wished to erase from my memory yet simultaneously would not have let myself forget for anything in the world. It was knowledge of the most terrible sort, knowledge that made me want to tear the world apart limb from limb, and yet I could not imagine how much worse off I would be had I remained ignorant. I could not afford to remain ignorant of this. Fate most certainly was no mere trifle.

I suppose this is how typical mortals felt when they were faced with the seemingly incontrovertible laws of nature. I

192 • Konrad Koenigsmann

must have felt this way at some point in my youth, but it grew harder and harder to remember with every passing year, every passing moment in which I had thought myself on top of the world. When I had come fully into my power for the first time, the world had lost some of its luster. It had given up all its secrets to me, and those phenomena which had seemed so inexplicable came to appear downright pedestrian when their inner workings were laid bare. I had thought I had come into the knowledge of everything there was to know about the world, everything I would ever *need* to know about the world, that there was nothing more for me to learn, ever. I had conceded that on that point, at least, I was wrong. As I had met and become acquainted with beings such as Rexdael, Yutigo, and Nuarti, I *had* learned new things, but even then, the political dynamics, the fighting techniques that I had learned remained within my grasp, within my direct sphere of control. But Fate? Fate was so far out of my grasp that I could have held an entire universe within my palm and still would have come no closer to reaching my goal.

Fate really, truly scared me. Even if I, unlike Rexdael and Nuarti, had not witnessed firsthand the products of Fate's bouts of whimsy, I carried within me a deep-rooted revulsion to any sort of control whatsoever. Yes, perhaps it could have led to my undoing in my most recent encounter with Yutigo, but then, after all, that encounter had also ended with me seconds away from ending Yutigo's life. No, what scared and repulsed me in equal measure was the possibility that I had never been in full control of my actions. Obviously, Fate probably didn't have the patience or time of day to watch over me at every instant or manipulate even the most minor of minor actions, but still…Rexdael had said that Fate had taken a special interest in me simply because I had defeated the Entity and in so doing had become the heir to a, even among beings, significant well-spring of power. I thought I had been doing good in recreating Earth, in recreating humanity, in hopefully creating a better version of the world I had grown up on, but what if I had simply done it because Fate had wished it so? Perhaps it had made my nightmares worse in the long run, to be surrounded by so many mementos of my past. But what if the nightmares had been induced in the first place by Fate? Knowing that Fate existed inevitably led to a questioning of every single decision that had been imbued with importance of any sort which I had made over the past six years. Particularly during the course of this series of events, the manipulations we had been subjected to became less and less subtle as my behavior and the behavior of my compatriots and enemies became more erratic and inexplicable. What if Fate wanted this? What if Rexdael had come to his epiphany precisely at this moment so as to render all of us paralyzed by fear and paranoia, easy prey for whatever was to come next? Now you begin to see the difficulties created by the simple act of having become privy to this crucial piece of knowledge. Fate occupied our minds regardless of our ability to hurt it, an enemy unseen and untouchable.

Perhaps all three of us were indulging our own cycles of doubt and paranoia at the moment, for the room could just as easily have been part of a morgue as it could have been part of a hospital, so quiet had we been since we had brought Yutigo to his bed. The events of the battle hung unresolved in the air, a series of swords of Damocles just waiting for Yutigo to awaken in order for each of them to swing down upon our necks. First Rexdael and then Yutigo had during the course of successive combat encounters awakened a beast of anger deep within me that I had tapped and unleashed in order to literally and figuratively pummel them into the ground. This I was certain was one of Fate's manipulations, for even while fighting the Entity I had never felt this way. It was intended as a taste of things to come if I did something Fate desired in the future. In those moments of anger, I felt exultant, one with my power as I had never been before. It was both glorious and terrifying to imagine what I could have done with such power had events not interrupted my emotional state in the aftermath of my victories.

Nuarti left me feeling uncertain as well. I had fought at her side, certain in the fact that we were united against a common enemy, but even now I did not know whether to call her friend or foe. I sensed a strength of will within her at least as strong as mine, though hers was thoroughly devoted to her code of ethics. This, at least, I could admire about her, for I respected a strong sense of right and wrong as much as the next being. But could Nuarti's moral compass really be trusted as being genuinely objective and unbiased? She had, after all, been Yutigo's close working partner since the inception of the Council of Realms, and it would not have been out of the ordinary for her to have developed a misguided sense of respect for him. She was only here now because she had been shocked out of her ignorance by a series of facts too undeniable and too horrible for her to ignore. Might not twinges of the heart override her moral compass, allowing her to retain a veneer of objectivity while in fact hijacking her for purposes entirely benefitting her? Or...or was this just my Fate-addled brain talking? Half of what I had just thought smelled like unfounded fearmongering, based upon the slimmest of facts and the wildest of conjectures. I gave a mental sigh of exasperation.

Thankfully, a flurry of sudden movement jerked me out of my train of increasingly morose thought. Yutigo had awoken, sitting up so suddenly that he had in essence flung himself bodily against the chains that held him fast. He smirked. "Well, this is certainly a first," he commented airily. "I've never been chained to a bed before. I suppose I should be honored that I'm receiving such…what do humans call it? Ah, yes, *VIP* treatment." Yutigo's chains rattled as he shifted himself into a more comfortable sitting position. Gingerly, he poked at his stomach, where recently pieces of an elevator car, thanks to me, had been lodged. "All healed up," he remarked. "I appreciate that you've done me the courtesy of leaving some scar tissue, at least." Rexdael, Nuarti, and I remained silent, gazing at Yutigo and each other with varying degrees of trepidation. Yutigo, of course, picked up on this as well. "In case you haven't noticed, *I'm* the one who's chained up here," he observed dryly. "Why is it, then, that out of the four of us, I appear to be the happiest at the moment? It's not as if you're attending a funeral or some other such somber event." He shot a glance my way, showing that for all of his seemingly carefree words, Yutigo had most certainly not forgotten the reason he found himself chained to a hospital bed.

"We need to discuss something very serious with you," Rexdael said curtly, vaguely looking as if he might be sick were he forced to talk much more.

"As long as it doesn't concern taking my head off, I'm all ears," quipped Yutigo. I noticed a vein begin to throb near

Rexdael's right temple.

"Yutigo, we, or at least I, have a question for you," said Nuarti, shooting glances at Rexdael and me as she did so. "Have you been feeling...*peculiar* lately?"

"*Weelll*," drawled Yutigo, drawing out the syllable in an exaggerated manner and grinning madly, "I do suppose being gutted like a pig with pieces of an elevator car falls into this particular category, so I—"

"Can the sarcasm, Yutigo!" To my utter surprise, Yutigo actually did shut his mouth. "I'm sure you know what I'm getting at, so stop playing dumb; it really doesn't suit you," Nuarti continued. "What I meant was: Have you been having any sudden mood swings, erratic patterns of behavior, thoughts you couldn't remember thinking lately?"

Yutigo's breathing stilled, though his facial expression betrayed nothing. "Perhaps I have, perhaps I haven't," he replied, somewhat terser than before. "What does it concern you?"

"It concerns us because the Boss Upstairs may have something to do with that," Rexdael replied sharply.

Yutigo's eyes let a flicker or two of fear run through them, and his skin perhaps paled a shade or two, but other than that there was no physical reaction to indicate he had even heard our words. Instead, he began to *laugh*. "You spared me so that you could tell me *this?*" he said between choked gasps. "Nuarti, your sense of justice is admirable, and considering what it has brought me in this instance, I'm feeling quite thankful for it, but really, dear. If that was all you wished to say to me, you should have just killed me then. This much I can ensure you of: you will never come so close again."

Nuarti looked bewildered. "I...I don't understand," she

said slowly. "Doesn't this revelation change anything?"

Yutigo scoffed. "*Think*, Nuarti. Even if the Boss is involved here, which I won't rule out as completely implausible, that doesn't change the fact that Rexdael and I have been at each other's throats from the moment the Council was formed. One revelation does not make us two bedfellows, I'm afraid. Even if this conflict is manufactured, you can't *seriously* be suggesting that every single one of our other conflicts has been manufactured as well, for I'm assuming that the reason the Boss would even take an interest in this case is dear Pierre over there. What reason do I have to ally myself with the three of you? You're not going to defeat the Boss, or even come close, so why should I lay down arms just because I might have been pushed further in a certain direction than I would have liked? Whatever has occurred, I can assure you it has not stemmed from the conception of entirely new sentiments but rather from the augmentation of long-standing, preexisting ones."

Yutigo even *talked* like a politician, and witnessing it made me somewhat nauseous. All this dancing around the intended point, this embellishment...what was wrong with good, old-fashioned directness? Had Nuarti seriously expected that Yutigo would consider whatever she thought we could tempt him with if we spared and imprisoned him instead of killing him? Yutigo *was* afraid, though whether it was simply a result of preconditioned reflexes, I was unsure. Nevertheless, his fear was not enough to overcome his pride, which meant any further attempts to converse were basically useless.

"What's to keep us from killing you now?" I asked brusquely. "You're defenseless and basically immobile. Do you really think you could stop me if it came down to it?"

Yutigo smirked. "Oh, Pierre. You forget that I know your companions better than you could ever hope to. You *are* correct, nothing I personally can do would stop you from ending my life once and for all this time. No, justice will do my job for me." Yutigo looked directly at Nuarti, who flushed slightly and began to stare fixedly at the floor.

I raised an eyebrow at Rexdael. He shrugged, as confused as I was. "What are you talking about, justice?" I asked skeptically. "Is it not just to repay you in kind for all the lives you have ruined, bodies you have left in your wake? What is there left to decide?"

"No, Pierre," said Nuarti softly. "It would *not* be just for you to kill Yutigo. He may have wronged you in this moment, but we can't definitively say that he was acting out of his own volition while doing so. And his other crimes, while surely grave and worthy of execution, have not been brought for judgment before a court of law. *We are better than our enemies.* We will not become judge, jury, and executioner here."

I opened my mouth to retort but was interrupted by a rhythmic pounding on the door. The four of us stared at each other, even Rexdael momentarily losing his mask of smug self-superiority. "Just to be sure," I began quietly, "none of you are expecting visitors of any sort, correct?" The three of them shook their heads as one. "Knowing our luck, it won't be anything good," added Rexdael.

Rexdael was, in a sense, correct. The rhythmic pounding stopped, but only because there was no more door to pound on, it having been turned into a shower of splinters. A group of what appeared to be three ordinary humans stood in the doorway. One held an automatic assault rifle, another a machete, while one simply held up his well-muscled forearms. Upon seeing us, the three humans advanced instantly, slowly but surely crossing the length of the room. Bullets sprayed from the gunslinger's weapon, and only a hastily erected force field prevented a series of minor but annoying flesh wounds. Calmly, I walked up to the gunslinger, twisted the barrel of his gun into a knot, and dropped him with a swift punch to the head. Nuarti and Rexdael each did the same with the machete-wielder and the unarmed one, respectively. "Was this your doing, Yutigo?" Rexdael asked accusingly. "Did you bring them under your thumb as well after Pierre had refused to do so?"

Yutigo rolled his eyes. "Yes, Rexdael, because I would command humans *I controlled* to attempt to harm me!" he replied sarcastically. "No, either these three specimens just happened to be walking by this room and decided they wanted to kill us, or someone else is behind all of this."

Nuarti raised an eyebrow. "So, if the Boss is responsible," she said with an edge in her voice, "doesn't that provide us with a more robust reason for you to join us?"

"Perhaps," Yutigo said dismissively, "but these humans seem like small fry, don't you think? I doubt you need *my* help to defeat them."

There was a clanking noise behind me. To my utter surprise, the man I had just dropped with a robust punch was climbing to his feet again, using the gun as a prop to pull himself up. Moreover, the tips of his fingers were *glowing with energy*. "On second thought," Yutigo continued amusedly, "this may be more entertaining than I thought it would be."

"*Shut up*," Rexdael growled at Yutigo. I advanced toward my man again, but this time I was stopped a few feet short of my target by a newly created force field. Sighing, I phased to a point behind the man and gave him another, slightly stronger punch to the back of his head. As he crumpled to the floor again, I wondered what Fate was going for with these relatively tame humans who were coming after us.

"*Pierre*," Rexdael warned. I turned toward him and ducked just in time to avoid being hit by a conjured scythe of energy. The man I had dropped had already gotten to his feet for the third time, and I was growing slightly worried. "You have to break the control, or they're going to keep coming," Rexdael continued.

Nodding, I focused my will into a single, razor-sharp point, just as I had when preparing to break the connection between Yutigo and Mr. Benton. This point, however, I aimed at the man's mind. But this time, instead of the man's mental barriers cleaving before me, I ran headlong into a barrier of solid shuritanium and found myself flying backward to land in a heap beside Yutigo. He laughed. The man whose mind I had just been forcibly ejected from shuffled to my position, towering over me as he raised a hand wreathed in glowing green energy...only for his head to be taken off in the next moment by a solid blade of light. Blood and gore splattered all over Yutigo and me as Nuarti went to behead the other two humans as well. I winced when I felt three of my creations die in that same instance.

"What are you doing, Nuarti?! They were completely innocent! It wasn't their fault! They didn't need to die!"

Nuarti simply looked at me. "It was kill or be killed, Pierre," she replied calmly. "This is the way it has to be unless we find a way to stop the Boss's meddling." With another wave of her hand, she resealed the doorway, and moments later, the sounds of pounding, more insistent this time, once again filled the room. "Yutigo, call an absentee meeting of the Council," Nuarti ordered.

To my surprise, Yutigo acceded to this. "Fine," he said evenly, "though it is a *bit* difficult to do that without having my hands free."

Nuarti scoffed. Scribbling a message down onto a scrap of paper she had conjured and stuffing it into a metal sphere that had appeared the same way, she tossed it at Yutigo. "Catch!" was all the warning she gave him. Reflexively, his arm shot upward, and even encumbered by chains, he managed to corral it in his grasp. Instantly, the sphere glowed blue and disappeared.

The ghost of a smile graced Yutigo's face. "And now? What else do you require of me? Or has my usefulness run to an end?"

Nuarti simply gave him a sidelong glance.

"What on earth are you talking about? Now? Now, we wait."

17

THE SCHISM

The Council of Realms

Even when no one was around to admire it, the meeting room of the Council of Realms continued to sparkle in all its magnificence. Fine traceries of color wound their way up and down the walls, across the ceiling, and down onto the floor. The Council table took up most of the space in the center of the room as it always did, a monolithic masterpiece of technological trickery. At a glance, everything would have seemed normal. But the more one looked, the more two particular features of the room began to stick out like sore thumbs. At the head of the table, an elaborate chair graced the table with its presence. At the moment, however, a red light pulsed rhythmically from within its headrest. In the center of the table, meanwhile, a blue light shone steadily from the indentation located there. A war was afoot, a meeting of the Council had been called to take place in the absence of its leader, and the bowels of the Council room had been locked away. What else could this indicate besides a crisis of the gravest sort?

The colors of the room's walls flared brightly as 5,269 portals formed within its bounds, and 5,269 beings stepped out of these portals in turn and calmly made their way to their seats. They were in varying states of disarray, some attired immaculately, some with merely a hair or two out of place, while others could have reasonably been assumed to have just rolled out of bed, though it was well-established that beings were not *strictly* required to sleep in order to achieve peak functionality. For this meeting, having been given no special instructions, they had all unilaterally decided to come in their natural, their original, forms.

Though surely the beings *must* have known what awaited them once they set foot in the Council room, a murmur of disquiet still ran through their ranks, particularly those of the non-elder members. The elaborate chair at the head of the table remained empty, though the red light in its headrest had ceased blinking. No, it was perhaps more surprising and more concerning that the two seats directly to the right of this chair remained empty as well. That Rexdael's chair was empty was perhaps not as surprising as it should have been; he was well-known to not look too highly upon these sorts of formal, elaborate gatherings. It was the fact that the other two chairs were empty as well in conjunction with his that elicited real cause for concern. Three of the most powerful beings absent, among them the head of the Council and its faithful recordkeeper, two of whom were staunch rivals? Nothing good could come of it—that was almost certain.

Some confusion ensued now, as there had never been an absentee meeting of the Council held before, and the one who would have known the proper rules and procedures, namely the recordkeeper, found *herself* absent as well. The beings thus fell to muttering among themselves, those who had had dealings with the illustrious head of the Council particularly concerned for what his absence could mean for them and their loved ones. Near the head of the table, Metixalos—an elder of the Council thanks to, among other things, the role he had played in helping to swiftly resolve the border dispute involving star nursery 223B-04-C—bent his head, leaning in closer to the center of the table in order to confer with his fellow elders. After a swift and furious discussion, another of the elders, who vaguely resembled a scarab beetle, seized the staff of the head of the Council, which was leaning against his chair, and pounded it on the table once.

Red beams of light, originating from the point where the staff had made contact with the table, raced their way down its surface, catching the attention of even those beings who had been too far away to hear the deep clang the staff had made as it hit the table over the sound of their own harried conversations. The room instantly fell silent.

"Thisss absssentee meeting of the Counsssil is called to order," hissed the scarab beetle, each word punctuated by a clicking together of his engorged mandibles. "Now, I'm sssure you are all wondering what exactly isss the purpossse of thisss meeting, asss well asss the reassson that our dissstinguissshed recordkeeper hasss sssealed offf the lower roomsss. The Mossst Honorable Head of the Counsssil hasss ssseen ffit to sssend usss a messsage to be read to the Counsssil in hisss absssence."

The beetle paused for a moment as his right pincer tapped along the surface of the metal sphere that had been sitting in front of Yutigo's chair. Eventually, his pincer found a small nib along the rim of the sphere. With a hiss, the sphere split into two halves, revealing a small sheet of paper curled inside. Unrolling it, he brought it up to one of his small, beady black eyes. "The reasson for thisss absssentee meeting of the Counsssil of the Realmsss isss asss followsss," he read off. "The..." His mandibles began to shake and click against each other. "The Bosss Upssstairsss," he continued in a quavering voice, "...the Bosss Upssstairsss hasss made movesss on New Earth, where Rexssdael, Nuarti, and I find oursssselvesss along wittth the Hartffford boy."

Even before the beetle had finished speaking, a veritable roar of noise had arisen from the ranks of the Council. If before some beings had found themselves in panicked states of mind, now a thrill of fear had run through even the foolhardiest of beings. Pandemonium ensued. Even the walls of the Council room seemed to dim in comparison with the full-on light show that was occurring in the center of the room as minute amounts of energy flared out from the beings in their panic. A deep clanging, far louder than before, caused everyone to freeze in shock, however.

"ORDER!" roared a voice far more authoritative and deeper-pitched than that of the scarab beetle. "THERE WILL BE ORDER IN THIS MEETING OF THE COUNCIL!" Metixalos had seized the staff from the inert pincers of the scarab beetle, who had at this point been reduced to a huddling mass of sharp extremities, and with one of his many legs

(Metixalos resembled a beetle of some sort) had almost driven a dent into the table with his concentrated pounding. The red lights of the Council table flickered erratically.

"Now," Metixalos continued gruffly, once everyone had become calm and sat down again, "we are not here to babble and bicker like little children. This imminent danger of the Boss Upstairs is, it goes without saying, one of the most perilous sort. So perilous, in fact, that our Most Honorable Head of the Council finds himself unable to grace us with his presence, together with two more of our distinguished elders, including our recordkeeper. We have obviously been brought together so that we can determine the best course of action to be taken in countering this threat."

A goldfinch-like creature emitted a squeaking noise that could have signaled anything from derision to complete and utter fear before clamping a claw around his beak in mortification. "Would you like to contribute something to the discussion, *Tulin?*" commented Metixalos acidly. "*Please* don't hold back on our accounts." Metixalos understandably did not view Tulin in the warmest of lights, having come to the conclusion that he was a naive little minion of Yutigo's after watching him introduce his dream pod proposal at the prior Council meeting. While this may have been a somewhat hypocritical stance for Metixalos to take, considering how he had gotten his position as elder in the first place, Metixalos did not believe that Tulin had needed to be coerced in order to work alongside Yutigo.

"Well," Tulin began in a high, reedy voice, "this is the Bo...bo...boss *Upstairs* we're talking about, is...is...isn't it? What are *we...we* supposed to do about th...that?"

A blue-skinned being with ears sprouting from the top of her head nodded in assent as well. "I think Tulin makes a valid point," she said in a more collected fashion. "What *are* we expected to do against the Boss? It's not as if we can very well declare that we are going to go to war over this, can we?"

Metixalos nodded his assent, though his mind was simultaneously elsewhere. He had been going over in his mind the recent series of proposals Yutigo had made at the last Council meeting, and it was, ironically, the proposal concerning New Earth that gave him the beginnings of an idea. Internally, he smiled evilly, a smile of revenge as he contemplated what he believed was a chance to break free of his past choices. "I believe I have a proposal which can at least temporarily solve our problem," he began. "It is quite obvious that this recent stirring of the Boss can be traced back to this human boy Pierre Hartford. In order to find some way to at least temporarily sate the Boss, then, we should eliminate Hartford and all that he has used his powers to create. I propose that we wipe out New Earth."

Tulin suddenly looked as if he had choked on a piece of overripe fruit and was attempting to spit it back out. "Des... *destroy* New Earth?" he managed, incredulous. "We *can't*! Our Most Honorable Head of the Council is still on the planet! If we were to destroy the planet now, he would be killed! How could we possibly allow that to occur?" There were many murmurs of agreement, especially toward the lower half of the table. Metixalos resisted the urge to snort derisively. Some of the elders, including him, had fallen into the habit of denoting many of the newest Council members with the moniker of "the Unspoiled Legion." These were the members of the

208 · KONRAD KOENIGSMANN

Council who had only seen the face Yutigo presented to the Council, his good face, so to speak. They had not been twisted, prodded, and pulled into submission yet and could not possibly understand the pain Yutigo wielded. A Council without Yutigo meant a world in which Metixalos could breathe easily, knowing his daughters were no longer in danger of eternal torture, a world in which the scarab beetle knew his brother no longer faced the threat of murder, a world in which so many Council members would be freed of the yoke of submission. Against that, the extermination of a petty little species, of several powerful Council members, or even the extermination of a singularly talented individual meant little. To Metixalos, the presence or non-presence of the Boss Upstairs on New Earth was not of any particular consequence, but it did serve as a wonderfully good excuse.

"I'm sure that the distinguished Council members would agree with me when I declare that the Boss Upstairs is far and away the biggest possible threat the Council of Realms could face, no matter the circumstances," Metixalos replied. "As grievous as the death of our Most Honorable Head of the Council would be, along with the deaths of the distinguished Elders Rexdael and Nuarti, it pales in comparison to the damage that the manipulations of the Boss could wreak if left unchecked. The surest way to nip this in the bud is to eliminate the source of this contagion before it has the opportunity to spread to other worlds, other realms." Metixalos swept the ranks of the elders with his gaze, noting with approval that at least a few of them appeared to catch on to what he was trying to accomplish, as well as what it would mean for them. They began to nod in agreement.

All opposition was not extinguished, however. "This talk of planet destruction is all well and good, Elder Metixalos," said a youthful red-skinned humanoid about halfway down the table, "but perhaps the Council could learn how exactly you intend to destroy this planet, New Earth? Recordkeeper Nuarti has sealed off the Records room, which in turn prevents us from accessing the armory and the planet destroying laser arrays stored within it. Did you have another weapon in mind?" Metixalos fought to keep his face stoic. That far, unfortunately, he had not developed his little idea before deciding to introduce it to the Council.

Luckily, one of the other elders who had caught on to Metixalos's idea, a reptilian being with angular yellow eyes and a long, pink sliver of a tongue, came to the rescue. "I do believe there is to be a meteor shower taking place near the star system to which New Earth belongs quite soon," she interjected smoothly. "To slightly alter its course is a trivial matter, I would think."

"Such a manipulation of matter requires a special dispensation!" protested the blue-skinned being who had earlier articulated Tulin's point about combating the Boss Upstairs. "Dispensation which must be signed by either the Most Honorable Head of the Council or the recordkeeper, both of whom are absent at the moment!"

Metixalos tilted his head in acknowledgment. "This is the normal procedure, yes. Yet is this not a time of dire need? A period of emergency? The Boss is no everyday matter, and the rules which serve us so well during those times must sometimes be circumvented so that the best possible outcome cannot be prevented. I'm sure an emergency dispensation could be granted at this time, to be retroactively approved by the successors of our Most Honorable Head and recordkeeper."

Tulin, sensing perhaps that he was on the losing end of this conflict, refused to be dissuaded. "Surely we can send a warning of some sort to the Most Honorable Head of the Council," he suggested. "The destruction of the planet could be scheduled to happen only after he and the distinguished elders in his company were safely off the planet!"

Metixalos tutted slightly. "To warn our Most Honorable Head, Tulin," he said in what was supposed to be a consoling tone, "would be to warn the Boss as well. That would just defeat the purpose of this entire proposal, so a warning is entirely out of the question. We must act now or never!" A majority of the elders began to murmur in agreement. "I propose a vote!" declared Metixalos. "A vote on this proposal, together with this exceptional dispensation that would make it possible."

"Seconded!" said the reptilian being almost immediately.

The votes began to flood in, and to Metixalos's practiced eyes, at least, it appeared as if this was as close a vote as he had ever had the opportunity to witness. For the first time in eons, perhaps, every member of the Council was free to vote as his or her conscience willed the member to. There were those who simply wished to see Yutigo destroyed once and for all, a fitting revenge for all the destruction he had threatened to bring down upon their heads, while there were others who simply quaked in fear at the thought of Fate being let loose on their realms. Conversely, there were also those whose fear of Fate was not stronger than their aversion to committing genocide, as well as the bloc of members who made up the "Unspoiled Legion."

When at last the votes had all been tallied, the elders momentarily were unable to see the vote count, for they had, as was typical, arrayed themselves in front of Yutigo's chair. Metixalos arose from his chair and walked over so that he was standing directly behind Yutigo's chair. The numbers were so close that at first he misread them and almost felt the breath leave his body, but on second glance, his body relaxed once more. "The proposal passes," he declared, fighting to keep the exultation out of his voice, "with 2,635 votes for and 2,634 votes against. Metixalos touched one of his limbs to the table, much as he had seen Yutigo do so often, and a series of lines on the table lit up green to confirm that the proposal had indeed passed.

Tulin, who had been struck dumb by the result of the vote, only seemed to realize what was happening when Metixalos opened the map of the realms and prepared to find the meteor shower whose intended use was now to destroy New Earth. In the depths of his despair, he would only afterward realize what a supremely stupid thing he had done.

Just as Metixalos was ready to redirect the meteor shower, Tulin conjured a knife and, clutching it in his right claw, hurled it at Metixalos's face. Metixalos was too caught up in his joy to notice that something was wrong, and by the time the other Council members had recovered from their shock, the knife had already buried itself halfway into Metixalos's brain. His body fell onto the table with a crash. All hell broke loose.

Luckily for Tulin, his allies were both more vigilant and in a better position to protect him than Metixalos's had been, or Tulin would have been skewered by twenty different knives, disintegrated by thirty different blasts of energy, or crushed like a small nut by fifty different sets of grasping fists. Instead, a series of overlapping energy barriers flew up to block all of these various attacks, as the Council members who had voted for or against the proposal broke into fisticuffs all around the room. The enchantments Yutigo and Nuarti had used to construct the table prevented it from taking even a little scratch, but this did not stop the Council members from climbing on top of, ducking under, or leaping over it. Now, the walls of the room really did seem dim and washed out in comparison to the deadly light show of death occurring in the center of the room. Elder turned on elder, councilor on councilor. Former political rivals became allies, and allies nemeses, all based off the result of a single vote. And for the first time since the creation of the Council, the number of beings went into sharp decline.

All the chaos, however, served to mask the actions of Metixalos's reptilian ally. The map of the realms had never been dismissed, and it still hung in front of Yutigo's seat, at the very edge of the fighting. The reptilian being slowly but steadily made her way over to the map, allowing her allies to deal with those who would have attacked her. Working quickly but surely, she found the meteor shower she herself had mentioned and redirected its course. The beep it caused caught everyone's attention immediately, but by then, it was already too late, for the reptilian being had already dismissed the map and locked in the changes. An inexplicable smile graced her face as she died, her shields overwhelmed by the sheer number of attacks launched against.

Tulin, realizing what a hopeless proposition it would be to continue to fight in the Council room, decided to open a portal. "To New Earth!" he cried. "We go to protect our Most Honorable Head!"

Quickly retreating, his surviving allies followed him with portals of their own. The scarab beetle, one of those who had sided with Metixalos, looked around at the remaining beings in the room. "Thossse foolsss mussst not be allowed to interfffere," he hissed out frantically. "Fffollow them!" And so they did.

In this way, the destruction of the Council of Realms commenced.

18

An Unconscionable Bargain

Pierre Hartford, New Berlin, Europa, New Earth

*T*hump, thump, thump, thump.

If I had wanted to, I could have probably used the sound of pounding fists on the door to the room containing Rexdael, Nuarti, Yutigo, and me to tell time, so rhythmic was the hitting. Operative phrase being "could have." It might have been possible had the sound also not slowly been driving me insane. At this point, I felt as if I had been sitting around for hours, but it could have just as easily been a few minutes or even seconds, so ingrained was the thumping in my mind. It had been occurring for all eternity, but it had also only just begun. However long it had been, I could not bring myself to simply wait, as Nuarti had blithely suggested, especially not with that constant reminder of what had been taken from me pounding on the door.

The stronger I became, it appeared, the more I lost. Though I could not hope to recapture them, I still remembered perfectly well the four years of obliviousness I had spent as a perfectly ordinary human being. They had been the happiest times of my life, even more so than the time I had spent trapped on Earth in Harkook's dreams. *Normalcy* was comforting. The moments when events in my life began tending toward the extraordinary were the times when everything around me went to pieces. The first time, it had been the world I thought I knew so well, the people I had thought could easily be defined as friend or foe. The second time, I had lost the majority of my friends and family. And now, here was the third time. What more would I, *could* I, lose before all would be said and done?

Perhaps this was it. Perhaps I was destined to finally lose my sense of self. This was not to say that I had never been under control before, but when I had, it had always been a fairly simple matter to distinguish between the times I had control and the times when I didn't. It had been a more basic, less insidious form of control. Moreover, it had always seemed as if I stood a chance, however slim, of beating my foes. This time, though… Did I *really* stand a chance? At times, I felt as if fighting Fate was like grasping at the wind: grabbing at it and having it perpetually slip through my fingers. I could never be sure that my thoughts were my own. A mental pathway could have been widened, another shrunken, and who was I to say that that hadn't been what I had wanted? Now my losses had only become more tangible. All that I had built up, all that I had done since destroying my creator, and, in a way, my father…all that was now being snatched out from under my feet.

The people were no longer mine, and the control I had never bothered to assert lay beyond my grasp, possibly forever. Was the very ground I had created to be next? The circumstances were different, for I had at least learned to assert my control over the ground to a certain degree, but I harbored no illusions over whose will was stronger. If Fate wanted the ground, Fate would have it.

The people...*the people*! My mother and Yuri! My friends! What had become of them? In the hubbub over Yutigo and the circumstances surrounding his near-death, I had completely forgotten about them. Could Fate have gotten control over them as well? My mother and Yuri were not my creations, after all, so perhaps that had protected them, but what about my friends? They *were* my creations and thus had no such protection.

"Where are my mother, Yuri, and my friends?" I blurted out suddenly. Yutigo fought to hide a smile of glee that nevertheless began to creep over his face, while Nuarti remained expressionless and Rexdael at least had the grace to look guilty. "In the room down the hall," he replied calmly. He caught the look in my eye, however, and hastened to add words of reassurance. "Don't worry, Pierre. This entire building is shielded so as to prevent any external mental influence from being exerted over anybody within these walls."

I raised an eyebrow. "The people at our door would beg to differ, Rexdael," I said disbelievingly.

"The building being shielded does not stop people who fall under mental control outside its walls and subsequently enter it from being mentally influenced," he responded. "I built this building to act as a defense against mental attacks and the physical attack of perhaps a single being, not a horde of hundreds or thousands of mildly powered humans."

"I believe the bigger question for dear Pierre here is how he intends to make his way down the hall to his human companions," interjected Yutigo. "After all, from our own experience it seems quite obvious that the only good way to stop these humans is to kill them. And judging from the sound of pounding on this door, there must be, oh…fifty or sixty at the very least simply standing outside. Is this the day they die, Pierre?" He giggled slightly.

My hand twitched as I fought the urge to attempt to take Yutigo's head off again. "I hardly believe that any killing will be necessary, Yutigo," I replied as calmly as I could. "My goal here isn't the elimination of a threat. This time, at least, I merely have to traverse it." Yutigo raised his eyebrows. I sighed. "Watch and learn," I said tiredly. "That is, if you can."

Phasing through the door proved to be more difficult than I had expected it to be. Nuarti, it appeared, had placed some quite hefty protections on it. I recohered on the other side of the door feeling as if I had just punched through a steel wall, bending over slightly and panting as I stumbled out of the phasing. Just in time, I put up a force field to protect myself from the humans, a significant proportion of whom had refocused their attention from pounding on the door to trying to pound on me. Luckily for me, there was only one other door in the long hallway, and it was relatively untouched. Only a few humans pounded on this door, which surprisingly was still in its doorframe, if only by the remnants of a hinge. Accordingly, phasing through this unprotected door proved to be far easier. I pivoted and reinforced the door just as a blow fell that would have surely taken it off its remaining hinge.

I heard a small gasp of surprise behind me and the sound of glass shattering as something hit the floor with a thump. I hadn't been looking particularly closely after I had phased into the room and before pivoting to reinforce the door either, but I thought that perhaps I had seen something being whisked out of sight out of the corner of my eye. I turned slowly to face the five remaining humans who knew me and were still definitely alive. Robert and Luka, it seemed, had blanched upon my entry into the room, while Max had his right arm upraised. I turned to look behind me and saw Max's personal communications device lying in a corner with some shards of shattered glass scattered around it. Yuri was holding my mother, who was covering her mouth with one hand. I looked at Max quizzically. "Everything all right here?" I asked, slightly concerned. "Of course, Pierre," chorused Robert, Max, and Luka. "Why not?" added Robert. "Well," I replied, "your personal communications device is over in that corner, Max, and I'm going to hazard a guess and say that it's broken."

I walked over to check. The personal communications device was indeed broken. So broken, in fact, that the outer shell was dented and whole chunks of glass had fallen out of the screen. "Yes, it does appear that way," said Max. "I threw it when you…appeared next to the door."

"You *threw* it," I repeated slowly.

"Yes," replied Max. "You scared us all pretty badly." A slight quaver had entered his voice, though whether it was because of fear of my phasing or something else entirely, I was not sure.

"Sorry about that," I said, feeling slightly ashamed. "It was the safest way I could come to check on you, which I'm also sorry for not doing sooner. You have seen what's been pounding on your door, though, right?" The five of them nodded.

"You don't need to apologize to us, Pierre," said my mother. Her voice was calm, though for some inexplicable reason her hands were shaking slightly. "We're fairly superfluous at the moment. Compared to everything we've seen today, a few people pounding at our door seems relatively tame. And we're sure you had much bigger problems that needed fixing. We understand. It's not as if we can provide much help at the moment."

"Don't say that," I admonished gently. "You're the only friends and family I have left! And I know that even with the limited powers you have, Mom, you can't possibly fight a being and live, but really, all of you, the information you gathered was crucial and provided us with valuable intel." There were slight smiles of appreciation all around at this last comment, though they seemed somewhat...forced. Something was off, even if everything appeared immaculate. "You're *sure*, besides me giving all of you a good scare, that you're all right?" Nods all around. "I'm just making sure because those people pounding on your door are being mentally influenced. You're absolutely positive that you are yourselves?"

Again, a series of nods, more assertive this time. "We're *fine*, Pierre," boomed Robert. "We know you'd protect us if anything nefarious were to be attempted against us, but until that actually occurs, I'm sure you have more important things to do than to continually ask after our well-being."

I raised an eyebrow. "You don't know how important all of you are to me, Robert," I said quietly. "None of those other things would matter to me the moment I learned that I had lost one of you." I paused. "In fact, if I didn't know better, I would think you were trying to get rid of me!"

A nervous chuckle bubbled out of Yuri's throat. My gaze flicked over to meet his, and he suddenly looked as if he wanted nothing more in the world than to give himself a sound kicking. Alarm bells began to go off in my head. "Something *is* wrong!" I insisted, all playfulness gone from my voice. "You keep insisting you're fine, but you're also behaving oddly. What are you hiding?"

"Pierre, we're just nervous for you," said my mother, looking confused. I noted that her hands had ceased trembling for the moment at least. "All this action, all this fighting has us on edge, and it's just making us slightly tense. And logically, what on earth could we know that would be worth hiding?" That made sense, I suppose. "You're right, Mom," I said. "I guess I'm just on edge too."

She smiled warmly, tenderly. "We know, darling," she said softly. "Now go protect us in the way you know best. Beat Fate and make us proud."

"Of course, Mom," I said, turning and walking toward the door, preparing to phase. "I'll try my...best." My voice trailed off as I paused a few steps from the door and turned back around. "What did you say, Mom?"

Her eyebrows scrunched together, but her eyes betrayed her, panic flitting across them. "What do you mean? I was just wishing you luck."

"No," I said, more sharply now. "No, no, no, no. You *specifically* mentioned the Boss."

"Whom?" interjected Yuri, this time I was sure in genuine confusion.

"*FATE!*" I roared back at him. An icy blast whooshed through the room, setting everyone's hair all askew. "The Boss is the euphemism we use to describe Fate," I continued more calmly, barely noticing the breeze I must have missed before when my mother had said "Fate" as well. "But that raises the question," I said, wheeling to face all five of them. "*Where did you learn about the Boss?*" I gestured with my right hand, and I could feel tremors running through it now. I was as scared as I was angry. Had Rexdael lied? What if Fate really *had* taken control of my parents, my friends?

"Pierre, I'm sure you told us about the…Boss last time," said Luka hesitatingly. More telling, however, was the fact that he was unable to look me in the eye. My mother's slip of the tongue had brought all the tension I had been sensing earlier out in the open. Everyone was pointedly finding a certain patch of wall or ceiling very interesting at the moment. My mother's hands had begun to tremble again. Max fidgeted uncomfortably. Yuri's neck could have been made of steel given how tense it had become.

"Yes, Luka, I'm so sure we talked about the Boss before," I said softly, "so sure, in fact, that I can't even *remember* the conversation we had about that." No one said anything in reply. "WHO TOLD YOU ABOUT THE BOSS?!" I yelled suddenly. Everyone jumped, and my mother gave a little shriek. A tear welled up in my eye, stubbornly refusing to go away no matter how much I blinked, though I wasn't sure if anyone else noticed. After all that she had gone through, I hated to inflict pain on my mother like this, but I *had* to know. I *couldn't* have them falling under Fate's thumb. It could not happen.

"Pierre, I think you should leave." Yuri had overcome his

fears enough to stand up at least, though he remained so tense that I thought perhaps his spine would crack from the strain. "I will gladly oblige you, Yuri," I began. "Once I have the truth, of course."

Yuri scoffed. "Tell me, Pierre, and be honest. Would it really stop at that? Or would you dig deeper and deeper, searching for something you could not name if prompted? You would tug at the rotten tree trunk, peel away its bark, dig your hand deep into its core, until the entire tree comes crashing down around you in all its glory. What *do* you expect to find at the bottom of all this? Nothing good, I hope. Because I am sure that when you finally dig deep enough for your liking, you will find yourself sorely disappointed. It would be best if you stopped now, before you pass the point where amends cannot be made."

I could never honestly say that I had *liked* Yuri, but now I could not help but feel a burst of hatred flow through me as I regarded him once more. "You would have this secret hang over me for the rest of our shared days on this earth?" I asked him coldly. "Perhaps I could ignore it now, in favor of going out and trying to win this conflict, if I did not think it so crucial. Do you know what I fear at the moment? I fear that you have fallen under the Boss's influence, and do you know what that would do to me? Do you?! I assure you, it would do far more damage than finding out that my own friends and family were hiding information from me, as can be the only other possible explanation. So tell me, Yuri, tell me quick and tell me true: Am I to be shattered or merely grievously wounded today?" Yuri stared at me unblinkingly, mutely, his eyes furious, fearful, and disgusted in equal measure. *"Tell me,"* I hissed. I did not scream or yell as I had before, but all the same, Robert began to shiver, and my other friends shrank in on themselves.

Yuri turned away from me to look at my mother and my friends. "Ladies and gentlemen," he began sarcastically, "I present to you your *hero*, your *idol*, the object of your unceasing devotion, Pierre Hartford! See how he makes you tremble in fear, how he brings you to the verge of tears, how he shouts and threatens! Does he seem the epitome of perfection to you now? Would you still die for him? *This* is the being you have thrown away your lives for, taken leave of your senses for, and how does he repay for what you have done for him? He *forgets* about you, abandons you in this dank, windowless dump of a room with a horde pounding down the door, and comes to find you only when it might have implications for the larger game he and his beings play. I say this now, knowing full well that I am right: *I told you so.*"

It was like watching two ships collide in slow motion. I had only intended to slap Yuri across the face, which was already a departure from my typical behavior in and of itself. He had made me that angry. But once my hand actually started to move, it became more and more difficult to stop it. It refused to simply brush past Yuri's face. Instead, the moment my hand made contact with his face, I began to...*push.* The next thing I knew, there was a snap and a pop, and Yuri's head was no longer attached to the rest of his body, while I was covered in a few bits of blood and other gore. My friends gave shouts of dismay, and my mother began to cry in earnest.

I could feel myself shaking as well. *What have I done? What am I doing?* I had just killed one of the few remaining people who had known me in my entirety, secrets and all. I had never loved him, but the past six years had shown that he was more friend than foe. I was angry, and justifiably so. Yuri had indeed said some very hurtful things to me. I felt insulted. But I did not feel bloodlust. Or, at the very least, my conscious mind did not. At the moment, I could not be sure that I was in full control of my physical actions. I screamed mentally but futilely, caged behind a barrier that left me merely an onlooker to what I dreaded would be a grisly spectacle.

I should have apologized, cried, shown some sort of remorse for the unfortunate accident that had just occurred. That was what people who were not psychopaths probably did after they accidentally committed murder. That was not what I did. "Look...*l...look* what you made me d...d...do!" I stammered. "This is what happens when p...p...people act like i...i...idiots! Why...why couldn't you have just *told* m...me?" Some tears rolled down my cheeks, but it would have been a stretch to call them tears of remorse. They were a reflex reaction to a traumatic event, nothing more.

My mother was fully shaking now, trembling like a leaf caught in an autumn wind. Her head was in her hands, but I could still see the tears coursing down her cheeks, the fat droplets squeezing between the gaps her fingers left and falling onto the floor with great big plops. My friends were still more shocked than anything else, staring at me as if they were just now meeting me for the first time, and none of them went over to comfort my mother.

"*Please*," I whispered, my own lips beginning to tremble. "Tell me." My mother just cried harder, shaking her head and causing tears to fly everywhere. "TELL ME!" I roared. The walls of the room rattled, for a moment drowning out even the sound of the ever-present pounding upon the door. My mother shrieked again, a high-pitched, keening wail which made me want to do nothing more than fold her into my embrace, though I knew that even the blood on my hands would have been enough to make her recoil from me, not to mention everything else.

"A message," she finally managed to get out between sobs, great, heaving ones that shook her whole upper body. "There was…*was* a…a *message*. A message sent…sent to…*to the mortals*. The h…humans."

"What did it say?" I asked brusquely. This time, only one long syllable answered me.

"*No,*" she whispered. Another set of sobs overcame her, but she simply continued to whisper that poisonous, that treacherous syllable.

"*What did it say?*" I repeated, more angrily this time. Head-shaking began to accompany the repeated "*No.*" From one moment to the next, I found myself no longer standing next to Yuri's body, but rather next to my mother, one hand forcing her head upward, the other holding a shuritanium knife that had suddenly appeared in my hand, wickedly sharp, against her chest. My mother's eyes were red-rimmed, her lashes thick with tears, and she looked positively ghastly, but she was still the most beautiful woman I had ever known. "Mom," I said in a tone far softer than the one I had used previously. "Please, tell me. What did the message say?" So close, I could feel her breath on my face, hesitant and stuttering, but nonetheless a pleasant warm breeze that made me think of bygone summer days I had spent with her and Yuri at our home on New Earth. *The best days of my life. Ones with a small, normal, happy family.* Even when threatened with a knife, having cried herself almost to pieces, she refused to break. For that, at least, I respected her.

"*For you,*" she whispered. "*For you.*" My heart almost stopped.

"What did it say?" I said again, more urgently than before. "Please, what did the message say?" Our faces were so close that it was a wonder the tips of our noses did not touch. Blue eyes met blue eyes, and neither pair liked what it saw in the other. It was then that I began to realize.

"*No,*" came the answer, as expected. "*No. N…no. Nooo.*"

The knife cleaved flesh as smoothly as if it were cleaving air. One gentle push, and it had already burrowed its way between two ribs up to the hilt. My mother gasped—a noise so gentle it might have been the sound of her falling asleep. I pushed the blade upward, felt it pierce heart muscle, and then her aorta. The gasp became a strangled scream, and the illusion fell away. Horrified, I pulled my hand away as if it had been scalded, but that only served to make things worse. The knife came out as smoothly as it had gone in, followed by a gush of blood.

A red spot welled up around the incision, staining the fabric of the plain white shirt she was wearing and spreading further with every beat of her heart. The knife fell out of my hand with a clatter, and I rushed to put my arms around my mother as the strength left her limbs. I laid her gently on the floor before attempting to staunch the wound with my bare hands. In that moment, try as I might, I could not summon my healing powers. The wound was too deep, my loss of control too complete, my guilt too overwhelming: Who was to say what was the ultimate cause of it? Blood washed over my hands, my attempts to apply pressure and stop the bleeding all for naught. With every beat of her heart, though, I could feel her weaken, feel the flow of blood lessen. Blood covered my hands, my arms, my mother's shirt, mixing with the tears of genuine pain I had begun to cry. My mother never said another word, but it was her eyes that broke me. They were so love-filled, so tender, so caring, emotions I no longer deserved, I, the son who was about to see through the act of matricide. All she had done, she had done for love, and I loved and hated her for it in equal measure. And so Lili Schwebler, the last person to know all my secrets, departed the world, leaving me all alone.

It was only then that I realized a piece of paper was lying next to her body, right near her newly unclasped fingers. Unfolding it, I realized it was what I had been searching for all along. The rage I had felt before was nothing compared to the inferno that raged through my veins upon reading the mocking poem in its entirety. This whole encounter, this… everything about this was planned. *I had been played.*

Only when someone coughed behind me did I remember that my friends were still in the room. Well, "friends." They could have just as easily prevented this. I was sure they knew the message just as well as she had. "Some friends you are," I said out loud. "But then, I suppose you inevitably had to be disappointing. As disappointing as your creator." In my rage, I couldn't tell how they died. Perhaps they, too, were beheaded, or stabbed through the heart. Or perhaps they simply vanished into clouds of disorganized atoms.

I fell to the floor and screamed.

19

HEADS OR TAILS?

Rexdael, New Berlin, Europa, New Earth (starting the moment Pierre left to find his family and friends)

"Nuarti," I began slowly after watching Pierre phase away and toward his human companions, "tell me, when did you find the time to lessen the protections on the door without letting the humans in as well?"

Nuarti turned to look at me, and I thought she might even be faintly impressed with Pierre, perhaps the first non-neutral emotion she had felt about him to this point. "I didn't," she replied. "He should have been unable to phase through the door, since the door's protections should have made it impossible for him to become unobservable when passing through its frame."

Yutigo merely scoffed. "The boy is more powerful than you would think, Nuarti. Were he more ordinary, the three of us would not be here in the first place, and neither would our welcoming party." He waved a hand at the door.

"It is one thing to hear of extraordinariness, Yutigo, and another entirely to witness it with one's own eyes. Quite often, it would seem, the results are...unexpected, no matter whether they are beautiful or ugly. Past experiences, at least, have taught me this one thing: first impressions are frequently misleading, for often the encounters they encompass tend to be ordinary, while the truly extraordinary ones take time to develop one way or the other." By this point, she was staring daggers at Yutigo.

"Pray tell me, Nuarti," he said playfully, with a hint of mock hurt in his voice, "what exactly about me is...*extraordinary*, in your opinion?"

"Your *amorality*!" hissed Nuarti in reply. "You are, without a doubt, the most sadistic person I've ever met. I thought you a staunch political ally! I *thought* you believed in a just system! You were perhaps somewhat overzealous politically, but that was not an irredeemable characteristic. Then I saw those records you sealed away. You make me *sick*! What's worse, I was your complicit ally all those years! And to me, at least, not knowing does not count as an excuse. I sacrificed, looked the other way whenever irregularities came to my attention, since I thought we were *this* close to achieving a system where none of that would ever be necessary again!"

Yutigo chuckled. "I beg to differ, Nuarti. Not about the amorality part. That I cannot deny. Rather there are some points in your theory of extraordinariness that I feel should be modified slightly. I do not think it is *time* that reveals the extraordinary characteristics of people, but rather it is the fact that the longer one knows somebody, the more likely it is that one experiences an extraordinary event with that person. For I believe that it is the truly extraordinary events that invite extraordinary characteristics to come out into the light. Of course, it is entirely possible for one's first encounter with another person to *be* an extraordinary event. I think the best example of that is, of course, dear Rexdael, who showed us all how destructive his genocidal tendencies could be upon the awakening of his powers. So extraordinary, in fact, was the event of Rexdael's awakening, so terrifying the extent of his abilities, that the Council of Realms was created *because* of him. On the other hand, the balance of probabilities dictates that one can also know a person for an immensely long period of time without ever experiencing an extraordinary event with that person and thus never knowing exactly what it is that distinguishes that person from the rabble. Such people often seem terribly disappointing, in my experience. Especially you, Nuarti. You, in particular, always disappointed me. I knew that only an extraordinary strength of will could have constructed the code of ethics you constantly touted, yet you seemed determined to be depressingly ordinary and boring. And now, now that we are finally experiencing an extraordinary event together, I see what makes you extraordinary, just as you saw what makes me that way. There is a fire within you, and it *burns*, burns so bright that it could easily blind. Unfettered, who knows how powerful you would be? If you would only choose to use it, you could have already achieved your goals! And therein lies the irony. The very thing you seek is what will ultimately drag you down. And you wonder why I find morals a bother."

I would not have thought it possible, but Nuarti's skin,

always such a pale shade when she occupied her natural form, was beginning to redden. The palest of pink shades crept across her neck, traced their way across her cheeks, brightened her ears. "Nuarti," I warned, "don't—"

"Rexdael, *shut up*." In her anger, her voice had quietened, a whispering coldness that did not hesitate to freeze, or even kill. I half expected ice crystals to begin forming on the walls. "You think I'm *weak*, Yutigo?" she hissed, her tongue darting out from between her lips between words. "You think I'm unable to accomplish my goals? I have seen far too many times what power does to those who wield it, and you are but the latest example. *Power* killed my people! I will not let it kill me, or the universe. I should kill you for everything you've done to me, Yutigo, all the lies you've told."

Perhaps Yutigo being chained up had turned him half mad, for instead of keeping his mouth shut, he began to laugh, a horrific cackle that made me want to screw my ears shut. He bared his throat for Nuarti. "Do it, then," he said between laughs. "Kill me, if you can." A sword of ice appeared in Nuarti's right hand and she held it to Yutigo's neck. It was so cold that Yutigo's breath came out in fine puffs of mist. "*Do it*," he whispered.

Nuarti growled.

"He's not worth it," I said. "Don't betray yourself for this."

Nuarti simply gave me a withering glance before turning back to Yutigo. "*Do it*," he repeated. "*Set yourself free.* Already one chance has slipped through your fingers. If it happens again, there won't be a third chance. Time is running short."

Nuarti's hand gripped the sword so tightly it began to tremble. The blade slipped slightly and made a small incision on Yutigo's neck. The wound did not bleed, however, leaving behind only a trail of ice crystals. Something about what Yutigo had said, though...

"Wait a minute," I said slowly. *"Time is running short?"*

Yutigo tore his gaze away from Nuarti to glance at me, and in his eyes danced pure manic glee. "Perhaps it is, perhaps it isn't," he said, giggling. "I flipped a coin. If Nuarti doesn't decide soon, *others* will for her."

My eyes widened. "The Council—"

The door was blasted off its hinges, interrupting whatever I had been about to say. It was much as I had feared. A being with the facial features of a goldfinch stalked into the room, blood dripping from his beak and clawlike hands. I could distinctly see a pile of bodies crowding the hall behind him. Of thumping on doors, at least in this building, I could hear no more. Several other beings entered the hall behind the goldfinch (it was now that I regretted not having paid more attention in Council meetings).

Nuarti wheeled around, but once the beings saw the sword in her hand, they panicked. "See how close the Most Honorable Head has come to death!" proclaimed the goldfinch. "And at the hands of the recordkeeper and Elder Rexdael, no less! How numerous the threats to his life are!"

Yutigo raised his eyebrows and his arms simultaneously, chains rattling as he did so. "Be so good and unchain me, would you, dear Tulin?" he drawled. At once, Nuarti attempted to rush over to Yutigo, only to bounce headlong off a barrier the other beings had suddenly conjured. With two snaps, the manacles fell off Yutigo's wrists. He sighed and stretched, shaking out his arms. "Thank you for that, Tulin. I have places to be, but these *traitors* most certainly do not." He waved a hand dismissively. "Kill them." With a snap of his fingers, Yutigo opened a portal and disappeared.

With the element of surprise lost, Tulin and his fellows proved no match for Nuarti and me. As a rule of thumb, the older the being, the more powerful he or she was. As such, the power difference between someone like me and someone like Tulin, whom I did not recognize but was sure sat near the foot of the Council table, might as well have been a gaping abyss. One punch was all it took to shatter his force field; the next took his head off. It was a similar story with his companions. They were all as weak or weaker than their insignificant little leader, and to watch them die was almost pitiful. Yutigo had known they would be fodder, but it had worked. He was gone who knows where, and Nuarti and I had been left high and dry.

I looked at Nuarti. "I fear the Council is no more," I said softly. Nuarti's face might have been carved from stone for all the expression she showed, but I saw her eyes dim just a little. Another dream, gone. Countless eons, wasted.

"You're right. Surely the elders would not have sided with Yutigo. It will be a bloodbath out there once they arrive."

"*If,*" I said, almost sadly.

"*When,*" Nuarti replied, more firmly. "The younglings would not have been able to slaughter them, and the elders would not stand to have them running amok on this planet." She made to cup her head in her hands. "Oh, Rexdael," she whispered in a tone of pure despair, "*what did we unleash?*"

Before I could answer her, however, an agonizing scream came from the room down the hall. Nuarti and I locked eyes.

234 • KONRAD KOENIGSMANN

"Pierre," we chorused. A pang of self-loathing shot through me. We had been so caught up in what we had lost here, but if Pierre was lost as well, we could already give up there and then. We ran down the hallway, carefully treading around the pools of blood and stray limbs, only to ram straight into Pierre's protections on the other door. A few panicked moments later, Nuarti and I smashed the door in, and we burst into the room. A macabre sight greeted us. Pierre's hands and face were drenched in blood, so much of it that his skin had turned various shades of dark red and black. The headless corpse of his mother's husband lay near the doorway, the head in question several feet away. Of Pierre's three friends, only shadows remained to denote where they had sat when they had died. Pierre himself cradled his mother's body, her chest one giant patch of red, wet and slick. A knife lay nearby, covered to the hilt in blood. Pierre shook as if a small breeze could blow him away at any moment, his body racked with sobs. He continued to scream, a sound so horrible, so filled with pain and despair that I, too, wanted to crumple to the floor and turn into a sobbing heap. It was as if Nuarti and I had not even entered the room.

I came up behind Pierre and attempted to place a hand on his shoulder. Pierre jumped to his feet, looking around wildly. I jumped backward, letting out a yell of pain and cradling my hand. Pierre's entire body had been roiling in raw, uncontrolled energy. The burns it left went more than bone-deep, though the pain soon receded to a more manageable level. Pierre's eyes found us and widened dramatically. He looked like some sort of abomination, but the look in his eyes more than made up for any grotesqueness. "Rexdael?" he said hesitatingly. "Nuarti?

THE REWRITING OF TIME • 235

What are you doing here?" At that moment, he resembled a child more than anything else.

"We're here for you," I said consolingly. "We heard you scream. We can't even imagine what you must be feeling right now."

Pierre's eyes sharpened, though he looked no less distraught. "You're wrong about that, Rexdael. It was *I*." His voice broke. "I...I...I'm the one who killed them. They were the last ones who really...truly *knew* who I was. It feels like genocide once more." Pierre let out another wail and made to cover his face with his hands again. Nuarti held his hands back, and Pierre struggled for a moment before he simply sagged to the floor, all the fight going out of him. Methodically, she rubbed away the layers of blood, grime, and tears with a featherlight touch, keeping care never to touch his skin directly.

"Pierre," I began, once he seemed a little calmer, "Nuarti and I can't help you unless you tell us exactly what happened here."

Pierre just shook his head in response. "I'm so stupid," he said miserably. "So stupid. All this over a stupid note." He brandished a bloody piece of paper. "I fell right into the Boss's trap." He held the note out. "I chose knowledge over my family. *Knowledge*. Was my family worth one stupid little shred of paper?! What kind of a person...what kind of a person goes and does *that*? I deserve to die!" He suddenly broke free of Nuarti's grip and lunged for the knife. It was all Nuarti could do to hold Pierre's arm back and keep him from stabbing himself through the chest. "*Let go of me! Let go of me!* I deserve it!" He began to cry again. "Even as I pushed the knife in, my mother stared at me with *love*. I killed her, and she still couldn't bring herself to hate me for it! What kind of a son does that?! I deserve death for that. I flipped the damn coin, and it landed on knowledge instead of family! *Knowledge!*"

Nuarti grimaced from the strain of holding back Pierre's arm, and her hands had begun to smoke. Pierre had let the note fall when he went for the knife. I picked it up and uncrumpled it. The blood had rendered it nigh illegible, but my hands still shook as I deciphered the message. The twisted poem certainly was in the Boss's style. To have turned Pierre into this...if the Boss wanted him so badly, why play with him? Why not open the door, let him in? I hadn't realized it earlier, so bloodstained was the note, but hidden in the red of the paper were traces of black ink. Coordinates? *Coordinates!* This...this whole horrific setup...it was to open the door!

"Pierre," I said slowly, "did you see the coordinates underneath the note?" The change that came over Pierre was just as chilling as the state we had found him in. Where moments before his knife-wielding hand had been juddering back and forth wildly, Nuarti staggering along the floor with it in an attempt to keep Pierre from stabbing himself, the moment I said the word "coordinates," the knife dropped out of his hand. As if on command, Pierre's tears stopped falling, his body stopped heaving, and his face turned still as stone.

"Show me," he said tonelessly, a stark contrast to his despair-filled cries of mere seconds ago. Tentatively, I held the note out. He took it from my hand calmly enough and stared at the spot that I indicated. Just as calmly, he folded the note up and placed it on the floor beside his mother. "I'm going to kill the Boss," he said. His voice was frighteningly steady. It could almost have been termed robotic. "I'm going to find the Boss, and I'm going to end this or die trying."

Nuarti and I glanced at each other, if anything, more concerned than before. "Pierre," Nuarti said, keeping her voice as even as possible. "Are you sure you want to do this?"

Pierre turned slowly to stare at her. Having just seen his eyes, it would have been stretching things quite a bit to call Pierre's stare fearsome, but nonetheless, after a few moments, Nuarti took an unconscious step backward. "What else can I do?" Pierre replied. "Every remaining human I ever knew is dead by my hand. There is nothing left for me here. This place…New Earth, modeled after my first home…I built it for *them*. For me, too, but always, it was more for them than it was for me. What is the point of its existence anymore if they are no longer here to enjoy it? *This* is what the Boss wanted, wasn't it? *This* is how I get drawn in. A severing of ties with the mortal realms, a map to the door…all honey for the trap. I will walk into it, but I *will* be prepared. The Boss dies today, and if I die too, then so be it. *I deserve it*."

Pierre slowly rose to his feet.

"Pierre—" I began, but he cut me off with a wave of his hand.

"This here is it, isn't it, Rexdael?" he said. "You, Nuarti, every single being, all of you have lived in fear of this nebulous entity that rules you all. The Boss has used an assortment of grisly little tricks to make you fear for your own skins, to fear being blasphemous. And it *worked*. The Boss *won*. But this, what the Boss is trying to do now, is a mistake. This invitation, this is as close as you've ever gotten to the Boss. I *am* special, and I intend to use that to my advantage. If you really, truly, want the Boss dead, if you want to live a life free of fear, *help me*. I've said this before, but I've killed one Entity in my time. How bad can another really be?"

Sadly, Pierre was right. I really, genuinely cared for Pierre now (no more trying to figure him out; he was special, and that was that). At the moment I was scared of *and* for him. He was suicidal, and going after the Boss *was* the textbook definition of a suicide mission. But…and it pained me to say this, but I was and would always be more scared of the Boss than anything Pierre could possibly do. If anything, I was more scared after this latest display of the Boss's power.

I looked at Nuarti and saw her reaching the same conclusion as I had. We nodded. "We'll help you, Pierre," I said.

"Whatever you need, we'll do," added Nuarti. She raised her hand high. "To ending the Boss."

"To ending the Boss."

20

HEADS IT IS, I SUPPOSE

Nuarti, New Earth

I wasn't sure if I had ever felt this confused in my life. At this moment, I felt rudderless. Sure, I had just made a solemn pledge to help Pierre take down the Boss, but that was *his* goal, not mine. *My* goal had most likely just gone up in a humongous conflagration, if the appearance of Yutigo's rescuers was anything to go by. Suppose Pierre, against all odds, really did manage to defeat the Boss. Where did that leave me? I felt older and more tired than I had ever felt before. Physically, of course, it was impossible for me to age, but mentally...never had my doubts felt more crushing, my mistakes more crippling. Did I have the will to try to create another just system? The perceptiveness to pick the right being for the job this time?

More troubling were the thoughts Yutigo had planted in my mind. He had called my goal impossible. Perhaps, just perhaps...he was right. If power was such a corrupting influence, then did that make it inevitable that any being handed absolute power, no matter how wise, how just, how kind, would be twisted, turned into a monster? Deep down, I suppose I had always known that even I could be turned. Yutigo had easily proven that. A few bruising words, and I had been ready to kill. Rexdael had been right. For the sake of one despicable being (though *how* despicable!), I had been ready to toss aside my entire code of ethics, the very chain to which my entire sense of self was anchored (those other beings whom I'd killed before could be said to have suffered at the hands of...natural selection). Worse, I knew that if the chance arose again, I would not hesitate to take my shot.

But was it really, *truly* wrong? I had been Yutigo's judge for so many years, tried so many of my fellow beings for crimes large and small in my quest for justice. Was I so wrong to want to judge Yutigo myself now for his various crimes? Yes, perhaps he had committed no crime directly against me, but every single thing he had done dishonestly as head of the Council was a personal slight against me. The revelation of his dishonesty had opened a wound deep and wide in my very soul. It certainly felt as if every crime had been perpetrated against me. It was a flimsy explanation, stretched far and wide from the truth, but it would have to serve. There was no other choice. One murderer had torn apart my society. I would not have the deaths (they were not, after all, murders, if carried out as a result of the judge's verdict) of Yutigo and his followers tear me apart.

A sudden rumbling sound drew my attention. I looked around the room, but there were only the dead bodies, along with Pierre and Rexdael, in it—in other words, nothing that could have been the source of the noise. The rumbling was coming closer from above, it seemed. Perhaps it was a falling object? It must have fallen quite some ways to be making such a noise. With milliseconds to spare, my eyes widened. "Move!" I yelled, pushing Pierre and Rexdael back with the aid of a force field from what I predicted to be the point of impact. Taken aback, they looked at me confusedly, only to jump as, with a crash and a bang, a meteorite crashed through the ceiling and continued straight on through the floor, leaving a hole just barely more than a quarter inch away from where Pierre and Rexdael had been standing and conversing.

More rumbling sounds appeared to indicate that more meteorites had fallen through the atmosphere, hitting buildings, trees, the ground. A meteor shower? There had been none scheduled in this location...but there had been one scheduled to occur just a few light-years away. Those stupid, *boneheaded* Council elders. As if they could sense when and where they were being thought of, a being that resembled a scarab beetle standing on two legs suddenly dropped out of a portal and into the room.

I rounded on him immediately. *"Are you insane, Elder Chinkro?"* I yelled. "The Council *redirected* a meteor shower?" Chinkro had the grace to at least look ashamed (or I thought he did; his mandibles had drooped a little). "If I ever see the idiot who thought this was a good idea," I muttered to myself. "There are *several* things wrong with this whole idea. A, there is a very good reason that weather manipulation requires special dispensation signed either by me or Yutigo! It is *dangerous*. It's a wonder you didn't cause any collateral damage while redirecting these meteoroids from their intended target! B, and this is partially my fault for giving Yutigo such a brief note to convey to the Council, don't act rashly when you don't have *all the facts*. There are a lot of things you could have done that represent taking action against the threat of the Boss without having to make it to the planet-destroying level! And now, these stupid meteorites of yours might just prevent us from beating the Boss once and for all. C, even if you were locked out of the armory and the true planet-destroying weapons, there are so many better ways to go about destroying a planet than sending a meteor shower at it! Heck, the meteorites might not even fully destroy the planet! You could have just altered the planet's orbit so that it would eventually fall into its sun, but *no*, you had to choose the flashy route! And finally, D, I don't even want to know how you started a scrum in the Council room, but those idiot younglings have Yutigo, and I just know that something bad will come of that!"

Chinkro had begun to quiver. "Really," he began in reply, "really, Recordkeeper, we were just trying to help. The Boss Upstairs is undeniably a fearsome proposition, and how were we to know that an opportunity might suddenly have appeared to do something about it? This is unprecedented."

I sighed. "Elder Chinkro, I expected the Council to send *aid*, not *meteorites*. I didn't expect you to run around like a bunch of headless chickens. And now? Now you've just come and mucked up a simple situation!"

"Well," replied Chinkro, "now that we're here, I suppose we could at least try to help you in whatever way we can, Recordkeeper. What would you have us do?"

"Ideally, stay well out of the way of anything that could be remotely dangerous," I snapped back irritably, "but somehow, I don't think that's an option. Yutigo will mass his strength should he come to attack us, so we must mass ours as well. Elder Chinkro, Elder Rexdael, Pierre over there, and I will teleport to a location from which we believe we will be able to strike at the Boss. You will spare as many beings as you can to start setting up a projectile shield around the entire planet and prevent it from being bombarded any more than it already has been. The rest of you will follow us to those same coordinates and defend us against whatever attack Yutigo may launch. Do not hesitate to kill."

"But how are we to know the location you will teleport to?" asked Chinkro.

"Hmm, I don't know," butted in Rexdael sarcastically, "trace the energy signatures, as Yutigo surely will be doing!"

Chinkro shrunk back a little at that comment, but it at least appeared that he understood what he was supposed to do. He opened a portal and quickly disappeared. I was as glad to see him go as he probably was to leave our presence, though I knew we surely needed him and his fellow beings who were opposed to Yutigo.

"OK, so what are the coordinates again?" asked Pierre, still utilizing his frighteningly calm demeanor.

"It reads 42.36 degrees north, 71.09 degrees west," said Rexdael. Pierre gave a dry little chuckle.

I furrowed my eyebrows in confusion. "I don't see what could possibly be funny about that," I said uncertainly.

"It's nothing," Pierre said, waving his hand in a gesture of dismissal. "Just an old memory. It only increases my desire to kill the Boss."

I shot Rexdael a look, but he simply returned my gaze with

a confused stare of his own. "OK, if it's nothing, let's go then," I said, conjuring a portal with a flick of my wrist.

The scene we exited the portal into was the very picture of desolation. The meteorites had not been kind to this location. I thought that it had perhaps once been a school or educational center of some sort, though of course there were no students walking around at the moment to confirm or deny my assumption. A big sign stood in front of us reading "M_T," with a small mound of shattered glass marking the place where the missing letter should be. In the span of the few seconds between my arrival and taking stock of my surroundings, two more meteorites had already fallen, dull booms echoing into the distance.

"Where to now?" asked Rexdael. "It's not as if the Boss posted a welcoming party to speed us on our way."

"Don't worry," replied Pierre calmly. "I know exactly where we're going to find whatever the Boss has left for us. This sick, twisted game was built with me in mind, after all." That, at the very least, was indisputable, particularly so after the incident involving those close to Pierre.

"Lead on then," I replied.

The ground was pockmarked with craters ranging from the size of a flea to the size of a cantaloupe. The bigger craters still contained the meteorites which had created the holes, some smoking from the heat of reentry. For so many meteorites to have fallen on a single location within such a short span of time was either incredibly bad luck or entirely intentional on the part of the Boss, I was sure. Rexdael, Pierre, and I had barely taken two steps, however, when the air in front of us shimmered and a whole host of portals opened, out of which stepped Yutigo and his younglings, a ragged host of perhaps fifteen hundred.

"I would say it's good to see you again, dear Rexdael, Nuarti, and Pierre," called out Yutigo, "but that would be telling a blatant lie. Because, you see, once again, the three of you have managed to ruin my day! I could be well away from here by now, gleefully enjoying the destruction of this planet from afar, and the continued existence of you three *irks* me. It just wouldn't be right for me to let you live after what you did to me. No one does that and lives to tell the tale if I get to have a say in it. So here I am, risking life and limb to put you down once and for all."

"Oh, Yutigo," I scoffed, "only one of us is going to die here today, and I don't intend to be the one who does. You may have brought your own little army to support you, but we have friends of our own as well!" There was a slight awkward pause between the moment I said this and the army actually deigning to appear, but thankfully for me, appear it did. I was glad to note that our numbers were significantly higher than Yutigo's, close to two thousand, and that we possessed far more elders than his band of younglings did. Yutigo, I knew, would not escape the battlefield until he had personally killed all three of us, or at the very least received proof of us dying. We had humiliated him, and that could not be allowed to stand, not now that he had regained his freedom. With our advantages in numbers and experience, that could only spell his death, for how could he hope to win this battle?

Yutigo's mouth tightened in rage. "Your coterie of followers won't be much help when they lie dead around your feet," he sneered.

"Pierre," I muttered out of the side of my mouth, "where

do we need to go?"

He chuckled wryly. "Directly behind Yutigo's lines."

By now, I suppose I should have expected that answer. The Boss refused to make things easy for us, even now, when we were so close. I looked around and found Chinkro standing near me. "Elder Chinkro, when Yutigo attacks, Rexdael, Pierre, and I must be protected at all costs," I ordered. "We are the key to defeating the Boss, and we need to make it to our intended location unscathed. Don't hesitate to kill the younglings. Yutigo has made it quite clear that either we or he will leave the battlefield in a casket." Chinkro nodded.

Yutigo became quite impatient when he realized that we weren't bothering to reply to his latest barb. "Well, what are you waiting for?" he snarled at the younglings. "Attack them!" With that, his army finally surged forward. Chinkro and the rest of our allies instantly formed an overlapping force field and advanced in turn. With satisfaction, I noted that the number of meteorites making impact was significantly lower than even when Rexdael, Pierre, and I had first arrived. One external stimulus, at least, would not be the deciding factor in this battle.

When the two armies met, it was with a harsh crash that reverberated across the landscape. Foolishly, the younglings had not, while charging, created an overlapping force field of their own (perhaps they lacked the discipline to do those two things simultaneously). It was hard to tell how many died because of that folly in the moment of first contact, but it certainly did not decide the battle. Fighting soon devolved into one-on-one combat all along the line, with only a few stray pockets of beings maintaining the cohesion to fight as a unit. It was hard to tell friend from foe at such close quarters, and I could not have said how many lay dead or dying on each side. Yutigo hovered like a terrible specter of death near the center of the line, laying waste to all those who dared oppose him (he *was* powerful and clever, a dangerous combination; it was just that I was even more powerful and clever than he). Rexdael, Pierre, and I did the best we could to skirt him.

The three of us had not been at the front of the line as it advanced, but we soon made our way over to one of the largest and most cohesive groups on our side. "We need to punch through the line!" I yelled at the group in general, unsure of who was the leader. "Our target lies some distance behind the enemy."

One of the beings near the front of the group, a surly-looking man with the face of a lion who had half an ear hanging off, nodded and barked commands to the rest of the group. Soon Rexdael, Pierre, and I found ourselves surrounded by a crude sort of wedge, slightly behind the front. The lion looked at me expectantly, and I nodded. "ADVANCE," he roared, and the entire wedge rushed forward at once.

Yutigo was too far away, the line held by inexperienced younglings running on adrenaline, and thus our wedge parted the line with little resistance. Once we had made our way through, the wedge became a circle around us, constantly in motion. Some opposing beings, however, had made it into the circle before it had managed to fully close up. It was up to Rexdael, Pierre, and me to deal with these intruders, for those maintaining the circle were busy enough with foes on the outside. Phasing in these quarters, surrounded by so many who had never even seen the technique before, was a sure recipe for disaster, so instead, my trusty sword of ice appeared in my hand. These younglings did not merit having any sort of complicated attack used against them. A simple stab wound would suffice for most.

The first being didn't even see me coming, so intent was he on attacking Rexdael's rear. My sword stroke cleaved him open from shoulder to hip, and he fell to the ground in two separate pieces. The second one managed to send a weak ball of fire at me, which I simply batted away with my free hand. She even managed to dodge my first blow at her neck, bending over backward, but before she could recover, my sword was already whistling downward, slicing through her legs as if they were nothing more than paper. This time, my blow found her neck as she fell. The third one thought it a good idea to punch me, only to find her arm cut off at the elbow when she reached out. As she reeled backward, I slashed open her belly. The rest died in similar ways, weak, worthless opponents to the very last. I could feel my blood beginning to sing. If only Yutigo would come to me now...

Almost as if my prayers were being answered, I turned to see Yutigo's line crumbling in disarray, some of his troops continuing to engage our main force, while the rest turned to chase us down, Yutigo among them. The lion saw this as well, and he looked perhaps a little less surly than before. "WHICH WAY?" he roared at me.

I looked at Pierre questioningly. "That building over there!" he yelled at the lion, indicating the largest and grandest building of the ones in our vicinity. The lion nodded to show that he had heard, and the circle immediately began to move in that direction. With every step, though, Yutigo gained on us, sometimes even throwing his own troops aside in his haste to reach Rexdael, Pierre, and me.

"FASTER," roared the lion, and the circle began to move slightly faster, though it seemed impossible to go any faster while maintaining any semblance of coherence. Yutigo caught up to us as we reached the door. His first attack, a trio of lightning bolts, almost broke through my hastily erected shield, but it gave Rexdael, Pierre, and me enough time to get through the door.

"HOLD THE DOOR," I yelled at the lion. Though surely he knew that what I was asking of him was suicide, the lion merely nodded grimly. I shut the door and added my own set of protections to it. It would not hold Yutigo for long, but hopefully it would be long enough.

Pierre, it seemed, had been correct. Now, at least, there was a beacon of light emanating from one of the rooms directly off the second-floor landing. "Lead the way, Pierre," I said. He did accordingly, and Rexdael and I followed him into the glowing room. There was a placard on the door that read "President." I wondered what it meant. Inside, there was a portal, merrily glowing a bright shade of red, but access to it was blocked by a shimmering, translucent white barrier.

"There's another note," said Rexdael, picking up a scrap of paper from a table near the door. He unfolded it and showed it to Pierre and me. Yet another twisted poem greeted us, shorter this time, though:

> *This far you've come, but one last door there remains to pass.*
> *One will advance, one will remain, and the last will expire, be they lad or lass.*
> *—You know who this is.*

I swallowed uncomfortably. "Obviously," I began, "Pierre is the one going through the portal. Which means…which means—"

"Which means one of us is the sacrifice," concluded Rexdael bluntly. "No need to mince words. We've come this far already. A little more blood spilled pales in comparison." His eyes had never looked as melancholic as they did now, and it was then that I knew.

"Rexdael, no," I breathed out.

"*Nuarti*," he replied, insistently but firmly. "You know it has to be me. I am no leader, and when this is all over, someone will be needed to initiate the rebuilding process, someone who is not only powerful, but also wise and just. The beings would not follow the war criminal, not as they would follow you, Nuarti. And besides, you and Yutigo have unfinished business. Third time's always the charm, they say." Rexdael had the audacity to wink at that last comment.

A single tear rolled down my face, and even Pierre looked less stone-faced than he had since he had learned of the co-ordinates. "Rexdael," he protested weakly. "Really, you don't have to do this."

"Of course I do, Pierre," replied Rexdael calmly. "You read the poem, same as I did. If we want a chance to win, one of us must die."

Pierre's face looked as if it were on the verge of crumpling again. "Goodbye, Rexdael," he said in a thick voice.

"Goodbye, Pierre Hartford," said Rexdael softly. "It was an honor to know and teach you." Finally, Rexdael looked at me again. "Take care, Nuarti," was all he said. It was all he needed to say. I had known Rexdael for so long, but I thought that it was only now, moments before his death, that I really saw his nobility, and not merely his emotional volatility. Another tear rolled down my face.

Rexdael turned away from both of us and, arms spread wide, walked calmly into the barrier. His body dissolved into a cloud of white sparks, and I could only hope that death had been a painless affair for him. The barrier dissipated, and Pierre moved to stand in front of the portal. "Good luck, Pierre," I said softly.

"Hold the fort down while I'm gone, Nuarti," he replied. I nodded.

Pierre stepped into the portal just as Yutigo appeared in the doorway.

21

DETERMINE YOUR FATE

Pierre Hartford, a place separate from the rest of time and space

The blackness of the space I stumbled into was a stark contrast to the vivid, rich red of the portal I had just gone through. It was an apt reflection of my mood, though. For now, it seemed as if I was losing companions with every step I took, both old and new. Yuri, my mother, Robert, Max, Luka, Rexdael...all gone, regardless if they had died by my hand or simply because of me. I had barely known Rexdael, but he at least had *understood* me, understood me in a way even my oldest companions could not have. He could have been my (significantly) older brother. He had taught me much, and his protectiveness had been endearing. His sacrifice would not be forgotten.

I was not angry. I just felt so...so...so numb and cold. The motivations behind my latest series of actions probably stemmed to some degree from hurt and anger, but I just couldn't feel it at the moment. Moving through the world felt like moving a great soup of molasses. Everything took so much effort. It was painful to have to maneuver my limbs. I was a murderer, and I in no way deserved Rexdael's all-too-noble sacrifice. Keeping somewhat emotionally distant was the only way to avoid dealing with the brutal reality of the world that, if I survived, I would come back to. I was destined to a life of perpetual loneliness. No one would ever know me again, know my history, know what I had felt and would feel. And I knew the one responsible for all this, the one responsible for handing me over to a tortured existence. Fate was the only reason I could bring myself to move, the only one that gave me a purpose I was willing to accept. *I needed to kill Fate.*

I took a step forward, and the space around me instantly began to come to life. Where my foot had landed, a pinprick of light appeared. As it expanded, I recognized New Earth. New Earth expanded until I could make out the cars on the streets of Boston before it zoomed into the distance behind me. Soon, the other planets of the solar system had zoomed past my feet and my arms as well. The sun, a ball of roaring orange fire, whizzed by my eyes so fast I almost missed it. The solar system became the local star cluster, the star cluster became the galaxy, the galaxy became a group of galaxies, and the group of galaxies became a supercluster. Still more and more features of the universe continued to whip past my arms, my legs, my face. The superclusters were complemented by voids, the star nurseries by black holes, the white dwarves by supernovas. I saw more scenes of galactic birth and galactic destruction, of star birth and star death, of planetary formation and collision than I cared to count. As such, I was almost scared half to death when a pair of hazel eyes, flecked with gold, snapped open in front of me. Like a shadow detaching itself from the darkness, the space around me rippled as a human body pulled itself into existence.

Fate was...a *woman* (somehow, I had never quite pictured Fate as being of one gender or the other). Her hair, strings of stars shining the brightest of blues, fell past her shoulders. Galactic phenomena twisted their way past her shoulders, down her back, across her chest. They twined their way around her arms and legs. Apart from her eyes, her only definitively human features, I was hard pressed to say whether Fate had a defined bodily form or not. The only thing that distinguished her from the rest of what I assumed was the universe swirling around me in real time was an inky blackness that surrounded her, darker even than the blackness of empty space. Finally, though I stood still, I could have sworn that the room was slowly rotating. But before I could open my mouth to say any-thing, Fate began to talk.

"Here I am, Pierre, in all my glory. It's what you've wanted all along. The source of your control stands before you. But really, how does it feel? Good? Fulfilling? Glorifying? Or does it change nothing at all? Do you just feel the same as you have always felt? Here's the catch: no one ever wins. There is no vic-tory. You win, people cheer, but for you? Nothing. No-thing at all.

"This was a test, and in one sense of the word, you've passed. You found the puppet master. Hooray! Here are some balloons. Have a medal while you're at it. But at the same time, you've failed. Just failed. There's no other way to express it all. Complete and ut-ter failure. You may be asking yourself, how could that be? I've found what I was looking for! I've found the path to freedom! No longer will humanity or any other interstellar race suffer again under the yoke of Fate, to be pushed and pulled to and fro, with no control over the future! I must say, after all this time, you are still surprisingly... *idealistic*. I would count myself impressed if you hadn't turned your idealism into this. Simply put, for all of your brilliance, you...are...a...*moron*!

"Ask yourself this. In all this time, through all the adversity, did you ever *once* stop and think: Might there possibly be a purpose to the existence of the one I'm chasing? Maybe, *just* maybe, there's something that lies beyond the obvious? But no, you just continued to carry on, uncaring, unthinking even of the consequences of your actions down the line. Have you even considered what will happen after I am gone? You think people will celebrate you for what you've done, revere you? Think again. No, they won't revere you, they'll *revile* you.

"Let me tell you a little something about any living creature that you, for all your study of humanity, have failed to grasp. There are only two things that dictate any person's life: selfishness and responsibility. One is an addiction, pushing people to do whatever they think necessary to further themselves. The other is a disease, striking down the weak and sapping the strength of the strong, stealing away their years like an insidious parasite. Because, you see, what humans fear most of all is *re-spon-si-bi-li-ty*.

"You don't believe me? Follow my train of thought. Suppose we have a child. Children are always learning and exploring their surroundings, and naturally, this means that at some point they'll make a mistake. So let's say that this theoretical child of ours, he or she goes somewhere he or she is not supposed to go, perhaps with one of his or her friends. When his or her parents discover this, naturally, they're not in a particularly pleased mood. They ask the child why he or she did this. 'It wasn't my fault!' is the unsurprisingly common refrain. The child blames it on his or her friend. The friend was the one who dragged him or her into this mess, and the child just followed along. The parents, however, refuse to accept this. You could have just said no, they say, done the right thing and turned around. Now, if we have a particularly precocious child, he or she might reply that it's his or her parents' fault. His or her genetics comes from his or her parents, and these genes are the reason he or she is naturally inclined to follow his or her friend to a forbidden place. The parents become even more flabbergasted and wave off this excuse as well. It is squarely the child's fault, they retort. Grudgingly, the child accepts this, bereft of other options. At that same moment, a small piece of that child withers up and dies. Why? Because he or she was made to accept the *responsibility* of his or her actions.

"During that whole scenario, everyone was passing the glowing coal of *responsibility* between each other. Whoever was touched by it heaved it off to someone else, anything to avoid the burning pain associated with that coal. And when the time finally ran out and the coal could no longer be passed along, the coal brought with it a tiny bit of death. The person holding it had a little bit of him- or herself perish. Now apply this concept to human society as a whole. Whenever there's a societal problem of any sort, no one wants to claim responsibility for that problem. Instead it is passed off. It's those dirty so-and-sos, people say, meaning whichever marginalized group has recently come to their attention. They're bringing poverty and disease to the rest of us! And their selfish desires for something leads them to assert their power over this marginalized minority and commit atrocities. When it suits them, people happily take responsibility for these horrific crimes. Why? They selfishly wish to advance in society, and admitting to these crimes helps achieve that. But then, when the tables turn, suddenly this isn't such a good idea anymore. Oh, Your Honor, they say when they're brought into court, I was just following orders. The responsibility for their crimes is simply passed off to a higher power, a higher authority. For what does it mean if they take responsibility? It means a life in prison, or perhaps even a death sentence. Taking on the responsibility would kill them!

"But even metaphorically speaking, this same concept still applies. Just look at politics! All politicians love to lap up responsibility whenever something good happens to their constituents or their country, but when things go awry? They're sprinting away as fast as they can from the wasteland of responsibility. Taking responsibility would kill them politically, maybe even put them in jail or strip them of their fortunes! And the faithful public servants, those who don't hesitate to take on responsibility? It *breaks* them! They come out of office having grappled with any number of problems, and what do they get for all their hard work? Ab-so-lute-ly *nothing*! They've tried so hard to tackle their responsibilities, take the blame when things go wrong, help others, and it simply steals away years of their lives! The pressure of fixing the problems they're saddled with shatters their spirits, and they're left broken, mentally and physically!

"Where do I come into the picture, you ask? Well, as Fate, sometimes *I* take responsibility for the issues no one wants to touch. People just say, oh, Fate willed it to be this way, and the responsibility disappears, falling squarely on my shoulders, since I can take it, unlike them. I can't die, at least not in the traditional sense, so it doesn't kill me but simply becomes a part of me that I can't feel. I give years back to humans and all the other interstellar races in the universe! Because of me, their lives are extended, and the quality of those lives is improved! Without me, do you know what happens to all creatures in the universe? They shrivel and wither away instantly under the gargantuan weight of the responsibility dropped onto their shoulders! It kills them, steals away their breath, disintegrates them into something less than nothing! Without me, life as you and I know it…it disappears! And I know that you of all people, Pierre, who fought so hard for good and for life throughout this universe and every other one, don't want that to happen.

"You have seen how it is to live in a world of responsibility. You have risen up as a hero to defend your ideals. But you know how your friend the Entity came to be in the first place? Originally, he, too, was good, benevolent, cared for his creatures. But he was too nice for his own good. Every time there was a problem, he claimed the responsibility for himself. Anything to keep his subjects happy. As time went on, people got more and more used to heaping responsibility upon him. And do you know what happened? The people created a monster they couldn't control! All that responsibility had corrupted the Entity's soul, turned it from white to black. And when they saw the result, they recoiled and sought to shackle it! And you, Pierre, you saw the solution, didn't you? You destroyed the whole realm! Because there was no other way! The responsibility that had corrupted the Entity tainted everything and everyone! Without me, the same thing would happen everywhere!

"However, there is a way to move to a post-responsibility society. Remove all free will. Why? Because it creates responsibility through its very existence! When people can control their actions, they are thus responsible for them! And from that moment onward, it slowly starts to kill them. But people living in blissful ignorance? They could live on happily until their bodies truly begin to fail them. Everyone would be happy forever!

"The catch, though, is that with no concept of responsibility in the universe anywhere but with us two, I would cease to be, because I am sustained solely by the belief that I exist to take the responsibilities of others. But for creatures with no concept of responsibility, there is no reason for my continued existence. That's why I need you. When I created you, I knew that you would be able to take on the responsibility of every single universe for all eternity, being the fairest judge of them all. I need you to take over my mantle as I fade away and become the shepherd of our new blissfully ignorant reality.

"You know why? Because otherwise, this miserable existence will continue for everyone! The game of life will continue in perpetuity. Because life really is a game, no matter what anyone says! Either you win or lose. You can choose not to play, but in the end, that really doesn't matter, because technically you don't lose, but you don't win either! And in the end, you do lose because without being in the game, you stagnate while others pass you by! But really, no one wins. Because the game as a concept survives beyond a single generation, and everyone always dies, leading to a new winner. In the end, only the game wins!

"Pierre, you yourself had ushered in a proto-post-responsibility society. But you *handicapped* yourself for a variety of reasons involving your own mental state, and guess what? It stopped! Things slid backward and society stagnated. Embrace the power rather than be repulsed by it! Pierre, you must understand that it's the only right thing to do. For you are incorruptible, as incorruptible as I am. I made you, and I know what you are! So join me, Pierre, and save reality once and for all. Be the unsung hero. Break the rules of the game, destroy it even! Do the *right* thing, not the *easy* thing."

Fate looked at me, her beautiful hazel eyes silently beseeching me. I gazed back evenly, nonplussed about what she had just told me. "Tell me, *Fate*," I said with an edge in my voice, "how long have you been rehearsing that spiel? How long have you been planning this? You talk about life as a *game*, but it was only the moment that you revealed yourself to me that life really started feeling like a game to me. *Your* game, in fact. You foisted this sick, demented, twisted series of events on me just to get me here, and you expect me to drop everything and help you after one little scripted speech? I was immeasurably happier when I felt completely in control of myself, when I felt responsible for my actions. It's only now, after you decided to take overt control of me at times, that I want to die. Maybe because you made me a *murderer!*"

Fate's eyes widened and she stepped backward slightly. "Oh, Pierre," she said consolingly, "I am so sorry, child. It pains me to see you so distraught." Her arm reached out, presumably to pat me on the back.

"*Don't!*" I said sharply, and Fate jerked her arm back as if I had scalded her.

"You have to understand this, though, Pierre," she continued. "There is a very specific reason none of your fellow beings has ever even come close to reaching me. When the universe decided to give itself a sense of sentience, it laid down a series of ground rules, one could say. I was to be stationed at my post here forever, keeping my lonely vigil and preventing the universe from bursting apart at the seams. Anyone who wished to reach me had to sever all personal ties to the mortal plane. Hence the deaths you caused and witnessed. Otherwise you wouldn't be here, armed with your opportunity to kill me."

My eyes widened. She knew? Fate scoffed. "Oh, come on, Pierre," she reprimanded, "what kind of a leader would I be if I couldn't effortlessly read minds? And even if we ignore that, your body language is giving it away."

I threw my hands up in the air. "Fine," I said shortly. "You got me. I do want to kill you. But please, you didn't really expect to endear yourself to me after what you made me do to get here, did you?"

Fate smiled. "Well, you might just be in luck, Pierre, because I *want* you to kill me." I gaped at her. "Yes," she continued. "Yes, I want you to kill me because I want you to *become* me. The reason I really brought you here is to 'join' me, which essentially entails killing me, and in so doing obtaining my powers, fulfilling my request, and taking over my position. Your bloodlust is sated; the universe gets a new and better caretaker."

Now it was my turn to scoff. "You really, truly, deeply think *I* would be a better caretaker than you? Surely when the universe created you, it could have easily created a perfect caretaker."

"Perhaps," Fate replied, "but if the universe itself is flawed, then logically the caretaker it creates will also be flawed. However, that doesn't mean it's impossible to build a perfect caretaker from within the system."

"Build," I replied slowly. "Are you telling me that I'm... designed?"

"No, no, no," said Fate, waving her hand around airily, "nothing so crude as that. I would call you the result of thousands of generations of evolution. I've been playing a long, long game. I didn't just decide yesterday that I needed a successor, you know. All beings can tell you that their powers were 'awakened.' Not a single one of them received those powers at birth. All of them were conceived in different scenarios, different sets of birth conditions, and their powers were set to awaken when a series of environmental stresses acted simultaneously upon them. The goal was to see how they would use their powers, with any differences presumably being the result of the beings' varying upbringings. It was hard to kill any of the beings outright. That would be stretching the bounds of my influence. This was an inherent flaw of my plan, I know, but I was confident that I could keep the awakenings of these beings separate enough so that the actions of the already awakened would not interfere with the rest. And so, with each new awakening, I examined what went right and what went wrong with the being who had just been awakened, and I adjusted the parameters accordingly. You, Pierre, are the last being I ever awakened because you are *exactly* what I was looking for.

"I know that I myself am weakhearted and corrupt at times. I'm not sure how much Rexdael or Nuarti told you, but there *are* horror stories of what I've managed to do to beings, to whole species. I got bored far too easily for someone who was supposed to watch over the universe for all eternity. My infatuation with the long game led me to have the ones I was supposed to care for play these little, shorter games with their array of ghastly endings. You are not like that, Pierre. You are perfect for this because you *care*. I don't anymore, and to be honest, I never really did. I *hate* the universe for creating me! I wish I didn't exist! But if this role must be filled, who better than you to fill it, Pierre? You care about everyone and everything, from the most powerful being all the way down to the puniest bacterium. The petty concerns of day-to-day life you would adequately be able to fulfill. When you are not faced with overwhelming strength, you have proven yourself *incorruptible*. You are smart enough, and you would have power enough to care for all, improve society for all, create an eternal peace and happiness. So, please, Pierre, consider it. *Consider what's best for the universe.* Let me end the long game."

Fate was almost pleading with me by this point, so desperate did she begin to sound toward the end. What she had done wanted to make me retch, but I could not deny that at least some of her words rang true. Responsibility *was* a killer. The universe had had free will for so long, but all it had done with it was try to kill itself over and over and over. Perhaps free will really was overrated. Moreover, from what Fate was telling me, I *would* be a better candidate to take over this position. Was I the *perfect* candidate, though? That was the real question.

"Suppose I accept your offer," I began, "what would I have to do?"

"It's simple, really," she replied. "You would accept the offering I made to you of my position and powers, I would transfer them to you, you would assert your control over everything in the universe, and then you would kill me. As a favor, of course. If you refuse, I'd simply wipe your memory, age you back down to a baby, and send you down to the mortal plane as a blank slate, free to restart your life. And I must warn you, once the power transfer begins, it cannot be interrupted for any reason whatsoever. So consider wisely."

As appealing as restarting my life sounded, I dismissed it as an option immediately. I was better than that! I would not leave Fate here to continue playing this abominable game and twist the universe to her own purposes. The power transfer could not be interrupted...which meant that once I accepted the offer, Fate could do nothing to prevent me from doing something she hadn't asked for. And the perfect solution popped into my head.

I took a deep breath and made my choice.

22

THE DANCE CONCLUDES

Nuarti, New Boston, Americana, New Earth (starting immediately after the end of chapter 20)

I wondered if Yutigo even noticed me as he stood in that doorway. For the moment, at least, his attention was completely taken up by the rapidly closing red portal through which Pierre had just gone. I would not call him panicked, but he phased while sprinting, appearing mid-stride a hand's breadth away from the portal. He loosed a stream of acid from the tips of his fingers, but it was already too late. The portal was gone, and thus Pierre was beyond his grasp. The acid instead rapidly ate through the opposite wall, which faced out onto the battlefield. The hole it left enabled me to see at least that the battle was far from over, though the fighting had moved away from Yutigo and me after he had decimated my rear guard. I had not even known the name of that surly lion, but nonetheless, he had trusted me, and in the end, he had protected me to his last breath. More important, and more pressing, was the fact that it appeared Yutigo and I were completely alone. The armies, as was often their wont, fought now only for the sake of fighting; their original purpose lay in a corner forgotten somewhere. With Yutigo, the reasons we should fight were all too clear.

I cleared my throat loudly. Yutigo wheeled around and only then seemed to notice that I had been standing in the room the whole time. "*Nuarti*," he said, rolling the three syllables around on his tongue as a child might with a lollipop perhaps. His lips curved upward in the facsimile of a smile, and his red eyes twinkled. "I am *delighted* to see you." He stalked toward me from the spot where the portal had been in the center of the room. "Of the three of you, I hoped you'd be the one I would encounter at close quarters. I wished to see whether the fire within you had awoken yet."

I began to circle to my right, never taking my eyes off Yutigo as I did so. He copied my movements. "Delighted to see me, or did you mean to say *kill* me, Yutigo?" I retorted.

Yutigo's lips parted, and he let out a peal of laughter, far fuller and richer than any laugh I had ever heard from him before. He really *was* enjoying this. "Degrees, my dear," he said. "Degrees. After all, it's possible that I see you and still kill you afterward, isn't it? Where's Rexdael?"

My lips tightened. "A sacrifice was required to open the portal to the Boss," I said shortly.

Yutigo's smile widened. "A pity I missed that sight. Now it seems with Rexdael dead and Pierre beyond my grasp, it is only *you* I need to complete the set." He spread his arms wide. "I said before that you would never have another chance to kill me. Allow me to revise that statement now. You will never have an *easier* chance to kill me. Assuredly, you have a chance now, but it is far smaller than it could have potentially been, and not so risk-free anymore. But fair's fair. Two of us will enter, and only one of us will leave."

I nodded. "Rest assured, Yutigo," I said acidly, baring my teeth, "this time, you will see the fire. Against you, I refuse to hold back any longer."

Yutigo nodded in return. "Good." He swept his hand out and to the side, taking an elaborate bow. "What do you say, my lady? Shall we dance?"

I didn't bother to return the bow. Yutigo and his ridiculous dramatics! I phased behind Yutigo and chopped at his outstretched arm, hoping to perhaps catch him off guard. This, unfortunately, was unsuccessful. A force field appeared around Yutigo's arm, off which my hands bounced, and he wheeled around and leaped back, gazing at me with an expression of hurt. "You dishonor me, my lady!" he called out even as he picked up an ugly monstrosity of a desk and hurled it at me. "But nevertheless, I see you have accepted my offer!"

I ducked, slicing the desk in two with a blade of air as I went and sending the resulting splinters of wood back at Yutigo. "Shut up and fight!" I snarled. "Stop trying to tempt me into doing something unwise with your words! We both know how that almost turned out last time."

Yutigo raised an eyebrow. "Even now, I fear my death no more than I did then. And after all, what kind of an opponent would I be if I did not choose to use every weapon at my disposal?" An arc of fire rose up around him, incinerating every splinter coming his way.

Fine, I thought. *Two can play this game.* "The opponent who fears me!" I called back, conjuring three large shards of ice from different directions and phasing to attack Yutigo from a fourth, conjuring another shard of ice in my hand as I appeared. Yutigo's arc of fire split into four separate circles, each hurrying to absorb me and my shards of ice. "See, you think that the only way you can beat me is by talking to me! You don't trust in your skills alone to defeat me!" I ducked under the circle of fire meant for me and hurled the shard of ice in my hand at the small of Yutigo's back. Viper-fast, Yutigo phased an arm behind himself to catch my shard of ice mid-flight and hurl it into the floor. The hole that formed now allowed me to see into the first-floor landing as well.

"Skills?" Yutigo said, scoffing, throwing a punch with the arm hovering in front of me. "You know, I think I only ever said you have a fire burning inside of you. Strength does not equal skill!"

I reached out to grab Yutigo's arm. However, just as I went to close my fist around it, the arm disappeared and Yutigo phased himself so that he instantaneously switched directions, having his other arm throw a punch as he did so. Badly caught out of position, I felt the whoosh of air redirected by his fist as I just barely leaped over it and then him. I landed lightly on my feet and watched Yutigo turn around again, this time without phasing. "Case in point!" he yelled out. "All those ridiculous acrobatics to evade one measly little punch! You're wasting energy!" I clapped my hands many times faster than the speed of sound. Yutigo's eyes widened as he realized there was no practical place to dodge my supersonic boom. Waiting until the last second, he phased directly through it.

A supersonic boom this strong did not merely shatter all the windows in the building. A six-inch horizontal gap appeared all along the wall behind where Yutigo had been. Stone and plaster rubble littered the floor and presumably the ground outside as well. Yutigo looked slightly worse for wear, with windswept hair and a long cut scoring one cheek. He brought his hand up to it and came away with blood, glistening as brightly as his eyes. "Am I wasting energy, though?" I asked Yutigo. "Perhaps it only seems that way to you because you are so much weaker!"

Yutigo raised an eyebrow. "I doubt the power imbalance would be so severe between the two of us. I know you, and I can guess at your limits! If this is the best you can do, then perhaps I was wrong in crowning you a worthy opponent!" He waved his hand, and I rolled to the side just as a chunk of the floor came out from under me and thudded into the ceiling, raining more wood and plaster down upon us.

"You *knew* me," I corrected. "I never showed you just how much I was holding back!"

I raised my arms, and a dozen copies of me, each made up of a contingent of flames burning bright white, flew up to surround Yutigo. Gleefully, I noted that Yutigo looked mildly impressed at this latest move. Despite this, though, I wondered if Yutigo really knew what he was in for. These flames were a special creation of mine. They burned hotter and brighter than most flames, and, if one only had the opportunity to investigate them from afar, looked completely normal. Perhaps a bit hotter and a bit brighter than typical, but otherwise normal. At the very center of each tongue of flame was a minuscule core of ice, cold enough even to extinguish the flames.

So long as I maintained a small pocket of air around these ice cores, however, I could use my powers to ensure that the flames would burn. When that pocket of air disappeared, on the other hand...well, Yutigo was in for one heck of a surprise.

Slowly, the copies closed the circle, conjuring a ring of fire within which to trap Yutigo. The flames were so hot that even at some distance I was beginning to sweat, and I could not imagine how Yutigo must be feeling at the moment. A boomerang-like object appeared in Yutigo's hand, dripping water, and he hurled it at one of the figures of flame. But the figure, engulfed in a sheet of freezing water the moment the boomerang made contact with it, was not so easily extinguished. The flames only grew brighter and more powerful, the roar of the fire stronger. Once the boomerang was out of Yutigo's hand, its path was not easily altered, and so each of the twelve figures I had created were struck in turn. Each time the heat and roar of the flames grew in intensity, to the point that a puddle of sweat was forming around me, and I could no longer see nor hear Yutigo inside the ring I had created. Surely, I thought, this he could not escape.

The flames had disoriented me as well, however, and so when Yutigo's mental probe shot at me, I staggered backward momentarily in my efforts to deflect it. The flames abated in strength just a tad, which was all the opening Yutigo needed. I blinked, and Yutigo stood beside me, covered in a thin sheen of ice crystals with patches of pale blue splotched across his skin, jabbing at my neck with a knife. I phased out of the way, realizing only afterward that doing so would mean losing control of the flames. Yutigo took the flames and hurled them straight through the ceiling. But this was a mistake on his part (he really *shouldn't* have been hurling the flames around without knowing what they actually did). The flames went straight through the ceiling and all the way to the roof. Every surface they touched, having not been shielded from elemental attack, turned into ice, which then proceeded to shatter.

When Yutigo hurled flames at the ice, it simply multiplied instead of melting away. A veritable ice storm formed as I gathered more and more of the falling shards around me, sending a few of them at a time at Yutigo, who found himself surrounded by an ever-growing amount of ice. Yutigo, I noticed with immense pleasure, was no longer bothering to even try to talk to me. I took this as a very good sign. He was on the defensive, reeling, having already made mistakes. All I needed was one good opening.

I should have remembered that desperation also makes gamblers out of some crazy individuals. Yutigo *phased* through the ice storm around me (imagine, for a moment, what would happen if Yutigo phased into a place at which a mound of ice landed simultaneously, and then remember that the ice was falling from above in an entirely random manner). Somehow he made it to a spot next to me without dying, though he was now bleeding from what looked like a thousand paper cuts, and punched me in the chest. Shocked that Yutigo was suddenly standing next to me, I had not even bothered to block, and I felt at least two ribs crack. I stumbled backward and almost directly into a falling office chair. Causing the floors to shatter logically also allowed for the things that had been standing on those floors to fall, and thus all the furniture had begun to fall as well, though up to this point, not much had fallen near the site of our battle. The office chair crashed right through the floor, and in my shock, I fell directly into the hole it had left.

I hit the floor below with a thump, luckily preventing myself from breaking anything else with a roll, though a good hundred bruises were forming all over my body. My fall broke my concentration for a few seconds, during which all the ice I had been controlling fell to the floor with a crash, the weight of it causing the floor to buckle as well. Just in time, I threw up a force field against the falling deluge of ice, wood, and office furniture, which left deep dents in the stone floor around me. Yutigo floated down after this bombardment, his smile firmly back in place. "How are we feeling now, my lady?" he mocked. "Don't quit on me now! Our dance has just barely begun, after all."

I ignored him and phased to a doorway on the other side of the room. Flinging the door off its hinges, I ran into the hallway that was behind it. Only after I was already quite a ways down the hallway did I realize that there appeared to be no doors, and thus no corridors or rooms, branching off it. I had trapped myself in a dead end. I attempted to blast a hole into one of the stone walls around me, but instead, my attack bounced off a wall of mental will. "Not so fast, dear," Yutigo said, appearing in the entrance to the hallway. "I'm afraid I can't let you do that." There was a shifting and creaking noise all around me, and the very walls and ceiling of the hallway began to constrict around me. Phasing meant going through Yutigo, for there was no other direction left to me, since a wall had suddenly appeared behind me as well. That was not an option. Any elemental attacks would do as much good against Yutigo's will holding the surfaces around me together as my attack of brute force had done before. The pain in my side was making it difficult for me to concentrate on mental attacks. "How does a stony tomb feel, my lady?" asked Yutigo. "Better or worse than one of *ice*?" He phased closer to me, presumably so that he could watch me die properly…and directly into the path of a falling meteorite. The clump of metallic rock crashed into Yutigo's right shoulder, with a resulting sickening crack, and he fell to the floor. The walls and ceiling stopped constricting around me, and immediately, I punched a hole through one of the walls, which luckily was on the outside of the building.

No one was fighting anymore, it appeared. The remaining beings were quite far away from Yutigo and me, but all of them were raising their hands up to the sky, trying their best to repair what I assumed was the broken force field that had been protecting New Earth from the full force of the meteor shower. They didn't seem to be having much success, however, as the meteorites continued to fall fast and furious, perhaps even more so than before. *Something* had ticked off the Boss. I wondered how Pierre was faring.

I took the moment's respite to repair my ribs and turned back to the building I had just emerged from to see Yutigo walking out through the hole I had created. His right arm hung uselessly at his side, his shoulder sticking out at an awkward angle. Behind him, the building crumbled to the ground with a huge series of crashes, too structurally destabilized by the effects of our fight and the barrage of meteorites falling on it and the surrounding terrain. Now it was, with certainty, far too dangerous to wantonly phase around. Even Yutigo was sure to see that, but if he didn't, I wouldn't give him the chance to go about doing it.

An ice sword once again appeared in my hand, and I leaped at Yutigo, swinging at his legs as I did so. Yutigo, who had been about to repair his shoulder, was instead forced to conjure a simple metal blade of his own and parry at an awkward angle. I danced away, and now, for the first time in this entire encounter, Yutigo and I *really* danced. It soon became clear that Yutigo, while quite good with a sword, was just the tiniest bit slower and less skilled than I was, and this disadvantage was only augmented by the fact that Yutigo was forced to compensate for his weaker right side and less able to parry blows directed there. He was further limited by the confined space in which we were forced to dance (I had conjured a localized force field to prevent meteorites from hitting us within that space, and neither of us wished to risk the elements) and, hampered by his weaknesses, unable to utilize his sword to its fullest.

Even fighting a losing battle, I could not help but admire Yutigo's tenacity and creativity. The broken shoulder had robbed him of his victorious smile, but the fierceness of him baring his teeth in a snarl fit his personality much better, I felt. In order to defend his right side, Yutigo was *tossing* his sword in the direction of my blow, waiting just long enough, and then phasing his hand to catch the blade and reorient it to most effectively parry the blow. Miraculously, I had never yet managed to strike at him before his hand caught the blade, but I was sure it was only a matter of time. There was only so much disembodied phasing a being as weakened as Yutigo could do before losing the strength of will to hold body parts in two places at once.

Sweat was pouring down Yutigo's face, and I could see his whole arm vibrating as he parried blows directed at his left side. It was time to end this. "Any last words?" I called out. Yutigo snarled instead. "I guess not," I continued. I flicked my blade up at Yutigo's left shoulder, which he easily redirected with a circling motion of his blade, but my blade never stopped moving, instead darting back down at his calf. Yutigo moved to parry this stroke as well, but it was only a feint. With all my strength, I pulled the blade back at the last moment and gave a two-handed swing at his injured shoulder. Yutigo desperately tossed his blade, but the distance was simply too great, and my blade caught his on the upswing, sending it flying away, as well as his hand as it phased to where Yutigo had hoped his blade would be. Gasping, Yutigo stumbled and fell to the ground. I smiled for the first time in the battle. "Now, Yutigo," I said triumphantly, "you have seen what it means for me to give my all." My blade whistled downward, heading for Yutigo's neck in a sweeping arc.

The blade had just barely pierced Yutigo's skin when a debilitating pain exploded from the very depths of my subconscious, and I knew no more.

23

PANGS OF CONSCIENCE

Pierre Hartford, a doorway to another place

Once again, I found myself in a black, void-like space, though this time, I was floating instead of standing. I gave a big, hearty yawn. Hadn't there been Fate in the room with me? At least, I think that was what the woman had called herself. Oh, what did it matter, though? I was so *tired*, so sick of the burdens I was carrying. Nothing would have pleased me more at the moment than a deep, fulfilling sleep. Even five minutes would be heavenly. My eyelids began to flutter open and shut, and though I desperately wanted to sleep, I knew there must be some reason for me to remain awake. It was just so *difficult* to remember! I continued to float and struggle with my fatigue when a face floated by. A *remarkably familiar face*. But that was *impossible*. "*Dad?!*" I blurted out.

The face stopped and turned toward me. Out of the

blackness of the surrounding space, the rest of Dad's body slowly appeared as well. He looked no worse for wear than he had six years ago before we had gone to battle against the Entity. He smiled, a regretful smile that spoke of a yearning for a time that could never be recaptured, of lost hugs and kisses, of lost moments simply spent enjoying life at peace. "Hello, son," he said.

"I...I don't understand," I said. "You're *dead*. How can I be seeing you here and now?"

"Well," said another all-too-familiar voice from behind me in a snide tone, "technically speaking, that's what you *are* right now."

And I remembered.

Flashback to the end of chapter 21

"I accept your offer," I told Fate. Her face instantly lost its pleading look, her eyes brightening immediately and her mouth breaking into an enormous smile. The stars of which her hair consisted perhaps shone even brighter for a moment, though I may just have been imagining that.

"Excellent!" she said. "Excellent, just excellent." She stretched out her arm, and I felt myself pulled closer to her. She stared deep into my eyes for a moment, as if to ensure that I was of purehearted mind and spirit and harbored no malignant intentions. Which I didn't. Technically.

After a few seconds, Fate pulled back and nodded. "Just to be sure," she said by way of explanation. "One can never be too careful with these sorts of things, after all. But I was right, as I always am. You will serve just fine." She spread the fingers of the hand attached to her still-outstretched arm. "Touch your hand to mine," she said. I did as she ordered. Already I could feel the power humming in the air around us. It emanated from Fate now in waves, causing the stars, galaxies, and other universal phenomena around us to grow hazy. It coiled expectantly, excited for what it sensed was about to occur.

"Do you, Pierre Hartford, accept this power, to be used in service of the position of caretaker of the universe, and only in service of that position?" intoned Fate. "Do you accept the duties that come with that position, to protect the weak, promote the strong, humble the arrogant, defend against evil, and maintain the peace?"

"I do," I replied simply.

"Then let it be done," Fate continued. "I hereby transfer the power of the universe to Pierre Hartford. Let it judge his worthiness, and if he be unworthy, let it strike him down and seek another."

As the words faded away, I felt a tingle start in my fingertips. Quickly, it spread through my fingers, down my arm, and into my chest. From there, it reached all parts of my body. My entire body felt like an enormous lightning rod, though I knew something significantly more powerful than electricity coursed through my veins. I could make out every individual nerve ending in my body. Other than that, though, I did not feel particularly different, and Fate looked much the same as she had. This couldn't really be it, could it?

The moment I said this, however, my entire brain exploded into one giant ball of pain. It felt as if the very neural pathways that held my brain together were melting away. Information was flooding my brain—species, planets, and stars flitting past my eyes faster than I could process them. My brain as it was presently constructed was simply too small to contain the information content of the universe, and it was too limited to process the requisite amount of data per nanosecond. It had to expand somehow, and so it did. There was a strange tingling sensation at the back of my head, and it suddenly felt surprisingly...*open*. I whipped my free hand to touch the back of my head, only to realize that I had no head left to speak of really. The last bits of my skull dissolved at the lightest of touches from my fingers, leaving only the bone that represented my face. I felt a pinprick of pain at a point on my head and let my fingers brush over it, only to realize that a star had made its way onto the back of my head. I looked at my outstretched hand again and saw it melting away as well. Skin, bone, muscle, and blood vessels melted away to be replaced by the inky blackness that denoted Fate's silhouette. As I lost skin, Fate gained skin in turn, and she began to gain a physical form to complement her eyes.

It was now or never, I realized. When my body was gone, it would be too late for what I had planned, and even though the transfer was far from complete, I had power enough for what needed to be done. I waited until I felt my neck disappear before initiating my plan. Fate was still smiling when the blade of power I conjured sliced through her neck and lopped her head off, so unexpected was my attack. *Technically*, I had done as Fate had requested by killing her. It was just that I had done so sooner than requested. The power that had not been transferred yet swirled out of Fate's body like a cloud of angry bees, the universe's way of telling me it was unhappy about what I had done. For now, at least, it possessed a small will of its own, but it was still beholden to me, the result of the uninterruptible power transfer that had been initiated.

I focused my will on finding the chain of command that determined the action of every single thing in the universe. It took several minutes of searching, during which the free power began to be siphoned off into me, but I found it. A thin multicolored line sprang into existence, originating at a point approximately six inches in front of me, immediately spider-webbing into a series of microscopically thin lines that each ended at a particular object or creature or sentient being in the universe. Using my newly enhanced brainpower, I quickly created a program that could determine the best course of action for every single thing in the universe. In its initial form, it was without a doubt imperfect, but it would learn from its mistakes as time went on and adapt to take only the very best courses of action, even if it meant making a less than optimal decision at some point along a larger route. I forced the vast majority of my power to focus on executing this program while I securely bonded it to the source of the free will chain.

The power did not like this. Its most natural state was for it to live and breathe freely; to flow through and around a body of indeterminate size, shape, and mass; to be used randomly, spontaneously, not in the service of a rigorous and regimented program, far away from the body of its commander. A flare of power rose against me and attempted to attack. With the little power that I had, I still managed to conjure a force field and batter this flare away. The power raged and seethed, but there was little it could really do against my iron will. I wished for it to carry out the program, and so it would, bound to it for all eternity…even if there was no longer a will to keep it in line.

With the last bit of power that remained in me, I consumed what little of my body still remained, ordering the power to kill me with my dying breath.

Returning to the present day

As the memories of what I had just done flooded back into my head, I wheeled around to face Karl von Liebnitz. "It's good to see you too, Karl," I replied. "But if this is where dead souls go, it's a wonder anyone would choose to die. The afterlife seems remarkably drab to me."

Karl laughed. "Oh, Pierre, don't you ever listen? Technically speaking, you're dead. You wished yourself dead, which is why you're here. But the only way you'll pass through to the afterlife is if you fall asleep here."

I frowned. "I *know* I didn't ask to end up in this…purgatory, so why am I here?"

Karl raised an eyebrow as Dad floated around to join him. "Guilt, I would assume," he said.

I furrowed my eyebrows in confusion. "I'm not feeling guilt over committing suicide, believe me." Now Dad raised an eyebrow as well. "I'm not!" I protested, nonetheless feeling a coil of guilt roiling in my gut.

"Pierre," Dad said gently, "if you were guilt-free, we wouldn't be here right now."

"In case you didn't get what your father was trying to say," added Karl, "not to mince words, but a guilt-free you would be lounging around in the afterlife right now."

My stomach was beginning to feel as if multiple snakes were twisting and twining around each other, but still I valiantly attempted to ignore the blatantly obvious signals. "If this isn't actually the afterlife, how are you two here right now?" I demanded.

"Well, technically, we aren't here," said Dad. "We're part mental projection of your soul and part mental projection of the afterlife. In other words, we have all of our memories, including those of the years we have thus far experienced in the afterlife, but our actions and behaviors are based entirely off what you remember them to be. We are here because it has been detected that there is an internal conflict within you that must be resolved one way or the other."

"The universe has sent us here to see whether we can talk you down from the ledge or not," added Karl.

"OK, OK," I said placatingly. "I *am* feeling guilty about killing my mother, Yuri, and my friends."

Karl tilted his head. "True," he said, "but not the reason we're here. Try again!"

"That is also something you're not really responsible for," added Dad. "It was part of what Fate had to do to get you to her."

Karl chuckled. "Yuri certainly didn't feel that way. Cursing up a storm when he fell into the afterlife, going on and on about how he was going to get you when *you* finally dropped dead as well! Then Lili came along and, as she always could, calmed everything right down." Both Karl's and Dad's eyes grew wistful at the sound of my mother's name.

I knew what the universe wanted me to say, but I was in a mulish mood and didn't feel much like cooperating. "I still don't understand why I'm here then," I said. "I don't think I did anything wrong!"

Dad smiled. "And what exactly did you do, Pierre?"

"I did...things," I replied awkwardly.

"What *things*, Pierre?" asked Karl more sharply. "The first step to overcoming this guilt is to actually *admit* what it is you've done that causes you to feel that guilt."

I sighed. There was no use in continuing to deny it. "I feel guilty about killing myself and leaving control of the universe in the hands of a program."

Karl gave me a mocking round of applause. "Oh, Pierre," he simpered, "I'm so proud of you! You did it!"

"Wow, I feel so good about myself!" I snapped back sarcastically. "Were you always this much of a pain, or do I just remember your worst moments too vividly?" Karl let a look of mock hurt suffuse his features, but he continued to laugh as he did so.

Dad stepped in. "Now, let's talk about how incredibly stupid you were," he said.

"Dad!"

"Oh?" he asked, raising an eyebrow. "Please, enlighten us as to how leaving the universe in the hands of a program was a good idea!"

"It was a perfectly well-thought-out plan!" I said in my defense. "Fate was an abysmally bad caretaker of the universe, at least in my book, anyway, and who's to say that I would have been perfect? I would have been better, sure, but for how long? How long before I would get corrupted and bored and started toying with people's lives for the fun of it? A program never would get bored! I took special care not to give it enough sentience to think independently beyond the parameters of the program. And additionally, it would adapt its stratagems for all eternity in order to seek and pursue the optimal strategy."

"Well, you've just revealed the fundamental flaw, haven't you?" asked Karl. I looked at him. "You said it yourself," he said. "You're imperfect. This is true, and it's undeniable, no matter how many pretty words Fate may have tried to whisper in your ear in an attempt to get herself into retirement. But if you're imperfect, then what about your program? You, with all your imperfections, created it, so logically, it *cannot* be perfect. And if it is not perfect, then that means that over time, errors will inevitably pop up. Who, in an automated system, will perform error correction? And so, over time, the power would become as corrupted, perhaps even more so, than Fate, and you've just screwed the universe over for good because this time you've put no mechanism in place to choose a successor! That is the doomsday scenario that will happen if you choose to enter the afterlife."

I looked down at the ground. Karl had given life to exactly those thoughts I had been thinking. "You're right," I said finally. "You're right, that's undeniable. I know that's an inherent flaw of my plan simply based on the assumptions I made. But I still think the program would do a much better job of taking care of the universe than I ever could. I don't think I could take the pressure. It would just be so hard...take, for example, the first time something reached the end of its natural life span, and I was forced to watch it, feel it die, to make it accept that its death was an inevitability. I would be reliving far too many painful memories." Tears began to fall from my eyes.

A hand landed on my shoulder, firm but tender at the same time. Gently, it kneaded my shoulder, letting the flesh roll between its fingers, the muscles uncoil and relax. For a moment, I could almost imagine that I was back at home before I had gone to MIT, and Dad and I were sitting in front of a big roaring fire. I was spilling my secrets, my wants and cares, and Dad calmly listening, providing the best advice I could have asked for. Here, though, there was no fire, and I was far too old and world-weary to truly believe that Dad alone could drive away all the evil that existed in the world. It didn't mean he couldn't try, though.

"Oh, Pierre," he said softly. "Oh, my son. There's so much pain, so much sadness inside you. Your sensitive soul cries out for solace. It is *that* which really makes you most suitable for the job of taking care of the universe. No matter how hard you try, you'll never be able to teach a program to really, truly *care*. Why should a program care what color lipstick a girl wears today, which girl a certain boy likes, whether a couple should wed? These and many more events seem so petty and insignificant in the larger picture, but they are so very important to the people caught up in them, and that is something you can understand, but a program can't. Yes, you *are* imperfect, but so is everyone! I was a selfish, conceited, arrogant fool back when I was eighteen, and it cost me my friendships. Karl formed a terrorist organization and tried to take over the world. Even your mother was working for the Entity. Don't trash the program. Keep it, listen to its advice. I'm sure most of the time it will be good! After all, you designed the program. Sometimes, though, listen to your gut, throw out whatever it is the program is telling you! Go back and fix the bugs accordingly. Take it one step at a time and try not to think too far in the future so that you don't become detached from the vividness of reality.

Go back and *embrace* the greatness. The universe needs you, and you're too valuable to lose."

Karl looked at me intently. "Even when you were my enemy," he said, "I respected you immensely. You always had the potential to be something I could never hope to be. You could be loved, not just feared. People would have loved you. People did love you because your sensitivity is such a magnetic character trait. But despite that, you have only taken the power thrust upon you unwillingly. You understand more than most the corrupting nature of power. You have seen it firsthand all too many times. You are not perfect, but you *are* great, and I can think of no better person for the job."

Tears filled my eyes as he finished. "Thank you, Karl, Dad," I whispered softly. "After everything I've been through, everything I've been forced to do, I really needed to hear that. Even if you're part projections of my soul, I know that at least parts of your real selves truly believe what you just told me. You have their memories, after all, and their reasoning skills. And I know that, more than anything else, someone needs to be there to hold down the fort."

Karl and Dad both smiled broadly, though both were beginning to tear up now too. "I suppose this is goodbye for good then," I said. They nodded. "Tell me," I continued, "is the afterlife at least stimulating?"

"Like you wouldn't believe," said Dad.

"So much to do, so many people to talk to, so many sights to see," added Karl.

I smiled sadly. "I would have very much loved to see it one day."

Karl and Dad inclined their heads, and then, simultaneously, they rushed forward and wrapped me into a tight hug. "Good luck, son," said Dad.

"Follow your heart," said Karl.

Slowly, agonizingly, I pulled myself away from the two of them and turned away before I could break down completely into tears. "I enjoyed this opportunity to see you two again more than the universe could ever imagine," I said finally. "When you see my mother again, I only request that you deliver my apologies to her for everything I did."

"She never hated you," chorused the two of them. I nodded in recognition.

Swallowing, I stepped forward, away from the last vestiges of my old life, and told the universe that I wished to stay awake for all eternity.

24

A NEW ERA

Pierre Hartford, New Berlin, Europa, New Earth

It was the year 2073.

I walked down the streets of New Berlin, humming the theme of Bach's Goldberg Variations under my breath. Some craters, aftereffects of the meteorite strikes, still dotted the streets, but on the whole, for a city that mere days ago had looked utterly ravaged by war (though really only one or two encounters had been fought within its confines), New Berlin was remarkably healthy. The Europan government was nothing if not a responsive social state. Aid had been given generously and without a second thought not just by the government but also from the personal coffers of government officials and the heads of the foremost companies of Europa and Americana alike. Upward of 40 percent of buildings had been damaged by falling debris during the War of the Extraterrestrials, as people liked to call it; 10 percent had been almost completely destroyed. Now, perhaps only 0.4 percent of buildings were still damaged, and none were completely destroyed. Construction crews worked around the clock, buoyed by the food, drink, and clothing provided by New Berlin's citizens, and the city soon regained its visual pride to go along with its spiritual one.

Once, I reflected, this had been my city, my very lifeblood. My love of the city had run deep, perhaps still ran deep on some level. It went beyond the Brandenburg Gate, Alexanderplatz, Friedrichstraße, or even the museums and other landmarks too numerous to name, too numerous to even think of. It had always been the small things, like the colors in which the subway stations were painted, the antiquated soundtrack that played over the speakers of city trains even though they were today all maglev and silent. It was the pattern in which the paving stones had been laid out, whether it was five or five hundred years ago, the beautiful simplicity of the slides, seesaws, and monkey bars of the city's playgrounds. For two years, my memories had depressed me too much to appreciate even the simplest of simple beauties. But for four, I had been happy as could be, surrounded by a veritable menagerie of familiar sights, sounds, smells, and tastes. Yet despite all this, I had never really found the unique character of the city's people to stand out to me. Now, by necessity, if nothing else, the situation found itself flipped completely on its head.

It remained an ordeal for me to ensure that people continued to walk normally whenever they were in close proximity to me. By necessity, the minds of all passersby were open books so that I could continue to make their decisions for them even as they brushed past me in the flesh. It was, however, disorientating in the extreme to process two separate streams of information about the same interpersonal encounter from two different perspectives all at once. My eyes saw the other person, but through that person I also saw myself so that I could decide what sort of an opinion he or she would formulate based on my physical appearance. Was I attractive? Did I seem a suspicious character? More simply, it was difficult to stand still and simultaneously feel the distinct need, the distinct urge to begin, continue, or stop walking. As the muscles in each leg of each person waxed and waned, it was a continuous process of deciding whether those muscles would continue moving in those manners, whether they would stop, or whether they would reverse direction. Even simpler still were the decisions along the lines of eye blinking. Should people blink or not? Should they pick their noses? Should they wet their lips? Should they scratch a particularly insistent itch? These days, deciding the thoughts of sentient creatures especially was a stop-and-go process, though the decisions I made for them occurred on such small timescales that they could not hope to possibly detect a delay between the conception of a thought and its execution or non-execution.

Time had ceased to play a role of any particular importance in my life upon my return from death's door. What was the meaning of a few seconds in the life of a man who was destined to spend an eternity frittering away seconds? Was there really a difference between day and night? What day of a cycle, of a month, it was? Which year? For every relatively decision-free soul, there existed a preponderance of decisions somewhere else in the universe. At this point, that was pretty much a given. The stream of information was unrelenting, and it no longer seemed important to make an attempt to measure the amount of time trying to surmount that same stream of information. I doubted that I could ever grow bored of this job, for when the universe is your playground, even the rarest of rare occurrences becomes a far more common experience than anyone with a typical life span and breadth of knowledge would think. Sometimes I wished I had decided to control not just the decision-making process but also the process of making thoughts. But it seemed simply a tad too draconian to me, and it would have deprived me of the true joy of my occupation. For within the unending, unrelenting stream of mundane decisions, it was truly the hidden gems that I lived for.

Take, for example, the first supernova I had had the honor of witnessing when I first entered my position. Just because the universe had hit on an optimum formula for determining how large supernovas should grow and when they should explode did not mean that I was required to be beholden to that formula. I *was* the lawmaker of the universe; the laws of chemistry could have bent over backward to touch their toes if I had wanted them to. Deciding down to the very atom when the fusion process would fail (the feeling of which was a thrill all its own), deciding if the degeneracy pressure of the neutrons would be enough to form a neutron star or not, deciding exactly how far and how fast the outer layers of the star exploded… every moment had been new and exciting, drastically different from anything I could have ever expected to experience as your garden-variety human or even as one of an exceptional class of beings that numbered in the thousands.

I sat down on a park bench, both so that I could more easily control the motions of the people walking past me without having to worry about my own simultaneously and so that I could lose myself in my thoughts. Sitting on the bench was an ordeal in and of itself. I had to decide whether the wood would mold itself (however slightly) to the shape of my buttocks or to maintain its shape; whether the metal and the wood wanted to squeak and creak, the likelihood of which also depended upon their respective ages...et cetera, et cetera. The only possible way I could have even handled all the sensory and mental information required to make the series of decisions a creature made every single day was by opening a parallel thought stream devoted solely to the decisions of that creature. You can imagine how many thought streams I required to cover the entire universe in this fashion! But it was my primary thought stream, the one from my own, one-stream mind, that managed to engage me. For this was the thought stream in which I collected all the interesting tidbits that occurred in the daily of each respective creature or being or thing and allowed me to investigate them at my pleasure. It was this primary thought stream and this greatest hits playlist that both kept me sane and gave me my dosage of sheer, giddy pleasure and wonderment at just how amazing the universe could be. It was always awe-inspiring to see how far the bounds of creativity could be pushed (this part of the decision-making I did not have control over, for I was only handed control after the universe had conceived whatever thing or creature or being it had been aiming for in full).

I was immensely glad that I at least had full freedom of movement within the entire universe, unlike my poor predecessor, who had lived and died within one extremely cool, intensely fascinating room, but still only a room. I only felt a pang of sadness when I donned a human form and realized that it would never quite feel like my own skin, my home. The human body was simply too weak, too small, too limited to contain all the characteristics and genetic code needed to construct a caretaker of the universe. Even now, as I sat on the bench contemplating other people, I could both feel and not feel the back of my head. This was always the most obvious part of my body that needed remodeling, for the true size of my brain likely spanned quite literally hundreds of light-years. The best way to describe it, perhaps, was that it felt as if I were constantly phasing the back of my head back and forth between two locations.

On a whim (see, I couldn't even control where my own thoughts came from!), I decided to visit the one being in the universe I could still talk to. Nuarti did not and would not know what exactly had transpired in my meeting with Fate, but she knew that Fate was dead and that I had survived, and that was good enough for her. The War of the Extraterrestrials had really done a number on the population of beings in particular. A disastrous battle that Nuarti had unwittingly incited with an ill-phrased note had resulted in the deaths of over four thousand beings within the room of the Council of Realms and on the battlefield of MIT. A mere 769 had remained when the meteors had stopped falling and I had taken on the caretaker position.

The Council of Realms was no more. I had "asked" Nuarti to at least consider retaining the name, even if the old structures, rules, and proposals were swept under the rug, never to be seen again. But doing that had resulted in an abnormally large number of mutinous thoughts coming from Nuarti (her exceptional strength of will before I had come into power still made it occasionally difficult to fully exert my control over her without becoming lax in my duties to the other things of the universe; oftentimes, it was easier to go with the thoughts most commonly generated by Nuarti than try to implant my own thoughts and ideas). And thus, the Beings' Congress had been formed.

Nuarti was Speaker of the Congress, which was the only formal, titled position in the body. There were no elders, no scribes even, as Nuarti could more than adequately fulfill that duty on her own, but simply representatives, a far more benign word than ruler. A ruler, by implication, did not need to worry much or even consider for a moment what his or her own creatures might wish of him or her, but a representative *represented* the will of the creatures he or she governed and was thus more pliable to the ideas and proposals the creatures put forth. Of course, the actual balance of power between the creatures and the beings had not changed, but it was amazing what the psychological effects of the name change did to the thoughts of the beings (which in turn made it easier to implement this new state of things).

On a more basic level, the awakening of beings was a thing of the past. Fate's horrific long game was something I vowed never again to repeat, and, if possible, to never think of again. There would no longer be any live experimentation or in fact experimentation of any type with respect to evolution, an amazing enough process on its own when given free rein without having higher powers twist it for their own macabre purposes. At Nuarti's behest, beings were now given a finite life span (but still eternally long relative to the average life span of one of the creatures they represented), so that she would perhaps feel less tempted by the enormous power she had never wanted to wield. In return, I had given beings the ability to breed, but only with each other, so that their species could continue. Despite what Yutigo had done, it did not diminish the sheer remarkableness of the beings Fate had created, and the small number who remained played a crucial, irreplaceable role in the universal ecosystem.

As I walked into the Congress room (simply a repurposed Council room; I had refused to let Nuarti allow a perfectly good pocket universe go to waste), I relaxed my control over Nuarti's decision-making to the degree that whichever thoughts came into her head first would control her actions and her words, the closest I could get to having a real conversation these days and not just a conversation with myself in a different body.

"Nuarti!" I said in a loud, booming voice. "How goes the dispensing of justice?"

Nuarti looked up from the latest sheaf of proposals that she was reviewing, and her icy blue eyes, bright with emotion, lit up as her mouth opened into a broad smile. "Pierre," she said in return, "a pleasure as always to see you." Nuarti had grown far more open with her emotions and had become far happier as well, having managed to finally achieve a balance between her code of ethics and the fire that burned bright inside her after killing Yutigo (though she had not delivered a killing blow, due in part to my dalliance with death, the coldness of her blade held against his neck had been more than enough to cause him to freeze to death).

"You seem happy," I remarked, not particularly insightful,

but I merely wished to see what reaction my comment would incite.

"I know," Nuarti replied almost giddily. "I'm in love with the feeling. It's all because of this beautiful, amazing Congress."

I smiled benevolently. "So the system is working as we hoped and predicted?"

"Even better!" Nuarti responded excitedly. "There has been not a single complaint about the abuse of power by any of the beings. With such a small number, I can check on them almost constantly as well, and I am more than pleased to verify these reports. I truly find myself impressed with what a few changes purely psychological in nature can do to a governing body. I have merely tweaked a few of the original rules that the Council was set up with, but the results have been drastically different."

"You should give yourself some credit, Nuarti," I said in mock reprimand. "I'm sure the Congress runs more effectively because it also does not have to deal with a prince of terror sitting in the seat of power and pushing his own agenda rather than that of the creatures of the realms. After the battles on New Earth, the beings that remain know you were not Yutigo's lackey, and after you manage to open up some more, I am sure they can love you for your personality as well."

Nuarti inclined her head. "You are too kind, Pierre. I am sure I can be thankful for much of this because of you," which was true, though with respect to the Congress, Nuarti really had provided the lion's share of new ideas, "and I feel that I rule in a particularly amenable atmosphere. The universe is at peace, and it desires nothing more than peace for a long time yet. There are only a few more rough edges to smooth out."

Uh-oh. If Nuarti was receiving reports of mishaps in the realms, those could also be laid at my feet. I, just like the program I had intended to do this job, could not be perfect all the time, especially not at the beginning when I was still inexperienced in providing the universe as a whole with a mutually beneficial outcome. There were bound to be a few mishaps along the way, and some of them were simply easier to fix than others. Instead of letting my discomfort show on my face, I quirked an eyebrow. "Rough edges?" I questioned. "That doesn't sound like good news."

Nuarti sighed. "I mean, yes, I suppose it isn't good news," she said, her good spirits dampening slightly, "but it really is such a dramatic improvement over the Council times that I find myself hard-pressed to curse a few bumps and bruises right at the beginning of the hopefully long and prosperous road ahead."

Perhaps that explanation was good enough for her, I thought, but I had promised Fate perfection (or as close as I could get to perfection), and I intended to do that because even if Fate had been a twisted creation of the universe, her words had not been false.

"At least let me see some of these issues," I requested. "I'm sure that I could help in some way."

Nuarti suddenly looked distressed and, endearingly, like a child who was being requested to hand over a cherished toy. "Must I?" she said pleadingly, almost whining. "You must be so busy, and these problems are so minor. I'm positive I could deal with them easily enough!"

"Double the hands make the work go twice as fast," I reminded her. Nuarti's face pinched as she acknowledged my point, but her pleading expression had not faded. "OK, fine," I said (as I had said, arguing with her remained a fraught proposition at the best of times), "at least give me *one* problem to work with. They're my creatures too. I just deal with them on a more...*micro* level." Seeing that she was not going to win any more concessions, Nuarti agreed, handing me the first memo from the sheaf of papers.

It was about a minor epidemic afflicting a population of what appeared to be "Minotaurs." Ah, yes, I remembered this incident now. While trying to purify their water supplies, I had accidentally engineered a scarily effective virus. Though the symptoms were (for now) mild, the virus's skills of hiding from immune system detectors, infiltrating cells, and replication were unparalleled. Were it to mutate and cause lethal symptoms, the consequences would be quite messy. Yes, it had been difficult for the time being to convince a virus whose sole goal in life was to replicate to build in a kill switch, and I hadn't been able to devise a way to surreptitiously create one during the replication process either. But really, if I simply opened up two or three thought streams, a solution would surely come to me sooner rather than later...

And so the new era began. Life continued much as it had before, but many familiar things had different names now, and a new aura of hope suffused the entire universe, a hope that the eternal peace long sought had finally come. Nothing had changed, and yet everything had changed.

It was the year 2073, and Pierre Hartford lived in New Berlin with his parents, Yuri Klatschnikov and Lili Schwebler, went to work at Energieforschung GmbH under the direction of Aloysius Benton, who had never had to kill a man, and had as his friends Robert Morrison, Maximillian Steinhardt, and Luka Prosek.

It was the year 2073, and Pierre Hartford was finishing his PhD studies at MIT under the stewardship of President Downs. Christian Roland enjoyed retirement from the now-defunct NSA.

It was the year 2073, and Will Hartford had never gone to MIT. Karl von Liebnitz, Lili Schwebler, and Will Hartford had eternally remained the finest of friends, and Lili had never married. Pierre Hartford was never born.

It was the year 2073, and Karl von Liebnitz was the leader of *Freiheit*, an organization that fought for the rights of those few unjustly incarcerated prisoners that remained. His wife, Lili Schwebler, and their two children, Wilhelm and Roland, were never far from his side, armed with the most incisive of legal minds and always willing to lend a hand. Yuri Klatschnikov, his brother in all but name, was mayor of New Berlin and the staunchest ally he could have asked for.

It was the year 2073, and Will Hartford was the CEO of Cybor Technologies, Inc. His wife, Lili Schwebler, and their son, Pierre Hartford, never strayed far from the premises of their Cape Cod home, the location from which Will worked, lived, and loved. Karl von Liebnitz was a beloved family friend and CTO of the same company.

It was the year 2073, and the being Rexdael had never grown up within a time bubble or under the thumb of the most terrible of dictators. He had never destroyed three planets or committed a single genocide. With his awakened powers, he gladly served the Beings' Congress and its Speaker, Nuarti.

It was the year 2073, and the being Yutigo had not almost

died at birth. He had grown horns earlier than any of his peers, and he was the best of friends with his nonalcoholic big brother, the leader of their clan. His powers were never awakened.

It was the year 2073, and who knows what had and hadn't happened in actuality?

Perhaps it really *had* all been a dream.

GERMAN GLOSSARY

Ach – Oh

Arthur Hausser in der 63. Minute! – Arthur Hausser in the
    63rd minute!

Autodiebstahl – car theft

Energieforschung – energy research

Entdeckung – discovery

Freiheit – freedom

fünf Jahre im Gefängnis – five years in jail

Herr – Mister

Komm rein – Come in

Mein Gott! – My God!

Quelle der Hoffnung – Source of Hope

Tor! – Goal!

Wandlung – transformation

Willkommen – Welcome

Wunderbar, nicht wahr? – Wonderful, no?